CW01659147

THE HIT

TEAM ZULU SERIES BOOK 1

JULIE WEAVER

Copyright © 2021 by Julie Weaver

First published by Epic Press

Edited by Donna Alward and Lyn Ruffian

Cover design by The Book Cover Boutique

All rights reserved

No portion of this book may be reproduced in any form without written permission from the publisher or author, except for the use of brief quotations in a book review.

This is a work of fiction. Names, characters, places, and incidents are products of the author's imagination or are used fictitiously. Any resemblance to actual persons, living or dead, events, or locales is entirely coincidental.

ISBN (paperback): 978-0-6452795-6-6

ISBN (special edition discreet paperback): 978-0-6459301-0-8

https://www.julieweaverbooks.com/

A NOTE TO READERS

This book contains adult content including sex scenes, violence, and swearing. Additionally, it contains reference to the following: drug addiction, PTSD, and neglectful parenting.

1

CAMERON

North Philadelphia, Pennsylvania

I wiped away a bead of sweat as it trickled down my neck. It was impossible to concentrate today, and it had little to do with the Indian summer turning the garage into a sauna. Or that my back ached from lying under this '71 Mustang all morning because the car hoist was on the fritz again.

No. This was all my brother's fault. My anxiety ramped up each day Justin continued to ignore my calls and messages. Most frustrating of all was I didn't know if I should be pissed off or concerned about his latest disappearing act. Flipping between the two states like Jekyll and Hyde was exhausting.

Damn you, Justin. Why haven't you called me back?

I'd throttle him if he was on another bender. He might have gotten off with a suspended sentence for illegal substance possession, but one positive drug test and his parole officer would have him locked up. Justin didn't have the fortitude to handle prison.

And what if he hadn't called because he was in some kind

of trouble? The prickling sensation shooting down my spine reminded me there were life situations worse than a correctional facility. Like being tossed into the Delaware with concrete shoes.

I shivered despite the stifling heat and relaxed my grip on the socket wrench. The last thing I wanted was to strip the thread on the Pony's oil pan. My boss would give me a solid ribbing if I made a rookie mistake like that.

The low rumble of a V8 engine approached the parking lot. I blew a stray lock of hair from my face and rolled out from under the Mustang to admire the '69 Chevelle as it came to a stop out front. Its cherry-red paint and chrome mag wheels glimmered in the sun. Still, it was no match for my ride parked two bays over.

After wiping my greasy hands on a rag, I tightened the messy bun on top of my head, then met the driver at his car.

"Morning. Can I help you?"

The man's eyes raked over me as though he'd never seen a woman in overalls. With fists propped on hips, he squinted while searching for something in the garage behind me. The buttons on his Hawaiian shirt looked ready to pop around his bulging gut. There was something about his beady eyes and wire-framed glasses that reminded me of the annoying character Newman from *Seinfeld*.

"Sure, sweetheart." He grinned while adjusting his specs. "I'm looking for Tom."

He did *not* just call me sweetheart. I shoved both hands in my pockets before he noticed me balling them into fists.

"He's out for a while, but I'm his head mechanic. Is there a problem with your Chevelle?"

Newman's eyes widened. "*You're* the head mechanic?"

I nodded but neglected to add that, apart from my boss, I was the only other mechanic who worked here.

He looked like a goldfish as his mouth opened and closed

without uttering a word. What a jackass. His reaction shouldn't surprise me. I'd seen it enough since I started here as a baby-faced apprentice almost ten years ago.

Hoping to dodge Newman's foot-in-mouth problem, I fast-tracked the conversation. "Why don't you tell me what's going on with your car?"

He scratched his head and looked between me and the Chevelle. "It's losing power, and the gauge says it's running hot."

"Mind if I take a look?" I strode to the front of his car before he had a chance to decline. "Pop the hood and start her up."

He did as I asked, then stood nearby while I leaned over the engine and ran a few checks. I glanced at Newman, whose eyes weren't on the car.

Ugh, what a creep.

My jaw clenched from holding in a smartass comment. Telling sleazeball clients what I thought of them was bad for business. Although, in this jerk's case, it might be worth it.

I dropped the hood and cleaned my hands again. "You can shut her down."

He did, then approached me once more. "Look, sweetheart, I think I'll come back later and get Tom to do a proper inspection." His insincere smile only added an extra foot to the crater he'd dug himself into.

Screw it.

I shoved the rag into my pocket and folded my arms. "Sure, you can do that. But I have to tell you, there's something seriously wrong with your head."

Newman recoiled and had the audacity to look shocked. "What did you say?"

Dude, please. As if no one had enlightened him before today.

I maintained my hard stare. "I think you heard me just fine."

"Listen, lady, I don't know who you think you are, but I'll be telling your boss about this." It was an effort not to laugh as Newman's second chin trembled with rage, and his face turned the same shade as his car. I really hoped he didn't have a coronary in the parking lot.

I held my palms up. "Hey, if you don't like hearing the truth, that's not my problem. But Tom will back me up on this." I gestured to Newman's car. "Your left cylinder head is cracked. There's coolant leaking into the block, and if you keep driving it, you'll destroy the engine."

He froze and blinked a few times. "The *cylinder* head?"

"Yes, the cylinder head. What did you think I was talking about?"

"I just thought you meant"—Newman cleared his throat and shook his head—"Never mind."

"Here are your options. You can leave the Chevelle here and I'll get onto it next week, or you can take it around the corner to Sean's garage. Of course, he'll charge you twice the price for half as good a job. It's your call." I focused on picking grease from under my short-trimmed nails while he decided.

There wouldn't be any negotiation. We were always busy because Tom's shop was the best in town for classic cars.

"I guess I'll leave my keys with you, then."

~

"HEY, KIDDO." Tom's voice boomed across the garage.

"Hey, old man."

I grinned as my bearded and tatted-up boss approached with a bunch of red roses in one hand and a grease-stained paper bag in the other. What would his badass biker pals think of the kind-hearted man he'd become since giving up the MC life?

"Aww, you brought me flowers?"

He gave me a knowing smile. "Shelley's been putting up

with my shit for twelve years to the day. I'd say she deserves them. This is for you though." He passed me the paper bag. "Got your favorite. Burger and fries from Marty's."

"Thanks, I owe you." I placed my lunch on the tool cabinet, but even the smell of the best burger in town did little to spark my appetite.

Tom eyed the recent addition in the parking lot while I packed away a few tools.

"The Chevelle just came in," I said. "Cracked head. I'll book it in when I finish up with the Mustang. Owner was a real charmer."

He picked up on my sarcasm and frowned with a concerned Dad expression that my own never had the care to use. "I keep telling you, you don't need to put up with that. Send them on their way until they learn some respect."

My lips twitched. "I handled it."

"I bet you did." Tom folded inked arms across his burly chest and nodded at my ignored food. "You feeling okay? Half those fries should've disappeared already."

I shrugged, reluctant to pretend everything was peachy because my boss would see straight through me. Not that I wanted to burden him with my problems.

"Are you worried about Justin?" Tom asked. "Has he still not called?"

"Five days and not a word." I sighed and returned a socket to its case. "But you know what he's like. Probably avoiding me because he doesn't want another lecture about getting his act together."

Tom grunted. "I think he needs more than a lecture."

I suspected my boss held back his harsher thoughts as a kindness to me.

"You're right." I shifted on my feet. "Still, I can't shake this feeling that he's in more trouble than usual. How much longer should I wait before I file a missing person report?"

"When's his next parole check-in?"

"Friday morning." Two days from now.

Tom scratched his bearded chin. "I guess if you're worried about causing a problem with his parole officer, you could hold off until then. He's screwed if he misses check-in anyway, so you won't be making things worse for him."

I nodded. "That makes sense. I'll wait." Justin was a grown adult. He could do what he wanted without telling his baby sister his every move, even if I was the only family he had. "Thanks for the advice, and the food." I grabbed the bag and sat on a stool by the workbench.

"Any time, kiddo. I'm always here for you."

~

As I PACKED up for the day, my phone vibrated in the pocket of my overalls. A sharp breath escaped me when I checked my cell.

It was Justin.

My stomach churned with both relief and anger as I answered. "You'd better have a damn good reason for not calling me back."

"Cammy, I don't have much time." His voice sounded muffled, as though his hand covered the speaker.

"Justin, are you all right?" I paced the workshop floor. "I've been going out of my mind worrying about you."

"Listen! This is important." His words flew out fast.

"Where are you? Why don't you meet me at home so we can talk about it?"

"No!" he snapped. "You can't be near me." Heavy metal music played in the background. Where the hell was he?

"Calm down and tell me where you are. I'm coming to pick you up." I grabbed my keys from the tool cabinet and dashed to my Camaro.

"No! There's no time to explain. You need to get out of Philly. Right now. Get in your car and go. I'm so sorry." His voice cracked as he broke down. "Oh, God. What have I done?"

He sounded so scared, but I'd seen him this way more times than I cared to recall. Justin's paranoia, extreme emotions, and frantic, rambling words led me to one conclusion: he was high. Worse yet, he'd probably been that way for days.

Justin imagined crazy things when his drug-induced thoughts turned delusional. Russians were poisoning the water supply, the neighbors were conspiring to kill him, the CIA had put spy cameras in his room. And yet, the sour cramp in my gut persisted, setting off alarm bells that were too loud to ignore.

I paused at the door of my car, heart pounding against my ribs. "You're not making any sense."

"Please, listen to me. Go somewhere safe and don't tell anyone. I gotta go. I love you, Cammy."

"Wait. Justin!"

The call ended. I stared at the black screen while clenching the cell in a death grip.

I tried to ring him back, but it went straight through to voicemail. "Dammit." I kicked a tire with my steel-capped boot, then checked up and down the street. For what? Now *I* was paranoid.

Tom's gaze remained on me as I walked back to the garage. I figured he'd overheard my side of the conversation.

"Was that Justin?"

I slipped the cell in my pocket and tried to calm my rapid pulse. "Yeah. He sounded totally fried. I bet he hasn't slept for days."

Tom rested his hands on his hips. "Is he in trouble? I could come get him with you."

"He might be, but I don't know where he is. Anyway, it was hard to tell if he was just high or in real danger." I released a ragged breath as unused adrenaline tingled along my limbs.

Tom frowned. "Perhaps he's racked up another loan he can't pay back."

It was possible. Justin had been in debt to dangerous people only last year. The trouble started when his habit spiraled out of control and he borrowed from one loan shark to pay another.

"I hope not." I pinched the bridge of my nose. "I don't want to use my savings to spare him from a beating again." Justin had promised to get clean and pay me back. I was a fool to believe him. "All I can do is wait until he comes home, then convince him to go back to rehab. And if he doesn't check in with his parole officer on Friday, he'll be doing time."

Tom stepped toward me. The pity in his eyes made my chest tighten. "Cammy, I don't say this lightly. Maybe it's time to distance yourself from your brother. I understand family is important to you, but I've watched Justin drag you into his problems for years. You don't deserve to keep paying for his mistakes."

"He's all I've got. And he's the only one who looked out for me when we were kids."

Tom knew about my rough upbringing. I'd shared many meals with him and Shelley. Sometimes we'd talk about the crazy things he got up to when he'd been the vice president of the Rogue Wolves outlaw motorcycle club, and on rare occasions, I opened up about how my father had been a solid contender for Philadelphia's shittiest dad.

My boss scraped a hand over his close-cropped hair. "I get that you want to help him, I really do. But with the trouble he's bringing into your life, seems like nowadays he's the one you need protecting from."

Those words were like a sucker punch to the gut. And yet... he might be right.

My eyes remained on the floor so Tom couldn't see the tears pooling in them. The bond I shared with my brother ran deep, and I wouldn't ditch him when he needed me most. "I've been taking care of myself for a long time. Thanks for your concern, but I'll be fine." I sidestepped my boss and headed for the bathroom.

I didn't cry at work, ever. And I wasn't about to start now.

2

SHEP

Center City, Philadelphia

I walked inside my city crash pad and closed the door behind me, muting the late-afternoon chaos of the busy streets. Silence at last. Too much silence, in fact, and the absence of a welcoming committee meant my only companion in this world was probably passed out on the sofa. Again.

After unpacking a bag of groceries in the small kitchen, I pulled the Glock from the band of my jeans. Through force of habit, I removed the extended mag and checked the chamber was clear before placing them both in an overhead cabinet along with my keys.

Quiet sounds from the TV drew me toward the living room where I spotted Ranger, all four paws aimed skyward and on *my* leather recliner. His dog bed, which cost more than any pet mattress ought to, lay ignored on the floor beside him.

Ranger's stumpy tail thumped hard against the armrest. Furry brows twitched as his brown eyes followed my approach, but the spoiled-ass pointer didn't move.

"No, really, Ranger, don't get up." I shook my head and

returned to the kitchen to grab a beer and a pre-dinner snack. Since Ranger sat in my spot, I relaxed into the three-seater sofa and popped the bottle top.

I flipped the channel to the evening news. The anchor reported a drug bust on a fishing trawler, a pile-up on the Delaware Expressway, and a decorated US Army veteran's suicide after battling PTSD. His widow wept as she told the reporter how her husband, a courageous war hero, had struggled to adjust when he returned home.

A knot lodged in my throat as I stared at the worn leather band tied around my wrist, a personal reminder of the horror show I'd experienced while deployed in Afghanistan. I took a long swig of beer and raised the bottle in salute to the fallen soldier.

Fifteen years serving my country in the Special Forces and then in Team Zulu, a black operations unit, meant I'd seen and done a lot of nasty shit. We all had our ways of dealing with it. I'd lost teammates—brothers—to the black dog. Me? I buried that baggage so deep it was never resurfacing.

Transitioning to life stateside was an ongoing struggle. I didn't miss the deployments, but I did miss the brotherhood. Now the guys from my team were all in different places, doing different things. Some were still operators, others had returned home to families and regular jobs.

Then there were the ones like me. Messed up enough to be misfits in the civilian world, functioning enough to avoid the psych ward.

On TV, the news anchor switched to a reporter with a breaking bulletin. Standing outside a run-down house in the North Philly Badlands, she told how Micky 'The Tank' Sherman, a notorious pimp and drug dealer, was missing and presumed dead in a case similar to other recent criminal underworld disappearances. She concluded by saying detectives were no closer to identifying a suspect.

I gave myself a mental pat on the back at a job well done.

No one would mourn that murderous son of a bitch.

Killing brought me no joy, but I took satisfaction in knowing that assholes like Sherman couldn't terrorize anyone anymore.

When I opened the packet of chips, Ranger flipped onto his stomach so fast he almost fell off the recliner. Nose raised, he sniffed the air to determine what was on the menu and joined me on the sofa.

I handed him the first chip and scratched the scruff of his neck. "You're a leech, you know that?"

Ranger's brown snout snuffled my jeans and nudged my elbow before he settled with his chin on my thigh.

The news finished, and I smirked when a commercial for Palermo Pizza filled the screen, complete with a catchy jingle and a smiling Franky Russo touting their latest specials.

Wearing traditional Sicilian folk garb—black vest over a white shirt, black slouch coppola hat, and a red silk scarf knotted at his neck—and sporting a cringeworthy fake handlebar moustache, Franky came across as a friendly, respectable middle-aged man dressed up to promote his large chain of pizza restaurants. Yet the public had no clue that the philanthropic owner of Palermo Pizza was also the ruthless leader of the Wolf Street Mafia. Franky Russo's upstanding citizen act was a clever mask, and one of many he wore.

The real Franky, the one who kept me well paid, couldn't be more different from his public persona. His illegal operation had emerged following the events of 9/11. When the FBI switched focus from organized crime to international terrorism, they left a gaping hole for savvy criminals to take back the streets. Led by Franky, the Wolf Street crime syndicate grew into a much larger and more sophisticated beast than Philly had ever known. No longer about protection money, loansharking, and theft, the Mob had evolved into a multi-billion-dollar empire with international links to drugs, weapons, and human trafficking networks.

Through bribery and coercion, Franky Russo was, as they say, untouchable, with a stranglehold on Pennsylvania from homeless street kids right through to the Governor.

If the mob boss had someone's loyalty and obedience, they were safe. If not, there were plenty of ways he could make them suffer.

I knew that better than most.

~

THE NEXT MORNING, Ranger sat at my feet licking his lips while eyeballing the omelet I ate straight from the pan. I tossed him the last piece, then opened my laptop.

The email with details of my next job had arrived. Franky had asked me to stay in town after taking out Sherman because he had another contract for me.

I'd agreed, but would be glad to get it over with. Both Ranger and I were itching to leave the city and get back to our true home—a cabin in the Appalachian Mountains. Far from civilians and the constant reminder that I didn't fit into their world anymore.

The only place I was at peace.

Franky's email was brief. A name and address, no more. My instructions from the mob boss were always the same. Make the person disappear for good and without a trace.

Franky sat at the top of a food chain filled with every variety of criminal imaginable. It took a lot of work keeping those scumbags in line, so his warnings were short and retribution swift. And if someone had pissed him off enough, payback might be delivered by me.

I pulled a new burner phone from the kitchen drawer and sent a message to tell him I was on it.

I turned to Ranger. "Stakeout? You in, buddy?"

He raised his head and wagged his tail.

Time to take out more of Philly's trash.

~

IT WAS late afternoon when I parked my car in the near-vacant school parking lot half a block from the address in Franky's email. You could bet that sometime within the next six hours the target would either arrive or leave their house.

I took in the quiet working-class suburban street. Kids rode by on bicycles, and the odd car passed with people coming home from work. A mature oak tree grew in most yards, some with a rope and tire hanging from a limb. The red brick bungalow I monitored wasn't the worst in the area, but the garden could use some maintenance and the house a coat of paint.

My usual ride drew too much attention, but the mid-size white sedan I'd rented remained unnoticed. Ranger sat next to me and provided the perfect cover. If I needed to get a closer look, we could take a walk without raising suspicion. Plus, he was good company. Stakeouts could be long and boring.

In the early evening, the peaceful neighborhood shook with the roar of a V8 engine. A shiny black '69 Camaro SS in pristine condition pulled into the target's driveway. The Chevy growled like an angry beast before the driver turned the car off and the street became silent once more.

I grabbed my binoculars for a closer look. The SS door swung open, and a woman stepped out.

Fuck me.

She was a sight for these miserable eyes. Mid to late-twenties, windswept dark blond hair that touched the middle of her back. Brown leather cowboy boots that reached halfway up her tanned calves, and cut-off denim shorts that showed off long, toned legs. A black Henley shirt had the top few buttons undone low enough for me to get a good idea of what was beneath. And there, on the side of her slender neck, was a smear of grease.

Interesting.

She made her way inside, closing the front door behind her. My mark's woman, I figured. Lucky man. Pity his fortunes were about to take a serious nosedive.

Ranger whined and stared out his window. That meant one thing.

"Seriously, you need to piss already?"

He let out a high-pitched yawn and shifted his weight from foot to foot.

"Fine. A quick walk. Think I need a closer look, too."

Ranger's floppy ears dangled as he tilted his head.

"Don't stare at me like that. It's got nothing to do with the woman. I want to get a feel for the house layout and security, that's all." I put on my Yankees cap and black hooded jacket before getting out of the car.

A neighbor mowed his lawn, and the smell of fresh-cut grass filled the air. I followed the sidewalk past the target's house. No cameras out front, no mesh or bars on the windows, and no lock on the side gate.

Continuing around the block, I found an alleyway running along the back of the property. It was wide enough to drive a car down. I peered over the fence into the yard. Overgrown lawn, faded outdoor setting, no dog, no lock on the gate, no cameras or other security devices on this side of the house, either.

Odd. My target was unconcerned about a break-in. It made me wonder if Franky had given me the right address. This job looked almost too easy.

We circled the rest of the block and returned to the car. No one else arrived or left. The only notable activity was when the woman came out in running tights and a Phillies T-shirt, her thick wavy hair tied up in a messy ponytail, and took off for a jog. Forty minutes later she returned, flushed and sweaty. It looked good on her.

That was it. Lights out around twenty-two hundred. No movement at the residence again until she drove off the next morning. I tried to ignore how she looked every bit as tempting as the first time I'd laid eyes on her.

Tired and frustrated, I pulled out the burner phone. There was a guy working at the DMV who I used to access records. He was paid well for his service and his silence.

"Davis," he answered.

"I'm after some details." I didn't need to explain who was calling or why.

"Fire away."

"I need you to do a run on a '69 Chevy Camaro SS, registration HEL 427."

"Nice ride." Fingers tapped on a keyboard. "Vehicle is registered to Cameron McKenzie, 159 Scottsdale Road, Upper Darby. Registration was transferred from Colin McKenzie about ten years ago. Wait, this is odd." His mouse clicked. "The owner has the cleanest record I've ever seen. Not a single infringement, or even a parking ticket. That's rare."

Didn't sound like Franky's usual target, but I was at the right house, and Cameron McKenzie was the name Franky had given me. The woman was driving my mark's car, but where was McKenzie?

"Can you pull up McKenzie's license?"

"I'm already looking at it." He let out a whistle. "Good-looking woman."

I sat up fast. "What?"

"Yeah. No one looks decent in their license mug shot, but this one's incredible."

"Send it to me."

More clicking. "Anything else?"

"Nah, we're good."

"Okay. Later." He hung up the phone.

I opened the screen shot from Davis, my eyes widening as I studied McKenzie's license.

What the fuck? The woman driving the SS *was* Cameron.

I stared at the photo. Upturned green eyes framed by long lashes, petite nose and natural bow-shaped lips. *Damn.*

I deleted the image and shook my head in a futile attempt to clear it from there as well.

This… this could be a problem.

Why did Franky want her killed? So far, nothing about the woman made me believe she'd be involved with the Mob. Looked to me like she lived a quiet life in the 'burbs. And her squeaky-clean record? Unheard of. What could she have done to piss Franky off so much that he'd order a hit on her?

Maybe there was a simple explanation. Maybe Franky had directed me to the wrong Cameron McKenzie?

Time for another call.

~

Franky answered on the fourth ring.

"Yes?" He didn't give his direct contact details to many, but sometimes Franky liked to have a brief chat over the phone with the target before I completed the job. A quick reminder of who'd paid for them to meet their maker.

I cleared my throat. "It's Shep."

"Mr. Shepherd." Franky's cool tone told me today I dealt with the professional business person. That could change in a heartbeat. "I assume you're calling to tell me you've completed the job?"

"No, not yet. I think maybe there's been some kind of… miscommunication." I chose my words with caution, hoping to keep the conversation civil. Franky didn't like being questioned. He'd once shot a guy in the knee for suggesting he'd been underpaid.

"I doubt that, but I'm listening."

"Cameron McKenzie. She's a woman."

A pause. *Shit.* "I am aware of this. Her insolent brother stole from me. I asked him to return the goods or his beloved sister would pay the consequences. Although it seems he doesn't care for her at all because he continues to ignore my request."

I dragged a hand through my hair. He'd never asked to have a woman, or anyone remotely innocent, executed before.

Franky continued. "I don't appreciate having to explain myself and I'm only doing so because I respect you, Mr. Shepherd. However, this level of unprofessionalism is tiresome. If you're unable to do your job, I'll get Mr. Tucci to do it."

Joe Tucci, aka The Butcher. No one deserved that kind of death. His targets ended up in pieces, mutilated beyond recognition. Forensic reports detailed how his victims sustained their injuries before death. When Franky wanted someone to disappear without fanfare, he called me. When he wanted to make a statement, he called The Butcher. Acid coated my throat at the thought of what that sadist might do to the McKenzie woman.

I needed time to figure out how to deal with this situation.

"Well?" Franky interrupted my thoughts. "I haven't got all day."

"Don't call Joe. The contract's mine. I'll message when it's done." My jaw tightened, and the phone shook in my hand.

"Good. It's always a pleasure doing business with you." Franky hung up.

I dropped the cell in the cup holder before I crushed it in my fist. "Fuck!" I growled, and thumped the steering wheel with my palm.

THAT NIGHT, with the lights off, I rolled the sedan down the dark alleyway and parked by the back gate of the McKenzie house. A knot formed in the pit of my stomach as I ran the plan through my mind another goddamn time. Why was I nervous? She was half my size.

Get a grip on yourself. This is not the toughest thing you've done in your life.

I slipped on a pair of thin leather gloves, donned my ball cap, and checked I had the tools I needed in my jacket pocket. I rolled my shoulders before getting out of the car.

Cool night air washed over me as I passed through the gate and headed for the back deck while clinging to the shadows. A dog barked a block away, but the house in front of me showed no signs of life. After picking the lock on the door, I slipped inside and closed it behind me gently.

A slight trace of her last meal lingered in the air. The fridge hummed a steady rhythm. On my right, a kitchen; on my left, a dining area. Straight ahead lay a long hallway. A faint light shone through an open doorway at the end. Her bedroom? I crept toward it, cringing each time the floorboards creaked underfoot.

I'd just uncapped the syringe that had been burning a hole in my pocket when my ankle caught on a tripwire, throwing me forward. I crashed to the floor hard, landing on my hip and shoulder. A metallic jangling noise came from above.

What the hell? A booby trap?

I scrambled to stand and checked the syringe. Somehow, it had survived the fall.

Bare feet thudded on the timber floor. I had to get to her fast before she called the cops. Already on my way to her room, I capped the syringe and put it back in my pocket before reaching for my Glock.

Beyond the doorway, a weapon cocked.

"If you come in here, I swear to God I'll blow your motherfucking head off!" she shouted, her voice wavering.

I pulled up short. Time to try another approach. "I'm not gonna hurt you, I promise, but we need to talk."

"Ever heard of a phone, asshole? Get out of my house!"

"Not leaving until we talk. Hold your fire. I'm coming to you unarmed."

This was a bold, risky move, but I needed to speed things along in case she'd already phoned for help. And if my judgment was decent, she wouldn't shoot an unarmed person, at least not right away. That she was yelling at me instead of firing warning shots supported that. Perhaps her gun wasn't even loaded.

I looped the trigger guard of the pistol over my thumb and held my hand high. Inch by inch, I moved my body into the doorway and hoped to hell she didn't shoot my sorry ass.

Cameron stood on the other side of the room wearing only a white tank top and cotton underwear. She raised the ancient shotgun higher on her shoulder, holding it tight in her grip.

She'd known someone was coming for her, and her archaic tin can alarm had been embarrassingly effective.

Her chest heaved while she eyed me over the barrel. I held her fierce stare and lowered my Glock to the floor slowly, then stood, keeping my palms high.

"What are you doing in my house?" Her shaking hands adjusted their grip on the twelve gauge. She held the thing all wrong, like someone who'd never fired a shotgun in their life. The kickback would knock her on her ass, but still blow a hole in me at this range.

"Like I said, I only want to talk."

"Wearing gloves and carrying a pistol?" She shook her head. "I don't think so."

"I'm not here to hurt you."

"Bullshit!" She shifted on her feet, but the aim of her weapon never left me. "Who sent you?"

I held still. "That's not important."

Her eyes narrowed. "Tell me why you're here. Start giving me answers!"

I showed her my palms in a calm-down gesture. "I will. If you lower the gun, we can talk."

"We *are* talking, jackass. Get your hands back up in the air and don't move!" Her nostrils flared as she glared daggers at me.

I did as she asked.

She glanced at her cell on the nightstand.

I took a step forward while her gaze was averted. "I wouldn't do that."

Her eyes whipped to me. "Stay back!"

I held my position. "Lower the shotgun so nobody gets hurt. Shooting an unarmed person will get you in a world of trouble." Doubtful since I'd broken into her home, but it was worth a try. "Listen, you're the only one here with a gun in your hands. You've got all the control. Don't do anything stupid." I used a soothing tone and took another small step forward.

Her brow creased. "I said stay back or I'll pull the trigger."

"Calm down."

"Do it, now!" She stared at me unblinking, the antique weapon trembling in her grip.

I lowered my chin. "Cameron, listen to—"

She froze, her pale face looking freaked at the sound of her name. Then she held her breath and closed her lids.

I dove to the floor.

Click.

The rusty shotgun misfired. Cameron's eyes snapped open.

Moving fast, I jumped to my feet. She hurled the weapon at my head. I deflected it with my forearm. *Ouch!* I growled and launched at her, but she lunged from my reach to snatch up a large wrench from her dresser. I grabbed her from behind, covering her mouth with my hand. She screamed and hit me on the brow with it. I grunted in pain.

I knocked the wrench out of her grip, pulled out the syringe and flicked the cap off. She reached behind and grabbed my ear, yanking my head to the side. I snarled and stabbed the sedative into her thigh. She jerked and screamed again, then thumped me in the jaw with her fist. I tossed the empty syringe to the floor and held her in a firm bear hug.

She still fought hard, bucking and kicking like a wild animal. Eventually, the drug took hold and her thrashing slowed.

Muffled screams became cries, then silence. I removed my hand from her mouth and turned her to face me. I shouldn't have. The fear in her stare was unsettling to witness and tugged on some long-forgotten part of me.

Long lashes fluttered as they struggled to remain open.

"I'm sorry it has to be like this."

3

CAMERON

Tires crunched over gravel. My head pounded like a bitch. I opened my heavy lids and squinted when glaring sunlight flooded through the window of a car.

Wait.

Why was I lying across the backseat of a pickup? I checked my aching wrists and found them bound firm with a zip tie. I tried to free them, but it was no use.

No, no, no! A scream threatened to escape my lips, but I wasn't ready to face my captor and didn't want him to know I was awake yet.

I glanced at the driver and blood drained from my face. It was the asshole who'd broken into my house and attacked me. A baseball cap sat low on his brow, obscuring his facial features except for a clenched jaw. The black T-shirt he wore strained against large biceps. One huge hand gripped the steering wheel so hard his knuckles were white.

Despite my terror, anger flared through me. *Damn you, Justin*. For once, my brother had been telling the truth.

The car lurched as it traveled over bumps and dips. Where was he taking me? The plastic cover on the seat crinkled and clung to my skin. My breath caught in my throat and my heart rate surged. If he was being careful to keep my DNA contained, it told me two things: he planned on killing me, and he'd probably done this before.

Hold it together, Cam. I bit my lip hard to stop myself from tumbling into a full-blown panic.

I had to try something, anything, to get away. Doing nothing was a death sentence. I didn't care if he was hulk sized. I wasn't going down without a fight.

The vehicle slowed, then stopped. A moment later, the engine shut down. I kept my eyes closed and remained still. The man exited the car, slamming the door. The sound of his footfalls quieted with each step.

I sat up to peer out the window and took in my surroundings. As I dreaded, we were in the middle of nowhere. In front of me was a log cabin set on a hill with a free-standing workshop on the right. Behind me, the ground sloped away to the woods below. All around was a multi-hued forest in the full grip of fall.

My kidnapper strode toward the cabin and up a set of timber stairs, a large brown roan dog following close on his heels. He unlocked the door, and the pair continued inside.

There wasn't time to think about it. I had to get the hell away from him. I tossed off the blanket covering my waist and legs. *Crap!* I had no shoes or pants. Modesty would have to go screw itself.

I pulled on the door handle. No luck. Must have the child lock on. Clambering over the center console, I landed in the front passenger seat. *Bingo!* The door opened, and I bolted downhill toward the woods without a backward glance.

Adrenaline filled my veins. Every footstep was loud as I sprinted deeper into the forest. My feet stung as they trod on sticks and nuts. I held my bound hands in front of me to stop branches from whipping my face. My heart pumped so hard I thought it might explode. Each wheezing breath of frigid air became more painful than the last.

Don't think about how much it hurts. Move!

A dog barked. *No!* I needed to run faster, but I was still woozy from the sedative. My feet kept slipping on the bed of moist leaves that covered the steep descent.

Footsteps thumped behind me and branches snapped. Birds squawked and took flight when my enraged kidnapper's curses echoed through the forest. He and the dog were closing in fast. I had to keep going, but my lungs burned and my legs were heavy and clumsy.

I tripped, hit the ground hard, and rolled before stopping at the base of a large tree. Winded and gasping for air, I curled onto my side. A searing pain stabbed at my ankle. I spat out dirt and felt something warm and sticky trickle over my brow.

The hound came into view first, followed by the man who slid to a halt before me.

My eyes traveled up and connected with an icy stare. He was tall and built like an NFL linebacker. The cool, damp ground sent a shiver through my bones, or perhaps it was from his shadow looming over me.

"Shit," he grumbled, not bothering to hide his annoyance.

I sat up and tried to stand, but fire shot through my ankle. With a groan, I fell back.

I picked up a fist-sized rock, the only weapon within arm's reach, and aimed it at him. "Get away from me!" I shouted between gasping breaths.

He held his palms out. "Calm down."

The asshole had told me the same thing last night. I didn't buy it then, and I hadn't changed my mind. I pitched the rock at him with all my strength.

He dodged. The projectile missed his head but still hit his shoulder hard.

Rubbing the impact site and wearing a pissed-off frown, he took a step closer. "That damn well hurt. Are you done yet?"

I shimmied back until I was up against the tree. "Not even close."

He crouched so we were at eye level. It made him no less threatening. "I'm not gonna hurt you, but you need my help." His deep voice was gravelly, but calm. The good Samaritan talking a jumper down from the ledge. Except he was anything but that.

Starting at my ankle, his eyes traveled the length of my body, then lingered at my temple. "You've got a nasty cut. I can fix that for you back at the cabin."

I touched the tacky wetness at the side of my forehead, then glanced at my shaking crimson fingertips. Nausea rolled through me.

If I was going to get out of this alive, I needed to pull myself together.

I swallowed, despite the dryness in my mouth. "Listen, you don't have to do this. People will know I'm missing and the police will come looking for me. Let me go, and I promise I won't tell a soul what you've done. I'm not stupid. I know you'd be able to find me again."

"Not letting you go. It's too late for that."

My stomach hollowed out. Too late? What did that mean?

"Is this about my brother?"

He nodded.

What had Justin gotten us into? And how the hell could I get us out of it?

"How much does he owe? I'll pay it back."

"Don't want your money."

"What do you want, then? Why are you doing this?"

"To protect you."

Huh?

"From *what*?" I snapped, needing better answers than the vague ones he gave.

"From..." He hung his head for a moment before meeting my eyes again. "From serious trouble. Look, there's a lot we need to talk about. We should do that back at the cabin before you catch a chill in your..." He averted his gaze as he waved a hand in my direction. "Underwear."

I folded my arms across my chest where the thin tank top did little to conceal the effect of the cool, damp air.

"Are you going to kill me?" My voice quavered, betraying my attempt at bravado.

"No."

"Rape me?"

Hazel eyes flared. "Fuck, no! I'm not gonna hurt you, all right?"

"Then why the hell did you drug me, tie me up, and drag me to the middle of a goddamn forest?"

"Because you would never have come with me otherwise. And that zip tie was a precaution, which proved its worth." He aimed me with a pointed look as if I were a bratty child.

I gritted my teeth, resisting the urge to lash out and bitch slap this guy across the face.

"Cutting pliers are in the cabin if you want your hands free."

Asshole. I hated conceding to him on this, but for now, I was out of options.

Before I had a chance to argue about it, he scooped me up. I flinched at the sudden contact. His chest was a solid wall of muscle and his callused hand under my bare thigh felt far too intimate.

My dizzy head pounded. A cold sweat spread over my clammy skin, and my entire body trembled.

He carried me up the steep hill as if my weight was no burden. A gentle breeze sent scarlet and amber leaves twirling to the ground. Apart from the sound of his footsteps and birds twittering, there was complete silence. No traffic noise, no aircraft.

That wasn't comforting.

"Where are we?" I asked.

His eyes remained forward. A perpetual frown creased his brow. "Can't tell you."

"Why not?" My temper flared with each of his evasive answers.

"Because I don't like being found, that's why."

Did that mean the cabin was his home? Not some temporary hideout? I wasn't sure if that was good or not.

Probably bad.

Everything was fucking bad.

Harsh eyes came to mine. "And the next time you think about leaving on foot, you might want to know you'll be walking for days to get anywhere. And that's if you don't get lost in the woods and die of hypothermia or dehydration."

Was he telling the truth, or hoping to scare me off another escape attempt? Either way, I wasn't walking or running anywhere on my ankle. At least not today. I hoped I'd stay alive long enough to try.

The cabin came into view as we emerged from the trees. His black pickup was parked out the front, the passenger door wide open and bing-bing-binging in protest. My captor used his foot to slam it shut on our way past.

He carried me up the creaking stairs and through the front door. Once the dog followed us in, he kicked the solid door shut, the hinges rattling with the force.

He lowered me onto a brown leather sofa. "Stay put." His footsteps on the timber floor echoed as he moved through the cabin.

Relieved to be away from his touch, I worked on slowing my breathing.

The hound jumped on the sofa next to me and I startled. He was some kind of hunting dog. A pointer perhaps. I sat still while he sniffed me from head to knee before flopping down and resting his chin on my lap. His stumpy tail wagged while big golden-brown eyes blinked up at me. He looked friendly enough, so I gave his floppy ears a rub even though it was awkward with my bound wrists.

The dog seemed okay with having a strange lady in his home. For all I knew, this was a regular thing and the previous visitors were buried under the house.

The big guy returned, tossing a blanket on the arm of the sofa and snorting when he noticed his pointer snuggled against my side.

"Ranger, get down."

The dog didn't budge, so his owner coaxed him to the floor by his worn leather collar. I wished he hadn't. Having the hound next to me had eased my anxiety, if only a little.

The man pulled a pair of cutters from his back pocket. I held my breath as he took my wrists in one hand and snipped the zip tie. Some idiotic part of my brain wanted to say thank you, but I'd be damned if I was going to show him any appreciation.

I draped the blanket around my shoulders and took a moment to pay attention to my kidnapper's features. Maybe I'd get the chance to describe him to a sketch artist if I ever made it out of here.

He had straight, light brown hair overdue for a trim based on what hung out the back of his ball cap. Frown lines were etched into his strong forehead. No surprise there. I doubted he ever smiled. His brows were slightly arched above hazel eyes, which were more olive green than brown. He had a well-proportioned nose, although it was a little bent out of shape. And the few days' growth on his jaw was a lighter shade than the hair on his head.

Fine, he wasn't hideous. I'm sure there were girls out there who were into the hulking, badass sort. He'd be much better looking if he hadn't drugged me and taken me against my will.

He caught me analyzing his face, so I shot him my filthiest stink eye.

Matching my menacing stare, he tossed his cap on the coffee table before moving to light the fireplace.

I took in my surroundings. This place was more than a hunting cabin. It was a home. Not grand like the impressive mountain abodes I'd seen on TV, but quaint and well cared for all the same. A well-stocked bookshelf stood against the side wall, and deer antler hunting trophies were hung for decoration. It smelled of the last fire that warmed the house and the timber that lined the walls. The decor didn't scream *I'm a psychotic kidnapper*, but I hadn't checked for a basement yet.

The most eye-catching thing about the otherwise modest cabin was the view through the large front windows. Mountains and valleys spanned all the way to the horizon, both magnificent and terrifying.

Perhaps he was right. Escaping on foot might be a foolish thing to attempt, but he had a truck parked out front, and if I could get his keys I stood a chance of getting out of here. And the sooner the better.

With his back to me, he watched the flames flicker and grow while grasping the stone mantle. Powerful forearms bunched with the strength of his grip. He could probably strangle a bear with those huge hands. His chest expanded with each slow, deep breath he took.

Something troubled him. Did he feel guilty for what he'd done to me? Or for what he was about to do?

I'd rather not stick around to find out.

Scanning the room once more, I looked for anything I could use as a weapon. My search ended at the solid wood coffee table before me. It held a few hunting magazines and a small cactus in a white ceramic pot. While his gaze was still averted, I reached for the pot and held it on my lap hidden under the tented blanket.

He threw one more log on the crackling fire before coming to sit at the coffee table in front of me. Resting his elbows on his knees, he hung his head while twisting a braided leather band around his wrist as though he struggled to summon his next words.

I willed myself to be brave. There would only be one go at this, so it needed to be fast.

Drawing the pot above my head, I slammed it toward his skull. He grabbed my arm and diverted the blow. The pot crashed to the floor, shattering. Quick as an asp, he was on me. His solid body pressed me flat onto the sofa as he pinned my hands above my head.

He scowled with wild eyes. "That wasn't very nice."

I brought my knee up to slam it into his balls, but he shifted his weight to prevent the impact.

Loose hair hung over his brow when he shook his head. "Uh, uh."

Oh, God. Did I think he was terrifying before?

My chest heaved with the effort to buck him off. "Get off me!" I snarled and tried to wrestle my arms free.

His eyes focused on where he held my wrists. Just as quickly as he'd pounced on me, he released me and backed away a few steps. The action stunned me into silence. He raked a hand through his hair, then scrubbed it down his face. I remained frozen and wide-eyed on the sofa.

"I'm sorry. I shouldn't have done that. But can you stop attacking me?" He gestured to the mess on the floor. "And my stuff. I liked that plant."

Without taking my eyes from him, I sat up with caution and waited for some kind of punishment—a slap, or worse—but it didn't come. Maybe he'd meant it when he said he wouldn't hurt me. At least not right away. But that was no reason to drop my guard.

His hands moved to his hips as he considered me further. "Knew you'd be trouble."

I almost choked. Trouble? This guy had no idea what a pain in the ass I could be. "If you've had enough of my company, you can let me go anytime now."

"Already told you, that's not gonna happen."

"If I'm your prisoner, can you at least tell me what I'm doing here? Without all the cryptic bullshit this time."

He scratched the back of his neck and took longer than he should to respond. "I'll answer all your questions after I get you patched up. You look like crap."

I let the insult fly past.

"No. We talk now. And whatever this is about, stop pretending that I'm not in danger here." My eyes narrowed. "It's obvious what kind of man you are. I can see it in your eyes, and it's written all over you."

He was an apex predator. I knew where I sat in the food chain.

His face froze. Must've hit close to home.

"I never said you weren't in danger."

"Whatever my brother has done, it's got nothing to do with me. There's been a big misunderstanding. You need to let me go."

"There's been no misunderstanding, Cameron. You're exactly where you're supposed to be." He blinked a few times and his stern expression softened. His cheeks puffed with the long breath he exhaled. "Fine. I guess we have to get this talk over with at some point. Let me grab something first." He sidestepped the sofa and went to the kitchen.

I reached for the blanket and dragged it over my lap, clutching it tight. My ankle throbbed like crazy, so I rested it on the coffee table.

He returned with a gel ice pack and a bag of frozen peas. After placing the items on the table, he sat facing me again, close enough that his thigh brushed against my propped-up calf.

Nope. I clenched my knees together and pulled my foot from the table.

"Leave it there. Keep it elevated." He took hold of my leg with a surprising amount of care and repositioned it so my ankle was on top of his thigh. Wrapping the gel pack in a cloth, he rested it over the purple bruise that was forming. "That ice is gonna get annoying, but tolerate it for as long as you can."

I wasn't sure about the ice, but I didn't think I could tolerate my leg resting on his for very long. He appeared clueless to the fact. I adjusted my position on the sofa, wriggling back as far as I was able.

He pressed the bag of frozen peas to the side of his head. It took me a moment to recall how I'd thumped him with the wrench during our struggle last night. My lips twitched as he grimaced in pain, and when he caught my smug expression, he sneered.

Get used to it, asshole. I won't make this easy for you.

As though determined to prove himself tough as nails, he tossed the peas on the table. "There's no easy way to tell you this, so I'm gonna come straight out with it. The Wolf Street Mafia has put a hit out on you."

I stared at him unblinking. The notion of a hit on me was absurd. I'd understand if I was being held hostage to force Justin into compliance. I'd even understand someone wanting to murder my brother if he'd screwed up bad enough. But kill *me*? That didn't make sense.

"You think the Wolf Street Mafia, as in, the Italian Mob, wants me dead?" I asked, staring at him as if he'd told me aliens were about to invade earth.

"The upper ranks of the organization are Italian, but they

recruit far and wide nowadays. I guess you could say they've embraced diversity."

How very woke of them. But he'd neglected the important part of my question. The part about them wanting to *murder* me.

"This can't be possible." I shook my head. "It has to be a mistake. You've kidnapped the wrong McKenzie."

"No. The contract is for you, not your brother."

"How? Why?" A cool sweat broke out across my skin. God, this conversation felt like a fever dream I couldn't wake from.

"Your brother pissed off the wrong person, and now they want revenge. Franky was using the threat against you to flush your brother out. It didn't work. Unfortunately for you, Franky's a man of his word, so he wants the hit done."

"Wait. Franky who?"

"Franky Russo. You haven't heard of him?"

I shook my head. The name didn't sound familiar.

"You've probably seen him in the Palermo Pizza commercials. Few know this, but he's the boss of the Wolf Street crew."

I racked my brain and came up with an image of a late-fifties man wearing wire-framed glasses, a fake moustache, and a cheesy Italian-inspired costume. If it was the same guy, I recalled his friendly, polite manner as he promoted a chain of pizza restaurants.

A choked laugh escaped me. Inappropriate timing, perhaps, but this had to be some kind of messed-up joke. "Are you seriously trying to tell me that the cheerful guy who owns Palermo Pizza is the boss of the most powerful organized crime syndicate this city has ever known?"

"He wears that mask well. I know him to be very different from the man on the commercials. But yeah, they're one and the same. Franky hides in plain sight." He shrugged. "I'm sure that's hard for you to believe, but can you think of any good reason I would make shit like that up?"

I guessed not.

"I still don't understand. Did Justin rob one of his restaurants?"

"Your brother did much worse than that. He stole drugs and cash from him. The order to take you out has come right from the top."

While the serious expression remained on my kidnapper's face, my stomach cramped like I'd eaten something rotten. "You really aren't lying, are you?"

He gave a subtle shake of his head, his lips pressed into a straight line. It almost looked like he felt sorry for me, and that unnerved me most of all because it meant he was likely telling the truth.

Someone had paid to have me killed. My heart rate rose with my terror. "Isn't there another way to settle this? How much does Justin owe?"

The ice pack slid off my ankle, so he shifted it back, applying light pressure to hold it in place. The unwanted contact seemed like the least of my problems now. "More than you'd be able to pay back. But it's gone past that now. They gave your brother a chance to return the goods in exchange for your safety. He chose not to."

I rubbed my eyes so hard I saw stars. How was I going to handle all of this? I'd been kidnapped, the Mafia wanted me dead, my brother was more of a screw-up than I'd realized and neck deep in shit himself.

Too much. It was all too much.

I took in the mountain of a man sitting opposite me and had a terrible, sinking sensation inside. "Tell me the truth. Who are you and why am I here?"

Steely eyes held my stare. "Name's Shep, and I've accepted the contract to kill you."

4

SHEP

Cameron jolted back and tried to pull her leg from my thigh.

I gripped her calf to keep her in place. “Not so fast. Hear me out.” I held her gaze and spoke slowly. “Already told you, I’m not gonna kill you.”

She stared at me unblinking, those glistening green pools frozen with panic. One hand clenched her stomach while her face paled to an ashen gray.

Perhaps I could have been less direct, but she needed to understand the gravity of her situation. Of *our* situation. I didn’t want to sugarcoat it, and I hadn’t lied, but my brutal honesty might have pushed her bad day one step too far.

A small nod was the only sign she understood me. She drew in a shaky breath. “You’re… you’re a hitman?”

“Yes.”

“For the Mob?”

I shrugged. “I take on some of their contracts, but I’m a free agent.”

“Holy hell.” Filthy hands covered her dirt-streaked face, muffling her words. “I’ve been kidnapped by a murderer.”

I'd already run this conversation through my head, so I expected to hear the horror in her tone.

"What if you change your mind and decide to finish the job?"

"I'm sure my word means nothing to you, but you've already tried to shoot me and knock me unconscious. If I were going to kill you, don't you think I'd have done it by now?"

Cameron scoffed. "Is that supposed to make me feel better?"

"Take it however you want, it's the truth." I released her calf to fold my arms and braced myself for the interrogation I'd been dreading since I decided to bring her here.

She pulled her ankle from my thigh and tossed the gel pack on the coffee table. "Why kidnap me and drag me to your home?"

"It was the easiest way to get you here. And you need to lie low. This is a good place to do that."

Judging by the suspicion in her eyes, that answer didn't cut it.

"You could've taken me to a police station."

"Nope. Franky has a bunch of cops in his back pocket. Also, detectives, judges, you name it. How do you think he gets away with all the shit he does?"

Cameron clasped her hands in her lap as though she had some harsh news to deliver. I might have found that amusing if I didn't suspect she was about to bust my balls. This probably wasn't a good time to pluck the twig from her tangled mess of hair.

She held up a finger. "First of all, there's no way that breaking into my home, attacking me, drugging me, and tying me up in the back of your car was the easiest way to get me here."

"Perhaps that could have gone smoother. But you did try to shoot me."

"You deserved that, and I'm not done yet. Second" —she held up another finger— "if you're telling me the whole truth, and I'm willing to bet my left tit you're not, then I don't need to lie low here with you. There are people I trust who I can stay with. Your concern is noted, but I can handle things from here. I want to leave right now."

I shook my head. "Not changing my mind."

Her nostrils flared with each heaving breath. "This is bullshit!" She spat the words with enough venom to take down a horse. "You're not trying to help me. Why the hell are you keeping me prisoner?"

I stood, then paced the room. "I *am* trying to help you. I'm keeping you here for your own good, which apparently you have no regard for at all. When I say *lie low*, I don't mean hide out at a friend's house. I mean you need to stay off the grid. Franky has people with access to bank transactions, security cameras with facial recognition, cell tracking. It would be so easy for them to find you." I ceased my pacing. "And you're not a prisoner, dammit. I'm going to let you go once I get some things sorted out."

She sat upright. "You will? When?"

"Two weeks, give or take. But I'll do my best to make your stay as short as possible. Trust me, I'm not enjoying this little get together either."

Cameron slouched back onto the sofa. The look of confusion on her face was a welcome change from the fear that had been there moments before. "Then why are you helping me?"

"I told you. To keep you safe." I headed to the fireplace to add more timber.

"Yeah, you keep saying that. But you're a hitman. It's not like you're some moral pillar of society. Did you change your mind and decide killing is wrong?"

"Hardly."

"I don't get it then. What's in this for you? I don't have much money to pay for your help." She froze. "Wait, are you going to sell me? Is that what this is? You'll let me go, but only once I've been auctioned to the highest bidder?"

I spun to face her. "No! That's not what this is. I'm a hitman, not a goddamn sex trafficker."

"You murder people for a living. It's not a stretch to think you'd sell someone like cattle."

It didn't surprise me she thought I was a piece of shit, but her accusation got under my skin.

"I'll tell you what's in it for me. The risk of being on the FBI's most wanted list if they somehow find out who I am and what I've done, and facing the wrath of Franky Russo if he discovers I've screwed him over." I took measured steps toward her. "Bringing you here has complicated my life more than you'll ever know, and if there were any other way to keep your ungrateful ass alive, I'd have jumped all over it."

Her upturned eyes never left mine, even when I stopped right in front of her.

I continued. "I don't enjoy keeping company, especially the kind that tries to knock me unconscious and break my property. So, if you think I've got something to gain by having you here in my home, disrupting my life and wrecking my peace, you're seriously fucking mistaken."

Cameron blinked a bunch of times and opened her mouth like she might argue the point, but then thought better of it.

I hadn't meant to raise my voice, but I was exhausted from not having slept since the night before and the long days of stakeout. And she had a talent for pushing my buttons. Not that I could blame her. I deserved her suspicion, even if I was trying to do the right thing. In any case, Cameron reminded me how terrible I was with civilians and why it was better if I stayed away from them.

She plucked lint from the blanket. "Why didn't you do it then? The hit?"

"Do you deserve to have a contract on your head?"

Her eyes cut to mine, chin angled low. "No."

"Well then, I guess I'm not a complete asshole after all." I rubbed my brow and sighed. "When I was first offered your hit, I accepted it. I assumed you were a guy and deserved to be put down if you'd been mixing with Franky. When I found out you were a woman, I wondered if Franky had made a mistake. He'd never asked me to do that before. I questioned it and he told me there was no error, that you were innocent and if I didn't do the job, then he'd get someone else to do it."

Her grip tightened on the blanket.

"I don't want to freak you out any more than you already are, but the guy next in line is a sadistic bastard who would've enjoyed getting his hands on you."

I let that sink in.

Cameron looked up at me. "You could've turned it down and moved on with your life. Why go to so much effort to help someone you don't even know?"

As the silence stretched, I faced the window and pinched the bridge of my nose. "I guess it seemed like the right thing to do. If I stood by and did nothing, I'd be as evil as them."

I wished I had a better answer, for her and for myself, but I couldn't explain why I'd set these actions in motion.

Was I doing the right thing? I wanted to help her, but I could've hired a private security agency to handle it. Instead, I'd opted to make sure the job was done right by doing it myself. Would I have made the same decision if I weren't attracted to her? I didn't think so, and I sure as shit couldn't explain that to her without inviting more fury. And now that she was demanding answers, I wondered if I'd messed up bringing her here. It was too late to dwell on that.

Cameron sat in silence but appeared no happier about her presence here than when she first arrived.

I turned to face her, thankful that she'd run out of questions for now. "Let's get you cleaned up. Then we can cover up those cuts."

She nodded.

"Can you walk?" I offered her my hand.

She looked at it like it might burn her and instead used the sofa for leverage while clutching the blanket around her waist. "I'm fine."

I headed for the hallway leading to the back of the house. "Bathroom's this way."

Cameron hissed, and I turned to find her balancing on her good foot without letting go of the sofa.

I moved to her side and didn't give her the chance to refuse my help. "Here, lean on me." Grabbing her around the torso with one arm, I hoisted her clear off the floor and carried her down the hallway. Thankfully, she seemed too stunned to fight me over it.

I eased her onto a wooden chair in the corner of the bathroom.

"I could've made it here myself," she grumbled.

"A simple thank you would've done the trick." Didn't expect she'd utter those words anytime soon.

Her eyes darted from the timber-lined walls to the clawfoot bath and through the large clear window behind it. Curtains were unnecessary when you had mountain views and no neighbors.

I began filling the tub, then rummaged through the bathroom cabinet for supplies. Once I'd found what I needed, I laid out soap, a washcloth, and a clean towel at the small stool next to the bath.

Cameron folded her arms and glared at me as if I'd just kicked a dent in that shiny black Camaro of hers.

"What?" I asked, resting my hands on my hips and stifling a groan. "If you don't scrub that dirt off, your cuts will get infected, simple as that." I wasn't fooling around here. She was a scratched-up mess and needed to get clean.

She sat up straight and pushed her shoulders back. "I don't need to soak in a tub to clean my cuts. A damp cloth will be fine. I can wipe down at the sink."

I took a hand mirror from the cabinet drawer.

"Look at yourself. You're filthy from head to toe."

She recoiled at her reflection. Her fingertips lingered over her dirt-covered cheeks, then traveled down the grazes and filth on her neck. Fresh and dried blood clotted at her temple and in her matted hair. The rest of her wasn't much better.

She sighed. "Fine. I'll take a bath."

An uncomfortable tension filled the room while we waited for the water level to rise. After turning off the taps, we stared at each other in silence. I should give her privacy, but after all the shit she'd pulled, I wouldn't put it past her to smash the window and climb through the damn thing if I left her on her own.

Cameron scowled and pointed to the door. "You can go on and leave now. I've been bathing myself since I can remember. I don't need any help."

I folded my arms across my chest. "Can't do that. You're a flight risk."

"I can't walk. How the hell am I going to run out of here?"

"You might be faking how bad that ankle is. Can't blame me for not trusting you. You've been a goddamn handful from the get-go. Get in the bath, and I'll keep my back turned until you're decent again." I moved to the doorway and faced the hall.

"Promise you won't turn around?" Her nervous tone made my throat tighten. Troublesome as it was, I think I preferred the fearless woman she'd been earlier.

I shoved my hands in my pockets and focused on the floor. "Yes, I promise. Whatever you think I am, I'm not a rapist. So you can get on with it already."

Behind me, the chair scraped along the floor. A moment later the bathwater sloshed followed by a deep sigh. I tried to ignore it and the fact it made me want to go back on the pledge I made seconds ago.

"You okay in there?" I asked.

"I'm fine. Don't you dare turn around!" she snapped.

Raising my hands in the air, I maintained my eyes-ahead stance.

The silence in the cabin was something I appreciated, but for once I wished there were other noises to distract me from the sounds of Cameron bathing.

I tried, I really fucking tried not to think of her naked and wet in that tub, but I was only human.

And a complete asshole.

5

CAMERON

I scrubbed dirt from my body, eager to get this over as fast as possible.

Shep stood with his back to me, arms folded and his black T-shirt stretched tight across broad shoulders. He almost filled the entire doorframe.

Aside from my wounds stinging a little, the scorching water was pure bliss on my aches and pains. I could've enjoyed this if my captor wasn't standing five feet away, and if he hadn't unleashed hell on my world with the news that the Wolf Street Mob wanted me and my brother dead.

If Shep told the truth, and I was starting to believe him, I was lucky to be breathing. Even so, shacking up with a hitman was out of the question. He might play the good-guy card for now, but a person capable of committing murder for money had a moral compass broken beyond repair. He could change his mind at any minute and decide I wasn't worth the hassle of keeping alive. I needed to escape. It was my only option, and the only way I could help my brother, too.

I submerged my hair and washed it while being careful with the cut at my temple.

"Nearly done," I called out, in case he thought to take a peek and get an update.

Shep scratched the back of his head. "I'm not trying to be funny here, but do you need me to help you out of the tub?"

"You're right, that's not funny. And I'll be getting out of this bath on my own if it's the last thing I do." *Bad choice of words, Cameron.*

"Suit yourself, stubborn woman," he grumbled under his breath and stuffed his hands in his pockets.

It wasn't easy climbing out of the bath, but I pushed through the pain and dried myself as fast as possible. I wrapped the towel around my body.

"You decent?" he asked.

"Sort of. I don't have anything clean to change into."

Shep spun around. "Right. I guess you'll have to wear something of mine for now. It won't fit, but at least you'll be warm. Follow me." He took two steps, then turned back. "Let me help you."

"No!" I thrust my palm toward him. "Lead the way. I'm fine." My ankle still throbbed, but the soak had helped enough that I could put some weight on it.

Limping down the hallway, I followed him to a bedroom. *His* bedroom. I paused at the door, keeping one hand on the doorframe while the other gripped the towel, my only barrier between decency and nudity.

This room also didn't give away that the owner was a kidnapping murderer. It had chunky wooden furniture and a rustic iron frame bed with Ranger's dog mattress beside it. The drawn curtains revealed the workshop and forest beyond.

The space was warm, homey... surprising.

Shep opened the top drawer of the dresser and pulled out a pair of cotton boxer shorts. From the wardrobe, he removed a red plaid shirt from a hanger. He tossed them both on the bed.

"That'll have to do for now. I meant to grab some clothes

from your house before we left." He scratched the stubble on his cheek. "Guess I got distracted when things didn't go as planned."

I arched a brow. "No shit."

"I brought your running shoes, though. They were on your back deck." He hooked a thumb over his shoulder. "I'll get them from my truck later."

I jerked my chin. That was as much thanks as he'd get out of me, even though I recognized decent shoes would be important for an escape.

He moved to the doorframe and stood with his back to me. Quick learner. Still, I kept the towel around my torso while I slipped my arms through the shirt and buttoned it. It was so darn huge it almost reached my knees, and I had to roll each sleeve up several times. When I pressed my nose to my shoulder, I smelled smoke. Not tobacco, more like a campfire. There was something else there too, a woodsy scent of timber and fresh-cut grass. It reminded me of the one time Dad had taken us camping. A rare happy childhood memory.

I dropped the towel to get into the boxers and rolled the waistband over a few times so they'd stay up.

"I'm done. Can I use the bathroom?"

Shep nodded, but didn't follow, thank God.

Entering the small room, I understood why he was more relaxed about letting me pee on my own, and it had nothing to do with preserving my modesty. The only window in here was high and too narrow to climb through. I finished my business and headed back to the bedroom.

"Out here!" he called from the front of the house. I was surprised he'd given me some freedom.

Calmer now, I hobbled along the hallway and took stock of the situation. I was still alive. Bonus. I'd pitched a rock at him and tried to smash a potted plant over his head, and he hadn't hurt me. Big bonus. He'd been five feet away while I was naked and vulnerable, and he hadn't tried anything creepy. Extra big bonus. Now I needed to convince him to let me go.

In the living room, I sat on the sofa to rest my ankle, unsure what else to do. Shep added wood to the fire. I didn't miss the head-to-toe scan he gave me on his way to the kitchen. His eyes lingered long enough to make me wonder if I looked silly in his huge clothes, but if he thought so, he didn't mention it.

He returned with a small medical kit and sat on the coffee table facing me. Being this close to him was intimidating, yet he didn't seem to sense how nervous it made me. Sure, he'd done none of the horrible things I thought he might, so I wasn't terrified like earlier, just wary as hell.

He took out a bottle of disinfectant and applied it to sterile gauze before glancing at me with a furrowed brow. "You know what's coming now, right?"

I nodded and braced myself for the sting. He leaned forward to inspect the cut on my forehead before dabbing with the antiseptic. I winced at the initial shock. Shep paused.

"It's fine," I said, and only then did he carry on with his task.

With him way up in my personal space, my senses went on high alert. It accentuated every sound. The tick of the clock on the wall, the crackling fire, my ragged breath as I tried to remember how to draw air into my lungs. And while Shep tended my wounds, I couldn't help but notice how gentle his hands were.

"It won't need stitches, but I should cover it until the skin knits over a little."

I nodded, scared that any words might come out a jumbled mess. After our heated interactions, his newfound kindness puzzled me.

He applied a Band-Aid and set to work disinfecting the grazes on my arms and legs, moving with an efficiency that made me think he'd patched himself or others up many times before.

He held out his hand. "Let me see your ankle again."

I hesitated, then raised it toward the table, but he reached for it and placed it on his thigh like he had earlier. Shifting in the seat, my eyes followed where his long fingers skimmed over the swollen area.

I wasn't sure what murderers' hands should look like, but his were well-groomed with clean, short-trimmed nails, although there were a few scars along his knuckles. My skin tingled as his fingertips brushed across my injury, but not in a painful way.

"I won't mess with that until the swelling comes down. Not much I can do for it now anyway, but at least you're able to walk on it. That's a good sign."

His eyes met mine and my heart rate sped up from the intensity of his gaze. The silence lingered between us. A flicker of emotion passed over his face, but it was too fast for me to read.

He cleared his throat and eased my leg from his thigh to the table. "I'll leave your hands unbound for now, but any more tricks like the one you pulled earlier and I'll have you in cuffs, got it?"

Great, we were back to threats, which wasn't such a bad thing. That version of Shep was easier to accept.

I held his stare. "Got it. I won't do anything stupid." Like stab him with a kitchen knife, the fire poker, or a broken bottle. All right, perhaps I *was* still considering doing something stupid. What I wanted most were his car keys so I could book it out of here.

"Stay here and rest up. I have to get some things from the truck." He stood and headed for the door.

Ranger trotted to my side once his owner had left the room. He sniffed my clothes while I gave him a pat. When I tapped the seat next to me, he hopped up and spun in a circle before resting his head on my lap. I smiled. At least he liked me.

Shep returned with a cooler and several shopping bags. He frowned at Ranger before he kicked the door closed behind him.

"You hungry?" he asked, then started unpacking fresh fruit, vegetables, and meat into the fridge.

He'd thought to bring supplies. It unnerved me he'd put so much planning into my abduction.

I shook my head. "No."

Although I should be. The clock on the wall said it was almost 4:30 p.m., and I hadn't eaten since the night before. My stomach wasn't ready for food yet. It churned, but not from hunger.

I stroked Ranger while his owner worked in the kitchen. A short while later, he approached with a toasted sandwich on a plate.

I huffed. "I told you I wasn't hungry."

Shep's lips twitched. "What is this? A hunger strike?"

"No." I folded my arms across my chest. "I don't want any food."

He held the plate out to me. "You haven't had anything all day. You should eat."

"Are you always this pig-headed? Or are you turning the charm on for me?" I flashed him my most insincere smile and made no move to take the meal.

He sighed, then laid the dish on the coffee table. "Suit yourself, but this is all that's on offer today. I'm heading to bed soon. Haven't slept since the night before last."

Now that I took the time to pay attention, his fatigue was obvious. His eyes were bloodshot and his footsteps fell heavily on the wood floor. All of this had taken its toll on him, too. So, the beast was human after all.

If what he'd said was true, maybe I should try to eat. After all, I'd need energy to escape. I reached for the sandwich and took a bite of the tasty-looking Reuben. It was amazing.

Perhaps my stomach had been protesting in hunger because my appetite was back with a vengeance.

A chuckle came from the kitchen. I paused my chewing, turned, then glared at Shep's infuriating, smug face. My right hand itched to flip him the bird.

I finished everything on my plate and took it to the kitchen sink. He might be my kidnapper, but I didn't expect any person to wait on me. And besides, I had questions.

Shep sat on a stool at the breakfast bar, staring at the laptop before him. It looked like he was scrolling through a news website. His eyes flickered between my face and the screen when I leaned against the counter opposite him.

"You said earlier I'd be here for two weeks. Is there any way to make it shorter?"

He rested his hands on his solid thighs. "Perhaps, but I have to make some inquiries. Organizing a safe house doesn't happen overnight."

My brows shot up. "That's what you're doing for me?"

"Trying to with the limited resources I have nowadays. I'm calling in some favors from people I used to work with."

Shep's gaze went back to the screen, but I continued to stare at him in surprise. Either he was genuine about helping me, or his bluff was getting more elaborate by the minute. Somehow, I didn't think it was the latter. But there was one problem.

"The Mob's after my brother, too, right?"

"They're looking for him, yeah."

"I can't sit around here for weeks while they hunt him down. I need to get to him."

He leaned back and folded his arms across his burly chest. "Not gonna happen."

"You helped me because my life is in danger, right? Why won't you let me help him?"

He held my stare. "Big difference. You did nothing wrong, but your brother has earned his situation."

"A life is a life, Shep. His is worth as much as mine." Although debating this with a murderer seemed like a futile mission, it wouldn't stop me from trying to make him see it from my perspective.

"Not true." His index finger tapped the counter as he leaned forward. "If a child and a rapist were tied to railway tracks and you could only free one of them from an oncoming train, which would you choose?"

I scoffed. "That's not what this is."

"Isn't it? If you leave here to find your brother, you'd be risking your own life for the sake of his. I won't let that happen."

"Do you want to know what I think?" I stared him down. "I think it doesn't matter what I say. You won't listen. Refusing to let me leave isn't about you being concerned for my safety. It's because you enjoy calling the shots, and my brother isn't a part of this little *save the day* scenario you've got going on inside your head."

Shep's expression hardened. "You think I'm doing this for the glory?"

"Maybe." I shrugged and feigned nonchalance because that part of my comment was a low blow. Shep's intentions were unclear, but I didn't believe he chased recognition.

"And you think your brother is a good guy?"

"Obviously, he makes poor decisions. But yeah, he's a good person."

"Not from where I'm sitting. He could have saved you. He could have done the honorable thing and handed himself over to spare your life, yet he chose not to. Your own flesh and blood screwed you over and fed you to the dogs. What does that say about his character?"

Shep's words were like a kick from a horse. I remained silent. Weak excuses for Justin's actions sat on the tip of my tongue, but I didn't insult either of our intelligence by voicing them. Plus, my brother's betrayal hurt so much, my defense would come across as hollow.

None of that mattered. I knew what I needed to do.

"What Justin did changes nothing. He doesn't deserve to die, and I still want to help him. He's the only family I've got."

Intense hazel eyes met mine. "Franky asked me to kill you, Cameron. And I'm not blowing smoke up my own ass here when I tell you I'm really good at my job. It would've been easy, so easy, to get away with it. Use your energy to keep yourself alive. You might need it yet."

My gut lurched.

When Shep took in my wary expression, he lowered his chin. "I didn't mean from me, all right?"

I swallowed deeply. "It's hard not to think that."

He rubbed his eyes before slamming the laptop shut. "It's pointless doing this right now. I'm so damn tired I can't think straight, and everything I say is coming out wrong. We can talk more in the morning when both of our heads will be clearer." He stood but remained facing me. "I'm sorry if hearing the truth upset you. I'm just exhausted and pissed about a lot of things."

Not knowing what to say, I blinked and nodded, accepting his apology without words. I still had questions for him. So many questions. I wished we could sort this entire mess out here and now.

Shep headed for the back of the house. "Come on, I'll get you set up."

I limped after him and paused at the entrance to the bedroom.

"Bed's yours," he said in a gruff tone that made me think he was uncomfortable dealing with the sleeping arrangements.

"Where will you be?" I looked behind me and down the hallway, but I didn't spot another bedroom.

"On the floor." He glanced at an area between the bed and the door.

"No." I shook my head. "Not in here."

He flinched a little. "Yes, in here. This is *my* room."

"That won't work. You have the bed. I'll take the sofa." I moved to grab a pillow from the bed, but he blocked my way with his massive wall of a body.

"Didn't ask for your opinion on this," he said.

I didn't back away. "Yeah. I'm noticing a theme here because you haven't asked for my opinion on anything."

A muscle twitched near his eye while he stared me down. "You're on the bed. I'm on the floor. End of story."

I folded my arms. "This won't go well if you keep being an overbearing jerk."

Shep mimicked my pose. "Never expected it to."

We held a five-second glare-off before I stomp-limped around him on my way to the bathroom. "Fine. Whatever."

I slammed the door behind me. With palms pressed to my hot cheeks, I took several deep breaths to calm my anger.

The bed situation sucked, but I could do it. It wasn't like I had a choice. Hitman or not, if he tried any funny business during the night, I'd twist his balls off.

After snooping through the cabinet and finding nothing strange, I gargled mouthwash, then used the amenities. When I emerged, I went to the far side of the bed, yanked the covers back, and hopped in.

Shep stood near the doorway watching me, his jaw locked firm. He should have more wrinkles for someone who wore a perpetual frown.

Facing away from him, I flopped my head on the pillow and refused to acknowledge that it smelled kind of nice, soap and a hint of pine. I picked it up and flipped it over before resettling.

Shep's footsteps thudded as he left the room.

He returned a short time later making an ominous jangling sound. My eyes shot open.

Oh, hell no!

I sprang up and shimmied back as far as I could, bumping my shoulders against the metal frame of the headboard.

"No, no, wait!" I held up my hands. "You don't need those. I can't run!"

He carried a length of chain and handcuffs. "Maybe you can't run, but I wouldn't put it past you to slit my throat in my sleep and steal my truck." He raised one brow, challenging me to contradict him.

"Slit your throat? Trust the psychopath to think of that. Keep talking, you're giving me some stellar ideas."

Shep took steady steps toward me. "If you're not planning on escaping, you shouldn't have a problem wearing these. It's insurance for me. Nothing kinky." He lunged and slapped one cuff on my wrist faster than I imagined possible.

I pulled against it and grimaced when my efforts only caused me pain.

"Stop struggling and it won't hurt. I haven't put it on tight."

He was right, but it didn't mean I was comfortable being chained to the bed.

I swung at him with my free fist and kicked his chest with my one good foot. It was like kicking a brick wall. Fighting him might be pointless, but I couldn't stop. Those cuffs were freaking me out.

His face remained stoic as he grabbed my flailing arm and held it at my side before shifting his weight over my body, incapacitating me for the second time today. It should terrify me that a killer held me pinned. Instead I was furious. I bared my teeth at him and growled.

Shep weaved the chain through the headboard before securing the end to the spare cuff. He gave it a firm tug to check its hold.

He released my arms, and when I kicked him away, he retreated.

I shimmied up to sitting. "Asshole!" I growled, my chest heaving. "You can't say you're trying to help me while holding me captive like this."

"Just did." He turned and headed for the door.

That son of a bitch. I slammed my fists into the bed as blind fury raged inside me. If I were free right now, I'd kill him. Except I had a feeling it would be as difficult as taking down the Terminator.

I had to get the hell out of here and away from him. With an exasperated groan, I tossed my head onto the pillow and yanked the covers up.

Shep returned carrying a blanket and rolled-up mattress. He laid them out on the floor in front of the doorway, blocking the exit before taking a spare pillow from the bed.

I breathed a sigh of relief when he headed to the bathroom, closing the door behind him. Seconds later, pipes creaked and the shower started up. For the first time since he took me, I had a moment to myself. I almost wished I didn't, because there were so many distressing thoughts rushing through my mind.

I was beyond pissed with my brother, but worried sick. Was he safe? Had he somehow evaded the Mob's search efforts? What the hell had he been thinking stealing drugs and money from them, anyway? If the dumbass needed cash, he could have asked me. God knows I'd helped him out enough times before.

It wasn't only Justin's situation concerning me. Tom would've worried when I didn't show up for work this morning. When he couldn't reach me, he'd call my friends, hospitals, and eventually the police. The same ones Franky paid off. They'd be no help at all. And did I want anyone to find me? My safety relied on Franky believing I was dead, so returning home wasn't an option. What a nightmare.

In the bathroom, the shower switched off and a few minutes

later Shep opened the door wearing only a pair of boxers. My mouth turned parched in milliseconds.

Holy hell. I wished I'd been facing the other way, or had a chance to school my features because I wasn't prepared for this. Shep was seriously built, but not puffed up like a bodybuilder. His physique was all coiled strength and sheer power. Cords of muscle stood out along his huge shoulders, chest and arms, and a ripped six pack led down to the vee of his waist.

The bastard knew he'd rattled me because he didn't walk through the door. He just stood there staring at me while I stared at him. I couldn't look away. My disobedient eyes drank him in despite it being wholly inappropriate. A heated flush crept up my neck.

Shep didn't seem to seek admiration though, far from it. It was as though he wanted me to see the real him. A predator and a seasoned warrior, if the many scars on his golden skin were any indication.

A muscle in his jaw flexed as our eyes locked.

Knowing who he was, what he was, had me frozen in place. Before me stood a murderer who I was forced to share a room with while being chained to a bed.

Nope, won't be sleeping tonight.

"Get some rest, Cameron. Got a lot to discuss tomorrow."

His words sparked me to action. I rolled over fast and prayed we never spoke of this awkward moment ever again.

Shep closed the curtains, blocking out what small amount of light remained of the day, then slipped into his makeshift bed. Ranger curled up on his dog mattress on the floor next to me.

It didn't take long for Shep's breathing to fall into a steady rhythm. I opened one eye to watch him. He lay on his back with the blanket pulled up to his waist, one arm behind his head, the other resting on his belly.

There was a boyishness about him as he slumbered. All his

harsh features softened the moment sleep took hold. Or maybe it was the gentle light seeping through the windows that made him look more like a regular guy than a cold-blooded killer.

I hadn't given up on convincing Shep to let me go. To do that, I needed him calm, so tomorrow I'd try to be more patient and less bitchy. And if I couldn't make him see sense, I'd find another way to get the hell out of here.

6

CAMERON

I stretched my limbs and arched my spine. My eyes snapped open when my ankle protested the movement, and something jangled at my wrist. It took a moment to get my bearings and remember where I was, who I was with, and the sickening realization that I'd awakened to an actual nightmare.

At least it was warm under the covers. The soft glow of morning light shone around the edges of the curtains. Outside, dew dripped from the roof and birds twittered in the trees. I imagined people paid good money for a remote cabin experience like this, but it kind of lost its appeal when you were chained to a bed by a hitman.

Hoping to hide from my reality a little longer, I burrowed into the blankets and pulled them up to my chin.

A warm body shifted at my back. I tensed.

What the actual fuck?

Shep had sworn last night he wasn't a rapist, but now that I was restrained in the goddamned bed, his true nature had emerged.

I winced and held in a whimper. I didn't want to find out

what his plans were when he woke up pressed against me. When had he moved from the floor into the bed?

He adjusted his position and something firm poked my rear.

Shit. Shit!

He stilled again and began a light snore. It ramped up from there and I worried he'd wake himself with the racket.

I steeled myself, peeked over my shoulder, and found a wet, brown nose inches from my face. My head dropped to the pillow, and I muttered a string of expletives, clutching my pounding heart.

I rolled over to give Ranger's head a pat where it rested on the pillow next to mine. He stretched and let out an annoyed groan. A relieved laugh escaped me. I'd mistaken one of his long legs poking me from behind for a giant, man-sized morning boner.

I continued running my hands over Ranger's floppy ears. He was a beautiful dog. "Boy, you scared the crap out of me."

Shep interrupted by clearing his throat. He stood in the doorway, leaning against the frame with a steaming mug of something in his hand. How long had he been standing there? The chain clanged against the headboard as I sat up. I wondered what mood he was in this morning. Couldn't be any worse than yesterday.

He was already dressed in casual jeans, a white T-shirt that fit tightly across his broad chest, and an unbuttoned blue plaid shirt, much like the red one I still wore. The rolled-up sleeves revealed muscular forearms. I averted my gaze quickly.

Shep appeared unamused as he sipped from his cup. "I see you two are friends. Sharing the bed, no less. Ranger should sleep on the floor. I'll make sure he stays off in the future."

"I don't mind if he sleeps here." I loved dogs and had always wanted one of my own. Besides, having Ranger close by calmed me.

Shep grunted, then approached, placing his drink on the nightstand so he could unlock my cuffs.

"Come to the kitchen when you're ready," he said, before turning to leave the room.

So Shep wasn't a morning person. I suspected he wasn't a midday, afternoon, or evening person, either.

I limped to the bathroom, testing my ankle along the way. It felt stiff and sore, but not as bad as I thought it would be.

Checking my reflection in the mirror, I almost didn't recognize the woman staring back. My fingers traced over the scratches on my face and neck. Dark rings under my eyes made me look older than my twenty-seven years, and my hair resembled a bird's nest since I hadn't combed it after bathing.

A clean, folded towel sat on the counter, along with an unused toothbrush, tube of toothpaste, bar of soap, and a bottle of water. It almost looked like a welcome gift to the hitman hotel. Still, I appreciated the gesture.

I washed my face and patted it dry. After finger combing my hair, I tied it up in a high, messy bun. I brushed my teeth and checked my reflection again. Still no better.

Exhaling a deep breath, I hobbled out of the room to meet with the enemy. Ranger jumped off the bed and followed me to the kitchen.

The cabin had a different vibe in the morning. Natural light flooded through the large east-facing windows, adding warmth to the space. The view of untouched mountains stretched to the horizon, valleys and peaks as far as the eye could see, and yet I couldn't spot a single man-made structure anywhere. Vivid splashes of crimson, auburn, and gold created a scene straight out of a travel brochure. But despite the incredible beauty, the extreme isolation made me uneasy.

The scent of coffee and bacon drew my gaze to the kitchen. Sir-Grumps-a-Lot leaned over a skillet, spatula in hand and a dish cloth slung over a shoulder. I did a slow blink, confused by this image of a domesticated contract killer. I hadn't pegged him as a guy who could cook, but then again, you didn't get to be his size and condition by eating garbage.

"Coffee's over there." Without taking his eyes from the stove, Shep pointed the spatula at the French press on the counter behind him.

I poured myself a cup of the heavenly smelling brew, then sat at a stool by the breakfast bar.

Bacon sizzled in the frying pan while Shep tended a pot of scrambled eggs and lowered bread into the toaster. Here was a guy who could multitask.

I sipped my coffee and a moan of pleasure escaped my lips. Only then did he glance over his shoulder.

"Is it okay?" he asked.

I nodded. "It's good."

"Spent a lot of years drinking awful coffee, or none sometimes. Only quality beans for me now."

We had that in common, if nothing else.

Shep placed a plate of food before me and another on the opposite side of the counter for himself. He remained standing to eat.

I picked up the fork and paused. "Thank you. This looks... delicious." And it did, but I hoped showing some gratitude might ease the tension between us. He seemed more relaxed than he had earlier, so perhaps he wanted to turn over a new leaf today, too.

"No problem. Figured you'd be hungry after, well, after everything yesterday." He bit into a slice of buttered toast.

I gave him a tight-lipped smile, remembering that I was trying to be nice, then sampled the eggs. Not bad.

We ate in silence while a thousand questions whirred through my brain. I dreaded asking Shep any of them, but this wasn't the time to wuss out.

I swallowed a mouthful of bacon and cleared my throat. "So, what happens now? With me, I mean."

"You stay here and lie low while I get things organized." He shoveled a forkful of eggs into his mouth.

I shifted on the stool. "Yeah, you told me that much last night. What things do you need to organize?"

"Well, I already mentioned the safe house. Plus, you'll need a new identity. I know a guy who does skilled work with document forgery. We need a passport and birth certificate as a minimum. I'll get you set up with an overseas bank account and plane tickets—"

"Whoa, wait up." I held out a palm. "Plane tickets? Passport? Surely you don't mean for me to leave the country?"

Shep paused with his fork halfway to his mouth and stared at me as if *I* were the crazy one. "Yeah, I do."

"That sounds kind of extreme, don't you think?"

He shrugged and continued eating. "Not if you know Franky. The *real* Franky. Not the schmuck from the commercials."

"I appreciate what you're trying to do, but I have an aunt in Illinois I can stay with. I'll lie low there until this blows over." I stabbed a piece of bacon on my fork and popped it into my mouth.

"No, you need to leave the country." He licked his fingers before taking a sip of coffee.

I chewed on my food and tried to remain calm while I pondered his request. I didn't want to argue with him again, but there must be some compromise to be had. "Mexico, then. I have a friend in San Carlos. I trust her. She—"

"It's not far enough away," he interrupted, then tossed a corner of toast to Ranger. "And you can't trust anyone anymore."

My fork clanged as I dropped it on the plate. "With all due respect, you're being ridiculous. This is my life we're discussing.

You can give your opinion on where I go, but the decision is mine to make."

Shep dusted toast crumbs from his hands, then braced them against the edge of the counter. "Listen, Franky needs to believe you're dead. The whole of America needs to presume the same. Your disappearance won't go unnoticed, Cameron. Soon enough, your face will be front and center of every news website in the country, so it won't take long for someone to recognize you if you show up in another state. And if one American tourist spots you in Mexico, it's game over." He raised one shoulder. "And I'd rather you go somewhere safe. It's not much good me saving you from the Mob only for you to be murdered in Tijuana by a cartel thug."

His concern for my wellbeing beyond this Mafia fiasco surprised me. My brow knitted. "You really think the Mob would cross state and international borders to finish me off? For revenge?"

"If Franky figures out you're alive, he'll stop at nothing to bring you down. His power is growing. He has links across the country. I've seen him crossed before, and I have never known someone as vengeful as that son-of-a-bitch."

"Tell me more about him."

"Franky?"

"Yeah." I shrugged. "I'm struggling to comprehend how the guy from the pizza commercials is some all-powerful crime boss I need to go on the run from." It was like trying to believe Betty White was an evil drug lord.

Shep sipped his coffee before answering. "Franky Russo was the youngest child in a large Italian family. They were poor, so he grew up tough. As a six-year-old, he witnessed the brutal murder of his father and eldest brother. Many years later, he avenged them. And ten years ago, his only son was gunned down by one of the rival families. His ruthlessness has always been legendary, but I reckon it was his son's death that shifted his brutality up a gear.

"Franky is hardworking, intelligent, and singularly focused on achieving his goals. He has the ability to wear any number of masks given the situation. He's a legitimate business owner whose lucrative nationwide chain of restaurants donates unused food to homeless shelters. That same business is a front for his illegal operations. Money laundering, drug distribution, and human trafficking."

My eyes narrowed on Shep. "How do you know all this stuff?" The identities of the Wolf Street Mafia's upper tier had always remained secret.

"I have an associate who's an intelligence specialist. And I'm always of the mind to keep my friends close, and my enemies closer. So, I can assure you, it would be unwise to underestimate Franky Russo."

A shiver rippled through me. "Since he's definitely not my friend, what else should I know about him?"

Shep leaned his hip against the counter and topped up our coffees. "He's a billionaire, yet he lives in a modest home in an upper-middle-class suburb. He might invite his neighbors over for a civilized dinner and later the same evening broker a deal to send a shipment of meth to the west coast. One day he'll attend a fundraiser for the Helping Hand Youth Foundation he established, the next he'll make a call to import a bunch of illegals, forcing them to work in one of his drug labs.

"Above all else, he demands obedience and respect. And when he doesn't get it, the real Franky comes out to play. The one who trapped four snitches in a car and set it on fire, burning them alive. The one who caught a drug mule sampling the product and forced him to overdose. The one who buried an undercover cop neck deep in a field, slashed his face and waited for the coyotes to smell the blood. Trust me, you never want to meet *that* Franky. And if he finds out what I've done, that's exactly who'll come for us."

Shep's pointed stare did nothing to ease my anxiety. The room remained quiet while I thought on his words, the only sound the crackling of the fire. The food I'd eaten curdled in my gut. "So, you're serious about me moving to another county?"

Shep nodded.

I sipped coffee to relieve the dryness in my mouth. "Where, then?"

"Australia," he said, while scooping up the last of his eggs with a piece of toast. Good to know all this talk of torture and murder hadn't affected his appetite.

"Of course." A nervous laugh escaped me. "To the other side of the damn planet."

"The choices were limited. The guy creating your new identity only has stolen passports from Australia or Russia available at short notice. I picked the more sensible option on your behalf." He moved his empty plate to the side, then took a sip of coffee. "Believe me, I've considered every scenario, and this is the only one where you have a chance of being safe. And by safe, I mean still breathing. There are risks involved, but this is your best shot."

My shoulders slumped. Shep acted as if we were chatting about my weekend plans, not escaping the Mafia and starting a new life.

"That reminds me, I have to call it in." He walked to the dining room and pulled a cell from a backpack.

"Call what in?"

"I have to tell Franky you're dead. That the contract is complete." Shep thumbed the keys on the rudimentary cell and sent the message, then threw it into the glowing embers of the fire. The acrid stench of melting plastic stung my nose.

"Eat up, Cameron. Your food's going cold."

It wasn't the only thing turning icy. I tried to suppress the tremor that ran through my bones at the prospect of being dead to the world.

When Franky Russo read that text, he'd believe Shep had murdered me, and I was only safe for as long as that lie was maintained. Shep had freaked me out with his warnings about the Wolf Street boss. It blew my mind, but I was starting to believe his plans weren't so crazy.

What about Justin? How he'd outrun the Mob so far was a mystery to me, but it was only a matter of time before they tracked him down. I wanted to help him, but I had no idea where he was. Hell, I didn't even know where *I* was. Leaving to search for my brother was a fool's mission.

Was I really choosing to stay in this cabin with Shep and go along with his plans? Sharing space with the hitman filled me with unease. And moving to Australia? That was too much to consider.

My head ached thinking of the unknowns that lay ahead. There was only one certainty.

Life as I knew it was over.

7

SHEP

Thank fuck. We'd had a conversation without it turning into an argument. It hadn't been an easy one for Cameron, and now she looked miserable. It would take time for her to accept where her life was headed, but I needed her on board with this plan because it would never work if she wasn't.

While she picked at her breakfast, I fired up my laptop at the dining table. I emailed Greg Peterson, a retired CIA officer down in Florida who made a pretty penny creating forged documents for anyone who had enough funds to buy his services. Cameron wasn't wealthy, but Franky was about to hand over a large sum for her murder. Seemed appropriate he should pay for the things she'd need. Once I knew how long Greg would take, I could plan the rest of her relocation.

It hit me then. Two, maybe three weeks alone with her in my home. There were so many logical reasons I didn't like that, and one foolish reason I did.

Never thought I had a type, but apparently easy on the eyes and feisty did it for me. Too bad she thought I was an asshole, not that I could blame her. I'd be wise to ignore my attraction to her and stay focused on the job. I couldn't afford to make any mistakes.

At the breakfast bar, she stared at the cooling scraps on her plate while shifting them around with the fork. No surprises that our discussion had killed her appetite.

I closed my laptop. "It's a waiting game now. I expect we'll hear about your documents in the next few hours."

"Okay." Her eyes didn't leave the plate.

"I've got some jobs to do today. I'm not comfortable leaving you unsupervised yet, so you can either tag along or it's back on the chain for a while."

That got a reaction. The way she stared at me, open mouthed and wide eyed, anyone would think I'd asked her for a lap dance. I knew she hated the cuffs, but she was still flighty. And I didn't want her snooping through my things.

"I guess you've got some company then." Cameron flashed me a tight smile that didn't reach her eyes. I suspected the chain would've been the easier option, but not her preferred one.

My life was fast becoming more complicated than a thousand-piece jigsaw puzzle of a clear sky. I hadn't expected this to be easy. I was shit at dealing with civilians, mostly because I had no filter for what was the right or wrong thing to say to a normal person anymore. Negotiating with an Afghan tribal leader or cutting a deal with the Mob? I knew how to talk to those guys. But having her here was a constant reminder of why I didn't do relationships or have friends. Not that we were either of those things. This situation was doomed to be uncomfortable from the get-go. Still, I didn't regret my choice.

"Put these on. We're going out." I handed her the shoes I'd retrieved from the truck and one of my warm jackets. Fall mornings were cool this high in the mountains.

Cameron slipped the runners on, wincing when she had to use her injured ankle to push her foot inside. She wrapped my jacket around her shoulders before following me outside to the large deck.

"Wow." She stopped near the railing and scanned the endless mountain scene before her.

There were no words to describe how amazing it was here. It was the most peaceful place I'd found on this planet. I drew in a lungful of crisp air and took a moment to appreciate the view myself. I couldn't say how many hours I'd stared over these peaks trying to put my life into perspective. Sometimes flashbacks and vivid memories from deployments became too much, but being out here made it better, tolerable.

The sun, now well above the horizon, sat alone in a cloudless sky. A light breeze blew cool air against our faces.

Cameron turned to me as awestruck as I was the first time I came here several years ago. "We're in the Appalachians, right? Which mountain are we on?"

"Yeah, that's the Appalachians, but I won't be more specific than that. Not a soul knows how to find me here and I wanna keep it that way. Sorry." I shoved my hands in my pockets.

"So, what is it you need to get done today?" she asked, filling the awkward silence between us.

"Gonna collect some firewood. I like to have a decent stockpile before the first snows arrive. It's a bitch of a job in winter, and I've heard reports we're expecting an early one this year." I didn't mention that the thought of spending the entire day stuck inside the house with her had me uptight. A dose of the outdoors and keeping busy was exactly what I needed. Might be good for her, too.

She followed me down the steps and to the workshop. The large barn doors groaned as I swung them open. On one side was my pickup and on the other were my tools, woodworking bench, quad bike, and trailer. Cameron watched as I loaded the chainsaw, added fuel to the bike, and hitched the trailer onto the quad.

Ranger joined us. He ran around with his stumpy tail wagging and nose already scenting for prey. I didn't have the heart to tell him we weren't hunting today.

I collected a rifle from the gun cabinet and secured it to the front rack of the quad.

"What's that for?" Cameron's gaze remained fixed on the weapon.

I popped a box of rounds into my jacket pocket. "Most likely nothing, but there's always the chance of coming across a territorial black bear. I've heard the odd report of cougars in these parts, not that I've ever seen any. And I guess I never like to go anywhere unarmed. Old habits."

Her wary eyes met mine. When my targets looked at me with fear, it never bothered me. But when it came from her, it made my gut twist.

She thought I might take her out to the woods and finish her off? That wasn't the impression I hoped to make. I wanted her to trust me, but it would be difficult for her to see me as anything other than a contract killer.

"It's not for you, Cameron. I won't change my mind about the hit, I swear."

She rolled her lips together and nodded, appearing a little more convinced this time.

"Look, I can promise you the rifle won't leave the rack unless it's needed, but you can still stay home if you've changed your mind. I understand if you're not comfortable heading out with me."

"No, it's fine." She exhaled a breath. "I want to come along. I guess I freaked out when I saw the gun. They make me nervous. I didn't grow up around them."

"What about the shotgun you tried to blow me apart with?"

Cameron scrunched her nose. "It was Dad's. I only pulled it out of the closet that afternoon. I'd never used it before. Don't think Dad had either."

"Remind me to teach you how to use a firearm before you leave here. And how to maintain them so they don't misfire." I gave her a pointed look.

Her brow furrowed. "You'd do that for me?"

"Sure. I want you to be able to protect yourself."

She blinked a few times, and I thought perhaps some color had returned to her face. "That sounds good. Thank you."

"Let's go then." I put on my cap, hopped on the bike and started it up. I patted the seat behind me. "You need any help?"

She shook her head before climbing on a little awkwardly.

"Shouldn't we be wearing helmets? How fast will we be going?" She raised her voice so I could hear her over the rumble of the engine.

"Only slow with the trailer attached. But hold on."

I pulled Cameron's arms around my waist. I wasn't thinking. She could've used the rear rack for support. Still, she held on tighter than I expected. No complaints from me.

"First time on a bike?" I asked.

"Yeah. Is it that obvious you've got a virgin on the back?"

I knew what she meant, but I glanced over my shoulder and lifted a brow.

Her eyes flared and jaw gaped. "No, not like that. I meant an ATV virgin. As in, never been on a bike before."

I couldn't hold back my grin when she shielded her eyes with one hand and said, "Oh my God. Can we get going, please?"

~

WE RODE to a spot where a few trees had fallen last winter. During the ride, Cameron's grip relaxed a little, but she never let go. Ranger ran along behind us, keeping pace with ease.

I hopped off the bike first and was a little shocked when she allowed me to give her a hand to get down, even though her ankle seemed better than yesterday.

She sat at the base of a nearby tree and released her hair, which had mostly escaped its bun. Messed-up waves and flushed skin suited her.

"So, you're a hitman and a hillbilly?" she said, splitting a blade of grass.

I almost tripped when I saw humor in her eyes. Perhaps the ride out here and the freedom of the outdoors had relaxed her.

Flashing her a wry smile, I unloaded the chainsaw. "Always thought I was more of a mountain man. And you wanna be careful who you go calling hillbilly around these parts. The locals don't take too kindly to it."

I inspected a fallen tree, deciding the red oak would be perfect for my needs since it had few knots and was dry.

"Did you grow up here?" Cameron asked. "You seem right at home in the wilderness."

"I've lived in a lot of places. Dad was in the Army, so we moved a lot. But when I was a boy, every weekend he could, he'd take me hunting or fishing. Think it was the only time my old man was happy."

"So, you two are close?"

I shot her a sideways glance. Why all the personal questions? I guessed if this was what it took to make her more comfortable with me, then I'd answer them as best I could.

I adjusted the brim of my cap and turned to Cameron. "He's been dead for some years now."

Her eyes whipped to mine. "I'm sorry."

I waved away her sympathy. "Even though we spent a lot of time together, I wouldn't say we were close. My old man was a hard bastard. I think he tried his best to raise me on his own, but home wasn't a loving environment. And look how I turned out. I'm sure there are plenty of shrinks who would love to analyze my upbringing, figure out how I got so screwed up."

I got down to work, hoping to avoid more questions. The air had lost its chill, so I removed my jacket and flannel shirt before starting up the chainsaw. I cut the tree trunk into foot-long sections, the tangy smell of sawn timber sharp in my nose. After each cut, I allowed myself a discreet glance at Cameron. Her eyes never left me as I worked.

I shut down the chainsaw and began loading the logs into the trailer. The hard work was still to come. I'd need to split and stack the timber when we got home, but I welcomed any task that would distract me from my house guest.

Cameron stood and limped toward the bike. "It's peaceful out here, but so isolated. Don't you get lonely?" She wriggled up onto the seat sitting side-saddle, her long legs stretching out in the sun.

"Nope. Best thing about this place is that there isn't another soul around for miles. I'm not good with people, as you've probably figured out. And I've seen enough depraved human behavior to last me a lifetime. I'd rather not see any more than I have to."

Her eyes narrowed. "What happened to you? Why do you hate the world?"

I shook my head. "I don't hate the world, just the people living in it."

"Me included?" Fair question. I hadn't exactly rolled out the welcome mat for her.

After dumping another log in the trailer, I turned to face her. "I don't hate you, Cameron. I hate the situation you've been thrown into. I hate that there are people like Franky who think it's acceptable to snuff out the life of an innocent woman so they don't look weak."

"But you admit to killing people yourself. Aren't you as bad as the rest of them?"

I shrugged. "Suppose so."

Her brow pinched. "All the disappearances in Philly lately, the ones the police have no leads on. Was that you?"

"Most of them." I didn't watch her reaction. For some reason, seeing the disgust in her eyes bothered me.

Cameron remained silent while I continued with my work. Eventually, she drew her knees up to her chest and shivered as though caught by a sudden chill.

"Are they out here?" she asked.

"Who?"

"The ones you killed. Do you bury them out here in the woods? I'm sure no one would ever find them." She looked around the landscape like maybe she'd find it littered with earthy mounds.

"I'd never desecrate this place with the likes of them. Trust me, they get the burial they deserve." A watery grave far out at sea. Weighed down and providing a nice snack for the local marine life.

Cameron released her legs and folded her arms across her chest. "Is that how you justify it to yourself? That their crimes are so bad they should pay for it with their lives?"

She didn't seem the sort to stick up for criminals, but I figured she was thinking about her brother. I cast her a sideways glance and moved to collect more logs. "If you knew what they'd done, maybe you'd agree with me. I'm not saying I'm a good person, and I'm not condoning what I do, but don't fool yourself into thinking any of them were decent human beings."

"I remember there was some big-shot lawyer who disappeared last year. Did you murder him?"

"Yep." I picked a splinter out of my palm and kept working.

Her jaw dropped at my callous response. Not sure why. She knew what I was. Guessed she hadn't expected such brutal honesty, but I thought it was best to earn her trust by telling the truth. And those bodies would never be found, so I didn't think discussing it was a risk.

"White-collar crimes don't deserve a death sentence," she said, still looking shocked by my admission.

"Agreed. But what the media never reported was that he'd killed three prostitutes from Franky's stable. I'd bet my life there were others, too. The sick fucker needed to hurt them to get off." I caught the look of horror on her face and spared her the details. "Franky got tired of replacing his girls and ordered the hit. I slept fine afterward."

Cameron swallowed with difficulty, perhaps wondering if this line of questioning was worth pursuing.

"What about that old man from New Jersey? The one under witness protection? Sure, he'd done time for murder, but he was, like, eighty-five. Why did you kill him in such a brutal way?"

I shook my head. "That one wasn't mine. Remember how I told you Franky's father and brother were murdered when he was a kid?"

Cameron nodded.

"The guy who killed them was convicted and sent to prison, but he didn't serve much time because he ratted out a bunch of mobsters, then got himself into WITSEC. Even though Franky has cops in his back pocket, it was still hard to get sensitive intel like that. Took a long time, but when he found that address, he made it count. Got The Butcher to make the old man suffer before Franky finished him off. Mutilation isn't my style."

She adjusted her position on the seat of the bike and folded her arms around her belly. "Right, your MO is to make them disappear. Like that crooked accountant who went missing a few months back. That one was you, right?"

"Yeah, but I didn't kill him."

"No?"

"No doubt he's a low life, but I couldn't pin him to anything that deserved a bullet between the eyes. He'd been cooking the Mafia's books for a few years, and something spooked Franky.

He didn't trust the guy anymore. So, I paid the accountant a visit. Told him he had two options: pack a suitcase and get out of the country before midnight, or stick around and I'd finish the job. He guessed who I was and knew who sent me. He grabbed his passport and wallet and walked out the door. Didn't even bother packing a bag."

"So, Franky thinks you murdered the guy?"

"No. I told him a half truth. Said I went to do the job and he'd already gone. That he must've got wind of trouble and taken off."

She blinked fast. "Why didn't you give me that option?" There was confusion on her face and perhaps a touch of renewed fear.

I lifted my cap to wipe sweat from my brow. "Cameron, if I'd turned up on your doorstep and told you to leave the country or die, how would you have reacted?"

"Not so great. Probably would've slammed the door on your face and freaked out."

"And then what would you have done?" I hooked my thumbs into the waistband of my jeans.

She puffed out her cheeks and looked to the sky for her answer. "Even if the idea hadn't sounded batshit crazy, I wouldn't have left the country since I don't have a passport. And I guess I would've gone to the police for help."

"Yeah, the same ones Franky pays off. Might as well have walked yourself right into his office at the strip club. Which would've landed me in a world of shit, too." I picked up another large log and loaded it into the trailer.

Cameron's shoulders slumped and she rubbed her eyes. "Point made. Maybe I'm understanding why your methods were a little extreme."

"I thought about this a lot before I decided to betray Franky and bring you up here."

She remained silent while picking at the hem of her shirt. *My* shirt. It sure as hell looked better on her.

After a short while, her gaze returned to me. "You're a real contradiction, you know that?"

"How so?"

Those upturned pale green eyes bored into mine. I swore she could see right through me.

"I don't know if you're my knight in shining armor or the most frightening person I've ever met."

After dropping a few smaller logs in the trailer, I faced her. "I may have done terrible things, acts you would consider unforgivable. And there are people in this world I would show no mercy. But I promise you this, Cameron. You never have to fear me."

She held my stare and not for the first time today, I wondered what was going through her mind.

I smirked. "I'm not sure what kind of fairy tales you were told as a kid, but I must make a pretty fucked-up version of a knight in shining armor."

"Sometimes the person who's supposed to protect you is the one who hurts you, so perhaps the opposite can be true." She shrugged. "Maybe the bad guy can be the protector."

That she thought of me as her protector gave me a strange sense of pride. It shouldn't. I only did what any decent person would if they had my resources and skills.

She chewed on a fingernail. "It's Cam, by the way. My family calls me Cammy. People who don't know me call me Cameron. Everyone else calls me Cam."

"All right." I nodded. "Cam it is."

I guessed that meant I passed the interview. That made me happier than it should.

A few minutes went by in silence while I collected more timber.

"Shep?"

"Yeah?"

She looked up at me from under long lashes. "Will you tell me your real name?"

She already knew enough to report me to the authorities after I let her go, but I didn't think she would. Plus, I sensed this was important to her. A leap of faith and something that could strengthen our mutual trust.

"Elias Shepherd. Asshole extraordinaire, kidnapper, hitman, and fucked-up knight in shining armor at your service." I raised the brim of my cap and gave a nod in her direction.

Cam chuckled and shook her head.

I wasn't used to it, but I enjoyed making her smile. Perhaps it was because she'd been having a shitty time, or maybe it was because she looked even more beautiful when her eyes lit up. Either way, I wanted to see it more and be the one responsible for putting it there. I was a goddamn fool.

"Thank you, Elias," she said with a tilt of her head and a cheeky grin.

"My dad called me Elias. People who don't know me call me a bunch of different names. Everyone else calls me Shep."

She nodded once, a smile still on her face. "All right. Shep it is."

Something tightened in my chest while I loaded the last pieces of timber into the trailer and tied the chainsaw to the rear rack. Cam wiggled so she faced forward, straddling the seat of the bike as I moved to sit in front of her.

Her hands went around my waist without me forcing them there, so I took that as my cue to start the engine and head home.

We made a slow descent to the cabin. I told myself it was to make sure the logs didn't fall out of the trailer. The truth was that I wanted to have Cam like that for as long as possible—

holding on tight, thighs spread around me, and hitting every bump along the way.

8

CAMERON

The brisk mountain air swept tendrils of hair across my face, but I didn't dare let go of Shep's waist to brush them away. Having his solid warmth at my front, blocking most of the wind, made the bouncy ride more comfortable.

A patch of flame-red trees on the side of the mountain drew my eye. As did the golden leaves that flitted across the trail on a gust. I was grateful for the unhurried ride back to the cabin. It gave me the opportunity to appreciate the stunning scenery, which I'd been too anxious to take in earlier. And the long journey allowed me time to sort through the conflicting thoughts consuming my mind.

Somehow, I was no longer nervous or frightened in Shep's presence. I wasn't ready to drop my guard, but I believed his intentions for bringing me here were honorable. He'd gone against Franky's orders once before by letting that accountant live, so this wasn't the first time he'd allowed a target to go free when he thought the punishment didn't fit the crime.

At his core, Shep was decent. What had happened in his life to turn him into a reclusive hitman with a conscience?

Shep stopped the bike in an open field, but left the engine

running. He tapped my hand at his waist and pointed up the hill. "A buck. I've seen him here before."

I spotted the deer camouflaged between trees. A strong beast with large antlers and smooth gray-brown coat. He stood statue-still with his tail raised on alert, watching us as we watched him.

I braced my hands on my knees. "He's beautiful. How can you tell them apart?"

"Look close." He leaned low. "See that scar that runs along his neck? And part of his left ear is missing. He's been in a few brawls."

The deer bolted, his white tail flashing as he dashed further into the forest.

When Shep noticed my smile, he returned it. Little crinkles at the edge of his eyes and deeper lines bracketing his mouth transformed his serious face. Perhaps it was because we were outside in the sunshine, but his irises seemed to sparkle a lighter shade of hazel. I couldn't lie to myself. I liked Shep's smile. What I didn't like was the way it made my belly flip-flop.

Back at the cabin, we left the bike in the clearing between the house and workshop and went inside. The clock on the wall said it was early afternoon. I hadn't realized we'd been away for so long.

Shep passed me a bottle of water and took one for himself.

"You hungry?" he asked. "I'll make us lunch."

"Sounds good. Can we have Reubens again?" They'd always been my favorite.

"Sure."

After the fuss I made yesterday, I was glad he didn't rib me about my request.

I watched Shep prepare lunch. He moved about the kitchen on light feet, even whistling a short tune as he toasted the sandwiches. This was... unexpected.

He placed our meals on the counter with a smile. It struck

me that I'd seen that look on him a few times today, and yet, I imagined that was rare for someone like him.

I shook my head and chuckled. "Who are you, and what have you done with the broody hitman?"

"What can I say?" He shrugged. "Being in the mountains makes me happy."

We ate the same way we had this morning, with me seated at the breakfast bar and Shep standing opposite.

"While you're here, grab whatever you want from the fridge or pantry. Don't want you wasting away. Try not to think you're my prisoner, because that's not what you are. And let me know if there's anything you need to be more comfortable."

That might be the most words he'd said without me asking a question.

I lowered my sandwich to the plate. "Thanks. I know you're trying to do the right thing, and I appreciate it. You can call it what you want, but chaining me up and not letting me leave still makes me your prisoner. Having my freedom taken away is a major felony, you know that, right?" I stared him down.

He nodded and swallowed his food. "I'm no stranger to committing crimes. Except this is the first one I'm not ashamed of. I'll do what I have to, to see this through."

I sighed. By *see this through*, I gathered he meant getting my ass out of this mess alive. I was reluctant to admit it, but his commitment to that cause was fast dissolving the lingering anger I harbored.

"And what if I told you I agree to stay and won't leave until it's safe? Will you back off with the cuffs?"

He lowered his sandwich and finished chewing. "I thought you were hell-bent on running off to save your brother?"

"I still want to help him, but he's gone into hiding, and I don't know where he is. Unless..." My fingers strummed against the counter. "Maybe you could locate him?"

If Shep had connections able to create fake passports and

organize overseas safe houses, then perhaps he could help Justin too? It was asking a lot, but I wasn't above trying, even if I had to beg.

He grunted. "For what purpose? So you can escape and find him?"

"I wouldn't have to if you went to him instead."

He frowned.

"Please, hear me out. The Mafia is going to track him down and kill him." I found it difficult to talk around the lump in my throat. "Justin has made a lot of mistakes, but he wasn't always such a screw-up. When we were kids, he was a good brother to me. I'm the only one looking out for him, and he's the only family I have left. I have to do something." Unshed tears stung the back of my eyes.

"It could take days to bring him in. I won't leave you here on your own."

"We could go together."

He shook his head. "And risk you being identified to help the asshole that threw you under the bus? No. This is serious, Cam. If Franky finds you, he'll—" He stopped himself from finishing that thought but held my gaze. The fear in his eyes shook me. "Trust me, there are worse outcomes than death if Franky gets his hands on you. Especially for a woman."

His words sent a chill through me.

Yesterday I'd thought Shep was cold-hearted. Yet here he was, visibly alarmed with concern for my welfare. It surprised me he cared so much, but that sentiment didn't extend to Justin. Was there any hope for my brother? My throat closed over as the tears I'd been trying to hold in spilled down my cheeks. I turned around and swiped them away fast. I didn't want to look weak in front of Shep.

"Come on now. Don't cry," he said in a soothing tone. I heard him yank two tissues from a box before coming around to my side of the breakfast bar.

"Sorry." I took the tissues and blotted my face.

"You don't need to apologize for being upset. Franky hasn't found Justin yet. Maybe he was smart enough to get himself south of the border already. That'll improve his chances."

Shep had a point. Whatever Justin did to stay off Franky's radar had worked so far. I wanted him safe, but that also meant I might never see him again. It would be enough for me if he lived through this, even if it hurt to imagine a life without my brother.

When another tear escaped, Shep leaned in and wiped it away with a shaky thumb. I drew in a sharp breath and my eyes snapped to his. Being this close to him made me nervous, but not in a fearful way. Not anymore.

His brow creased. "I'm sorry, Cam. For your brother, for Franky, for having to turn your life upside down like this. I'm sorry for all of it."

I blinked several times, taken aback by Shep's honest apology. It disappointed me he wasn't willing to help Justin, but I wasn't angry with him. Not after everything he'd done for me. To ask for more was selfish, even if I had done it out of desperation.

I was awful to Shep when I first arrived because I'd been terrified, but now I regretted some of my actions and words. This man had saved my life while risking his own. His efforts to help me were staggering, and I couldn't think of anyone more dedicated or suited to the task. Shep was lethal. He knew the enemy, and he had the means to keep me safe. He was the perfect protector and had made my personal security his top priority.

I shook my head and gave him a wan smile. "You really are my fucked-up knight in shining armor." I reached for his hand, the one that had wiped away my tears moments ago. His skin was warm and comforting, even though I knew what those hands were capable of. "Thank you, Shep. I mean it. I owe you my life."

I wasn't sure how I mustered the courage to touch him, but it was important I conveyed my gratitude.

He nodded, averting his gaze to our joined hands as though the contact made him uneasy. It wasn't my intention to make the situation awkward, so I released my hold on him.

He cleared his throat before shoving both hands into his pockets. "So, I gotta split those logs now. Why don't you pick a book from the shelf and come sit out on the deck? Might do you good to get some fresh air."

I couldn't blame him for wanting to redirect our conversation. Weepy women made me uncomfortable, too.

"Okay, sure."

Shep did the dishes while I checked out the bookshelf. He had a few classics, but most were crime and thrillers. I settled on a worn paperback copy of *The Count of Monte Cristo* and held it up to show Shep. He gave me a nod before heading for the front door.

I followed him along the wrap-around deck to the side of the house where there was a single Adirondack chair. I sat, and Ranger stared at me like I was in his spot before he spun in a circle and laid on the floor.

Shep jogged down the stairs and retrieved an ax from the workshop. I watched as he placed a log on a large timber slab, then made quick work of splitting it into smaller pieces. He stacked them in a pile under the deck.

Although not overlooking the ranges, the view from this side of the cabin was still stunning. The fresh earthy scent of the woods was heaven to this city girl. Beyond the workshop, the tree line sloped down the mountain where the sound of flowing water caught my ear.

"There's a river down there? Why didn't I hear it yesterday?" I asked.

"Yeah. It's always louder this time of day when the breeze carries it. Good fishing spot."

I tried to read, but found myself distracted. It was hard to take my eyes off Shep and the way he wielded the ax with ease. The force behind each stroke made it look like he was slicing through honeycomb. I'd tried chopping wood once, so I knew it was difficult.

I gave up trying to take in the words on the page and settled on pretending. As Shep got through the logs, his brow glistened and his tee clung to his abs.

He put the ax down for a moment to remove his sweaty shirt.

Don't stare, don't stare, don't stare.

Why weren't my eyes listening to my brain? It might have something to do with how every muscle in Shep's arms and torso bunched with each powerful swing, or maybe it was the way his jeans hung tantalizingly low on his lean waist.

Ugh! What the hell is wrong with me?

Ogling Shep was all kinds of messed up, but you'd have to be a week-old corpse not to notice.

He glanced up, but I was quick to avert my gaze to the book. I needed to remember to flip a page once in a while.

Why were lines becoming blurred with Shep? Perhaps it was his assurances that his targets were awful people who deserved their fate. Perhaps it was the kindness he'd shown me today. Or perhaps it was that he had gone to extreme measures to save my life, because somehow, I was able to look beyond his checkered past and see a person who didn't horrify me. I was still cautious, but warming to him with each passing moment. And that scared the heck out of me.

When the last of the wood had been stacked, Shep walked up the stairs, the sound of his heavy boots thumping on each tread. He snatched his shirt from the railing and flung it over his shoulder before coming to stand next to my chair.

My skin prickled at his nearness. Oh, God, he smelled good, like leather and sawdust. The heat radiating from his body was overwhelming, and I stifled the urge to squirm in my seat. I kept my nose buried in the book because if I looked up now, he'd notice that his shirtless presence flustered me.

He panted. "Good book?"

I took my time answering and did so in a lazy tone, even though my heart hammered in my chest. "Mmm hmm. Riveting."

I turned a page and continued pretending to read. He stood so close I could reach over and poke him in his stupidly perfect abs. Damn him to hell.

"It's a good one," he said. "What part are you up to?"

Crap! I didn't realize there'd be a quiz.

"What part? Ahh... the part where they send him to prison." My voice picked up at the end making it sound like a question rather than the answer it should have been. *Idiot.* It was lucky I'd seen the movie in high school.

I checked to see if Shep had bought the fib and found him smirking. "Fast reader."

"I am, actually."

He headed for the front door with a boyish smile still on his face. I closed my lids and swore under my breath.

"It's getting cool out. I'm gonna head on in and wash up. You should come in, too."

If it was chilly, I couldn't tell. I used the book to fan my heated cheeks. "Okay." I followed him on unsteady legs that had nothing to do with my injury.

He held the door for me as I hobbled in with Ranger close behind.

"How's that ankle?" he asked.

"Still sore, but much better than last night." I moved to the sofa so I could sit with it elevated on the coffee table.

Shep loaded the fireplace with kindling, then lit it. "If you want to wash up before dinner, I could run a bath for you."

I shifted back in the seat. "Will I have privacy?"

His mouth tilted up into a half smile. "I reckon you could have some time to yourself. I might've been an asshole last night. Sorry."

"Then a bath sounds nice, thank you."

9

SHEP

While Cam soaked in the tub, I prepared dinner, a pasta sauce with beef, tomatoes, and mushrooms. I turned the heat down low, covered the pot, and ducked off for a quick shower.

When I returned to the kitchen, she still hadn't emerged. Was she upset about her brother? She might resent me for my stance on him, but I wasn't about to change my mind.

I knocked on the bathroom door. "Dinner will be ready in ten. You all right in there?"

"Yep. Be with you soon."

She sounded upbeat, which was a relief.

Water sloshed from within, so I figured she was getting out. Before I thought too long about what that might look like, I busied myself with finding her some clean clothes.

The day had gone better than expected. Cam didn't seem to hate me anymore, which was as much as I could ask for. Foolishly, I wanted more—a whole lot more.

My eyes were drawn to her far too often. The hint of toned thigh beneath the boxers, her slender neck as she sipped coffee, those feline eyes that somehow made me want to say yes to anything she asked. I needed to stop staring so much because I didn't want to freak her out. Besides, my priority was her safety, and I had to stay focused to do my job. Why did I have to keep reminding myself of that?

I grabbed her clothes, which I'd washed first thing this morning, and placed them on the bed. I added a clean pair of boxers and another of my shirts. Until now, I'd never understood why guys liked women to wear their clothes. It must be some Neanderthal marking bullshit, and apparently I was right into it.

Back in the kitchen, I boiled the pasta, threw together a green salad, and dug out a dusty bottle of red wine from the pantry. I finished setting everything out on the dining table as Cam emerged from the hallway.

A smile tugged at my lips. She'd found a leather belt to cinch around her waist, so my shirt looked like a dress on her. With bare feet and wet hair hanging over her shoulders, she looked... beautiful.

Two weeks and she'll be gone. Sort your goddamn head out, soldier.

She sniffed the air and followed her nose to the kitchen. "Mmm, smells delicious. What did you make?" At the stove, she peeked inside the bubbling saucepan.

I scratched the back of my head. "Nothing special. Just pasta and sauce."

"Looks great. I'm starving."

I served up two plates and took them to the table. Cam followed, her pace slowing as she approached her seat with a confused expression. And then I saw it. It looked like I'd set up a romantic dinner.

What was I thinking? The only things missing were candles, low lighting, and cringeworthy violin music.

"What's all this?" she asked, her gaze shifting between me and the table.

A nervous laugh escaped me. "This isn't what it looks like. It's only dinner. No big deal." I couldn't stop babbling like a goddamn teenager on a first date.

"Really? Because you've gone to some effort here." Delicate fingers thrummed against the back of the pine chair as she stared at the table.

What could I say? Part of me wanted to do something nice for Cam. Impress her, even. Only now did I realize how stupid that was.

Her eyes came to mine. "I thought... I thought maybe this was—"

"You can eat wherever you want." I interrupted. "I didn't mean to make you uncomfortable." The coward in me didn't want to hear her say that I'd gone too far and was a fool.

Her brow pinched. "Don't be silly. I'd be happy to share a meal. I was going to say, I thought maybe this was a pity dinner."

"A what?"

"You know, my life's a disaster. You feel bad about dragging me here like a caveman, so you've made a nice meal to cheer me up. Is that what this is?" She pulled out the chair and sat down.

"I guess. Sort of."

"Well, it's working." She smiled. "Hurry, sit. I want to eat." She rubbed her hands together as she eyed the steaming plate in front of her.

All right, a pity dinner. Let's call it that and move on.

I sat across from her and wiped my clammy hands on my jeans. I needed a drink. Cam had already started on her salad when I reached for the bottle of red. "I've had this for a while. I don't really drink wine, but it should be decent. It's Chianti from Italy." I showed her the fancy label. "You want some?"

With her mouth full, she covered her lips with one hand and nodded. "Mmm hmm."

I didn't own wine glasses, the unsophisticated animal that I was, so I opened the bottle and poured it into two whiskey tumblers.

She didn't mention anything about that as I passed her a glass. Instead, she sniffed the contents. "Was it a gift?"

"A gift?"

"Yeah. You said you don't drink wine, so I figured it must've been an unwanted Christmas present or something."

I chose not to tell her I couldn't remember the last time someone gave me a Christmas gift. How I acquired the wine wasn't any easier to talk about. "I sort of... found it while working. It's sat in the cupboard because I don't have people over much. Well, ever, if I'm being honest. Apart from Ranger, you're the only other person who's been up here."

Hearing his name, Ranger's head popped up over the back of the sofa.

Cam chuckled. "I like that you think of him as a person. There's so much intelligence in his eyes. He's special."

She didn't know the half of it. Some days, Ranger was the only thing connecting me to this world. He was my constant companion, hunting partner, and accidental therapy dog. His presence had pulled me back from some of my darkest moments. "Yeah, but don't let him hear you say that. He already thinks he runs the show."

Cam smirked, proving she was firmly on team Ranger. I wasn't sure what to think about how fast they'd taken to each other.

We both took a sip of wine, and Cam nodded her approval. She rolled her lips while considering the red, her brow knitted in concentration. "Shep?"

"Yeah?"

"I'm not drinking a dead man's wine, am I?"

I shrugged. "He didn't need it anymore."

Her eyes bugged out. "Oh God, you're serious." Her face

twisted as she placed the glass back on the table. "Please tell me he was a terrible person."

"One of the worst, believe me." I sipped my wine without an ounce of guilt over where it had come from. It was decent, too. Should've known a captain of the Mafia would drink quality red.

She smiled and shook her head. "You know, I can categorically say this is the weirdest date I've ever been on."

I nodded. Perhaps she didn't realize what she'd said, and I sure as hell wasn't about to call her out on it, but it couldn't be a good thing that it sent a small thrill through my blood.

We both dug into our food, and even though neither of us spoke for a time, the silence didn't feel awkward.

Today, I hadn't been short tempered like I often was around people. It surprised me, but I was comfortable around Cam. Even talking to her was easy. She intrigued me and I wanted to know more about her. Not technical details like I'd already gathered from my investigations, but personal things: what made her tick, what made her smile. We'd be spending a lot of time together, so it only made sense that I was curious. At least, that's what I told myself.

"So, an automotive mechanic is an interesting career choice for a woman."

Cam rolled her eyes, then pointed her fork at me. "Don't you start with that chauvinistic nonsense. I was just starting to like you."

Her last comment almost made me choke on my food. "I didn't mean it like that. It's awesome that you work on cars." I didn't mention I thought it was sexy as fuck. "What got you interested?"

"I've loved cars since I was a kid. Helen, the Camaro, she's mine now, but she used to be Dad's. He wasn't much of a parent, but he let me help polish her, change the oil, that sort of stuff." She smiled and our eyes met. "That's where my passion for classic cars started."

"You named the Camaro Helen?"

"Not me. Her original owner, before Dad got her. The guy obsessed over her. Story goes he named her Helen, as in 'Helen of Troy,' the most beautiful woman who ever lived." She arched a brow. "Odd name for a badass car, right? But it seemed wrong to change it. Dad won her playing cards. Must've been the only decent thing he got out of his gambling and get-rich-quick schemes." She twirled spaghetti on her fork and popped it in her mouth.

My eyes followed the tip of her tongue as it slid over her top lip.

"This is delicious," she said, scooping up more pasta. She'd almost cleared the plate.

"There's more if you want it."

"I'm good, but thanks. Who taught you how to cook?"

I finished chewing before answering. "Self-taught, I guess. Growing up with my dad, we ate simple meals. He wasn't much of a cook. When I got older, I taught myself how to make a few different things. And I've only ever lived on my own, so if I wanted to stay in good condition, it became important to look after myself. I'm thirty-six. There's only so long a guy can live off pizza and frozen meals."

"You've never lived with a woman?" Cam reached for her wine.

I shrugged. "It never fit into my life. And now, being tangled up with the Mob, it's too risky. If Franky has a vendetta, anyone close can become a target." I gestured to her. "Case in point."

Her head dipped in agreement before she stabbed at her salad.

"And when I was younger, I spent a lot of time deployed. My head was never in the right space for a relationship. I think women could read that and kept their distance. And let's not forget that I don't get along with... well, almost everyone. I may as well have a tattoo on my forehead that reads 'doesn't play well with others.' Guess I'm not considered very good boyfriend material. Can't understand why." I gave her a wry smile and sipped my wine.

She chewed on her lip. "Military, huh?"

"Fifteen years."

"Don't know why I didn't pick up on it earlier. What were you? A Marine or something?"

"Just an infantry grunt." I didn't want to lie to her, but I'd rather not talk about the places I'd been and the stuff I'd done. Plus, much of it remained classified.

She snorted. "I'm not sure I believe that. You seem more capable than a regular Army guy."

"You hang around long enough, you learn a few skills."

Cam sipped her wine. I don't think she bought my story, but she didn't question it any further.

"Well, maybe you don't have much experience with women, but I can honestly say that this" —she gestured to the table— "is the nicest thing any guy has done for me."

"Really? I don't know which of us is the sadder case. If this is the nicest thing a guy's done for you, what kind of assholes have you been dating?" The notion of past boyfriends who treated her like crap didn't sit well with me.

"It's true. I have terrible taste in men. Jerks every time." She sighed before straightening in her seat and flicking her hair over her shoulder. "Enough about my poor life choices. What made you join the Army?"

I pushed my empty plate to the side, then leaned back in my chair. "Dad was in the Army most of his life, and he raised me in a way that made me think it would be a decent path to follow. I was keen to get out of the house, so when I finished school, I enlisted the very next day. I wasn't interested in sitting behind a desk all my life. And being a teenager, I craved action and adventure. Seemed like a good move."

"Was it?"

"Yes and no. I was good at it. All those years hunting with Dad gave me decent natural instincts and good marksmanship. I had a level head on my shoulders and didn't scare easily, so ended up spending a lot of time in combat in some shitty places."

"Afghanistan?"

"Mostly, yeah."

Cam swished wine around her glass. "Sounds intense. Is that why you left?"

It was why I accepted my next military role, but I couldn't tell her about Team Zulu. Outside of the guys in that unit and the senior government officials who gave us our missions, not a soul knew what we'd been a part of.

"Yeah. It got harder to go back after each deployment. The things I saw were burned into my brain, and there was only so much I could handle before my head was fried. I sensed it was... changing me. At first, I had problems sleeping. I knew something was up when I'd be stateside and certain sounds would trigger me into automatic fight readiness. I couldn't switch off the hyper-vigilance of the combat zone. It wasn't normal. I'd seen a lot of guys discharged with severe PTSD, and I didn't want to end up there. All I wanted in life was a bit of land, some peace, quiet, solitude. So I quit. Spent some time living at my uncle's ranch, helping around the place, keeping to myself."

"How did you become a hitman, then? Sounds like you'd had enough of death."

"I had. I saw too many innocent people killed by invading forces, or even by their own. Sometimes we could help, but not often enough. And sometimes we weren't able to save them at all."

Cam sighed. "That's awful."

"Did what I had to." I shrugged. "Others had it plenty worse. At least I walked away with my life and all my limbs."

She adjusted her position in the chair. "What was it like being there?"

I groaned. "I don't like to talk about that stuff. And anyway, it'll only upset you."

"It might help me understand you better."

"Why would you want to do that?"

Her mouth hung open as though taken aback by my question. "I don't know. I guess you're not the person I thought you were when I first arrived. You must've been through a lot in your life to get to this point, and if we're going to be spending two weeks together, I'd like to learn more about what makes you... you."

I glanced at my wrist and realized I was spinning the worn leather braid. Could I tell her how I got it?

I stopped fidgeting. "I don't know, Cam. Are you sure?"

She nodded. "I'm sure."

"All right." I paused and considered my words. "There's this one day that plays over in my head. My team was deployed to the Kunduz Province in Afghanistan on what should've been a straightforward mission. They assigned us to protect a bunch of overseas doctors working at a local hospital. We'd escort them wherever they needed to go and also be on-site at the clinic to provide security. Easy work compared to being on the front line, but there were a lot of kidnappings and suicide bombings happening, so it was justified."

She remained silent, nodding from time to time and giving me her undivided attention.

My mind drifted back to that day. It was easy to do; those images were never far from my thoughts. The run-down hospital with its basic medical facilities, boarded-up windows, and exterior walls peppered with bullet holes. Hell, I could almost still taste the dust that was stirred up every time a vehicle passed.

"There were these orphan street kids always hanging around. A bunch of them would run up to us giggling, and then one would tie a leather band on our wrist before they'd all run off again in fits of laughter. They'd hold out their palms to see what we'd give them in exchange for their gift. We'd hand over chocolate bars and gum from our ration packs. I suppose we shouldn't have done that. Perhaps then they wouldn't have kept coming back. It became a bit of a game between us. Must have collected about twenty of the damn things myself. This is the last one they put on me." I held up my wrist to show Cam. I doubted the tattered leather would survive another year.

I was about to continue, but hesitated when Cam folded her arms around her belly.

"I'm fine," she said. "Please, keep going."

I nodded before downing the rest of my wine. "It's so stupid, some of the that've stuck in my head from that day. I'd been patrolling the perimeter with two guys. Sinclair was on his first deployment and nervous as hell. The poor son of a bitch checked his watch every few minutes as if he couldn't wait for the day to be done. Rodriguez and I had been teammates for years. He'd been telling me a story about how his brother's pit bull knocked up the neighbor's poodle. He laughed so hard the cigarette fell right out of his mouth." I smirked at the memory, but it dropped away because that had been the moment it all turned to hell.

"Then the rebels mortared the hospital. Did a lot of damage before I could even call in support. It was their own damn people in there. The old, the injured, women and kids. They did it because they didn't want the locals to be grateful for what the doctors and our military were doing." I released my grip on the glass before it shattered in my hand. All these years later, the anger I harbored for those cowards was still raw.

"We called in the Dust-off—the evac helicopters—and got the medical staff out. They were our mission's priority. But the bulk of the casualties were locals. There wasn't room to take anyone else, and it wasn't safe to send more of our doctors back in to help the ones left behind. It was our fault the place got bombed, and we couldn't even stick around to help. Just bailed on them like it wasn't our problem to deal with. It was a fucking mess. The things I saw as we left that hospital..." A painful knot formed in my throat. I stared at the table where my thumbnail pressed hard into the grain of the timber. "Those kids didn't make it."

"Shep, that's..." She shook her head. "I don't know what to say."

Maybe I shouldn't have told Cam that. Maybe it was too much.

I grabbed the bottle of wine, topped up her glass, and refilled my own. We both took a long drink.

"Killing a man who's aiming his AK-47 at me or my brothers was one thing, but seeing women and children injured and dying and not being able to do anything to help them? That shit stays with you. I never want to feel like that again."

She blinked fast and pushed her plate aside. "I'm so sorry you went through that. God, those poor people."

I hadn't meant to go into so much detail, but once I got started, it kept rolling out. There was something about Cam that made me drop my guard.

"We were supposed to be there to help, but sometimes we were making things worse. How can you beat an enemy that's willing to manipulate and sacrifice its own people to get what they want?"

She reached across the table and squeezed my hand. "It wasn't your fault. You know that, right? Their blood, it's not on you. It's on the psychos who bombed a hospital with innocent people inside. Your team and those doctors were doing something good in a place most would be too damn scared to walk into."

Perhaps she was only trying to lift my spirits by saying that, but I was too distracted by her hand on mine to care. Her skin was smooth and warm, and when I looked her in the eyes, she didn't glance away.

"Thank you for telling me. That can't have been easy." She removed her hand and leaned back in her chair.

I nodded. "Plenty more where that one came from, but you get the idea."

Before she could ask any more, I stood and went to the kitchen. There was a bottle of sixteen-year-old single malt I'd been saving. Now seemed like a good time to try it. I brought it back to the table with two glasses and sat across from her.

"I need something a little stronger than wine. How about you?"

She nodded.

"And don't worry. I purchased this bottle myself." Well, purchased with the funds from murdering assholes, but we didn't need to go into that.

I poured us each a dash. The smooth, strong amber liquid erupted in my mouth, the heat spreading down my throat.

Cam downed hers fast. She coughed and her eyes widened. One hand fanned her reddening face.

"Oh boy," she wheezed, her eyes red and watery. "It burns."

"Yeah, a little. Haven't you had whiskey before?"

"Only mixed with cola." More coughing. "Oh, wow. That's strong."

"You can leave it."

"No, I'm fine. I think I drank it too fast. On TV, they always throw it back in one shot. That's clearly the wrong way to do it." She laughed, finding the situation funny now the heat of the whiskey had lessened.

As easy as that, she made me smile. Those hard memories

from moments ago were pushed aside and replaced with something beautiful. Something worth saving. A surge of protectiveness rushed through me. I hadn't been able to help those people in the hospital, but I'd do everything I could to stop Franky from getting his hands on Cam.

She spun the tumbler on the table. "So, you still haven't told me how you became a hitman."

That part of my life was easier to discuss.

"I wanted a place of my own, but being in the military didn't pay well enough to afford the space and privacy I needed. A brother I served with who knew my situation approached me. He'd done some work for the Mob and they offered him the job, but didn't want it. He asked if I was interested. Turns out my particular skill set is well suited to contract killing. Wasn't long before I could afford this property."

Cam chuckled. "Crime pays then?"

"You have no idea."

"You've got the thing you wanted." She shrugged. "Why are you still a hitman?"

"It's complicated." I scratched the stubble on my jaw, not sure how much I should tell her.

"Go on."

"Years ago, when I enlisted, all I wanted was to make a difference, fight to protect our country and those unable to help themselves. I may not have achieved what I wanted to in the Army, but perhaps I can make a difference stateside, one asshole at a time."

She nodded, but whatever opinion she had on the matter she kept to herself. I never expected her to approve of what I did. Hell, even I didn't like this thing I'd become.

Cam's silence urged me to justify myself further. "And what else is someone like me good for? I've spent so many years in war zones I can't unlearn my reactions to certain sights and sounds. I'm not wired like a normal person anymore. The civilian world is difficult for me to tolerate. Only place I belong is up here on my own, where I can't freak out other people, and they can't bother me."

Her eyes shined with pity. I didn't want that.

She wriggled in her seat. "I'll admit you're not the emotionless murderer I assumed you were. But Shep, you can't play God. You shouldn't get to decide who lives and who dies in this world."

My eyes snapped to Cam's. "I did with you."

"And I'll be forever grateful. I mean that." A small smile formed on her lips. "You know, under that gruff exterior and moodiness, you're a sweet guy. You just have a unique way of showing it."

I swirled the whiskey in the tumbler. "Choosing not to kill someone isn't sweet."

"Maybe not. But you did a lot more than turn down my contract. I'd be dead right now if you hadn't stepped up." Her green eyes turned glassy. A heaviness pressed on my chest at her expression.

I nodded, but didn't take my gaze from hers. "Are you all right?"

"Yeah, I'm fine. I guess it's hard to contemplate how close I came." She braced her hands on the dining table and stood. "Thank you for dinner. Dishes are mine. It's the least I can do."

"Wait up, I'll help."

She managed a small smile. "Okay."

I helped her carry the plates to the kitchen and filled the sink with hot, soapy water. I washed and she dried. We worked in silence while she seemed deep in thought. I should say something to cheer her up, but I was useless at that sort of thing.

After packing the dishes away, Cam moved to the sofa to read while I fed Ranger. Jobs done, I returned to the dining table and opened my laptop. I searched through some news websites and found no mention of Cam's disappearance, but it was coming. It wouldn't take long for her boss or a neighbor to notice her missing, and since she wasn't a notorious scumbag, there'd be a big-scale manhunt starting soon. Pretty young woman disappears? That gets nationwide coverage.

I also wanted to know if there were any leads that might implicate me. It had been a clean job, but with so many people having security cameras out the front of businesses and homes these days, it was difficult to predict what blowback there might be. The excuse I'd given Franky for taking some time off, that I was staying out of town to lay low, was legit.

I pulled out the weapons case to give my Glock some love. It needed stripping down and cleaning, a task I always found therapeutic. Some people meditated to relax. I cleaned my guns. When I finished, I returned the case to the locked cabinet in the utility room.

Back in the living area, Cam had passed out on the sofa with the book laying open against her chest. Damn, she had the sexy girl-next-door thing going on. It wasn't only that. If she were a bitch, there was no way I'd be this taken by her.

Nope, apart from having poor taste in boyfriends and being too loyal to that jackass brother of hers, there wasn't much I could fault in her. I wished there were so I wouldn't be standing here staring at her like some creeper.

You're a grown-ass man. Act like one.

Instead of waking her, I scooped her up and headed toward the bedroom. She stirred and nestled her cheek against my chest. One hand grabbed a fistful of my shirt. I tried to ignore how much I liked that. The red wine and whiskey must have knocked her out good. If I was being honest, I was a little affected by the alcohol myself.

I laid Cam on the bed and pulled the covers up to her shoulders. She stirred again and rolled onto her side, dragging the blankets higher. I should put the cuffs on, but I didn't want to disturb her. And she seemed on board with the overall game plan, so she wasn't as much of a flight risk now. Besides, she'd still have to climb over Ranger and me to get out of here. Well, Ranger wouldn't wake up, but I was a light sleeper.

I used the bathroom and brushed my teeth. Ranger trotted into the room and hopped onto the bed next to Cam.

"Look after my girl." Lucky son of a bitch.

My girl. I had no right to call her that.

I turned the lights off before stripping down to my boxers and getting into my makeshift bed on the floor.

I punched the pillow a few times before folding it under my head and tried to think about anything but the gorgeous, totally off-limits woman curled up in my bed.

10

SHEP

I woke at dawn, and my first instinct was to check on Cam. She was still asleep, lips parted, hair fanned across the pillow, and an arm draped over Ranger's neck. In the last few days, I'd somehow become the third wheel in their relationship.

The cabin was chilly, so I snuck out to the living area to light the fire. When I returned to the bedroom, neither Cam nor Ranger had stirred, so I took a quick shower.

As I washed, my mind wandered to dinner last night. I hadn't expected Cam to want to get to know me. What surprised me more was that she hadn't withdrawn after I'd shared some harsh realities about my life.

Perhaps she had a fascination for broken people. Her relationship with her brother suggested that. If she thought she could fix me, she didn't realize how damaged I was.

I hung the towel on the drying rack and froze when I heard the front door slam.

What the fuck?

I tore out of the bathroom. My stomach lurched.

The bed was empty. *Goddammit!*

I bolted for the front of the house, feet thudding down the timber hallway and heart pounding in my chest. When I reached the living area, I came to a skidding halt. By some miracle, I didn't land on my bare ass.

Cam stood in the kitchen with her back to me, stretching to reach a large mixing bowl on the top shelf.

Relief washed through me and I almost dropped to my knees.

She turned at the commotion I'd made with my entrance. "Hey, good morn— Oh!" She covered her mouth with both hands as she took in my nakedness. She didn't shield her widened eyes, though, or avert her gaze. Nope. She stared right at my cock.

I snatched a cushion from the sofa and used it to cover myself.

Cam's face and neck turned bright red. Her hands moved to her cheeks as if they burned. Her eyes came to mine, a look of confusion on her face. "What the hell, Shep?"

"I heard the front door, and I thought... I thought that maybe you'd..." My throat dried up. I grimaced as I tried to swallow.

"You thought I'd run off?" she asked, appearing calmer since I'd covered up.

I dragged a hand through my wet hair. "Yeah."

Cam wouldn't get far on foot, but if she'd found where I hid my truck keys and left, I'd have been stuck here with no way to go after her. Being out there alone was a death sentence for her. It made me sick to consider it.

She's here, I told myself. *She's safe.*

"I woke up when you were in the shower. I thought I'd make us pancakes for breakfast. You've been doing so much for me I wanted to return the favor." Cam looked between me and the kitchen counter where the ingredients and a fry pan were laid out. "Ranger scratched at the door. You must have heard me letting him outside."

I nodded while my pulse steadied. "Sorry. I hope I didn't make you uncomfortable with" —I glanced at the pillow covering my junk— "that."

Her lips rolled before a small smile emerged on them. "I'm a grown woman, Shep. I've seen a naked man before. You surprised me is all."

She still hadn't averted her eyes. They moved from my calves to my thighs, then lingered on my abs and chest. She was giving me a decent eye-fuck. Did she like what she saw? Being a bastard, I decided to find out.

I made my way toward her slowly. As I drew nearer, she shuffled back, and when her ass bumped into the kitchen counter, her hands flew behind to steady herself. I didn't think it was possible, but her flush deepened. My eyes were drawn to her mouth when her tongue darted out to moisten her lips.

Oh, darlin', you shouldn't have done that.

If it weren't for the pillow covering me, she'd know the true nature of my thoughts. I moved with a speed that gave her the chance to tell me to stop, or even hold up a hand, but she didn't. Another two steps brought me way up in her personal space, right where I wanted to be. Her shallow breaths were warm against my chest. Long lashes fluttered as her chin tilted up, and those feline eyes remained glued to mine.

Still holding the cushion with one hand, I reached up with the other and retrieved the mixing bowl, placing it on the table next to her. "Pancakes would be great, thank you."

Cam's mouth opened and closed without making a sound. Instead, she nodded. Damn, she was cute when flustered.

I took a few retreating steps. She remained unmoving with her lips parted, her eyes flicking between my chest and smug face. I turned, threw the pillow back on the sofa, and headed for the hallway. She'd seen the front, so my rear shouldn't shock her.

As I reached the bedroom, I thought I heard Cam mutter something about my ass, or maybe she called me an ass. I couldn't be sure.

A smile tugged on my lips while I dressed, and the prospect of spending the day with Cam excited me.

When was the last time I'd felt like that?

11

CAMERON

The butterflies in my stomach had guzzled an energy drink. I was sure of it.

A choked laugh burst free. "That man has one fine ass."

Also noteworthy were Shep's abs, chest, and arms. And, of course, his cock. In my experience, most dicks were weird looking, and some were downright ugly. His was neither of those things. Far from it. With that unhelpful observation, I rubbed my eyes until I saw spots.

He'd been standing so close with only a small cushion concealing him. If I hadn't forced my hands to stay glued to the counter, they would have ended up on Shep. To push him away? I sure hoped so, because doing anything else was the very definition of stupid. But I'd wanted to.

My head was all over the place. Time to refocus. Shep had been doing everything for me since I'd arrived, and I needed to pull my weight. But it wasn't only out of obligation. I wanted to do something nice for him. He was breaking down my defenses, one sweet gesture at a time. So how could I repay the person responsible for the fact I was still breathing? By filling his belly with carb-loaded, syrupy goodness.

Could I even remember how to make pancake batter? My brain was as scrambled as yesterday's eggs. I threw all the ingredients into the bowl and mixed them around. There must be some clever tricks to make them taste amazing, but my mind drew a blank. Who needed an electric beater when you had trembling hands and a whisk?

I worked it out in the end. While cooking the second pancake, Shep returned wearing a snug-fitting black Henley and faded blue jeans. Damn, he looked almost as good with clothes as he did without. The shirt hugged his muscular torso in all the right places. The top two buttons were undone, exposing a hint of the smooth, sculpted chest underneath.

I poured him a coffee as he sat behind the breakfast bar and opened his laptop. We both liked our java the same way—strong and black—except he took no sugar and I loaded mine with two heaped teaspoons. I had to search deep in the pantry to find the container.

The rest of the cupboard's contents were boring as batshit. It couldn't be good for someone to be so healthy. And I wasn't sure what to think about how organized the space was. Tin cans stacked in a row. Pasta, rice, and cereals in labeled airtight containers. Perhaps it was his military experience showing through, or maybe he was raised that way.

I watched for his reaction as he took his first sip of the brew.

"Mmm, it's good. Thank you."

I smiled. "You're welcome."

Shep glanced up from his laptop, lifted a brow, then refocused on the screen. I was a little self-conscious wearing only his boxers and my white tank. I'd ditched the plaid shirt once the fire warmed the room. Still, he'd seen me wearing less when he first brought me here.

Shep looked up again, and this time stared right at my tits. Didn't even try to hold back his grin. What the hell?

"You got a little something on your... ahh." He pointed at my chest.

I glanced down. *Great.* There was pancake batter on my top, clinging to the underside of my breasts. It must have happened when I'd been working the lumps out of the mix.

"Dammit!" I wet the kitchen towel and used it to wipe at the sticky mess. That made him laugh, and I realized what I was doing. Giving my boobs a good rub down while wetting my white top.

I scowled at Shep, who tried in vain to straighten his face.

"Breakfast and a show. It's my lucky day." His laughter burst through and he gave up hiding his amusement.

"Jackass!" I stomped across the kitchen and slapped him on the arm with the spatula.

"Ouch!" He grabbed his bicep, feigning injury. "Geez, who says I'm the violent one around here?"

I covered my tits with one arm and pointed the spatula at him with the other. "You better not teach me how to use that pistol of yours, or you'll regret it."

"I don't doubt that." He shook his head while grinning.

It was the first time I'd seen him laugh with abandon. He looked ten years younger and like a weight had lifted from his shoulders. It made my chest tighten with affection for the big guy.

Flirting with Shep was intoxicating, but I needed to stop reacting to him. We were both feeding off this energy between us, and it was getting out of hand.

I went to the bedroom to change into a shirt of Shep's, then headed straight to the laundry room and rinsed my tank since it was one of the few things I had here that fit me.

Back in the kitchen, I loaded Shep's plate with two odd-shaped pancakes that I hoped tasted better than they looked. I set them down next to his laptop with maple syrup, butter, and cutlery. He was absorbed in what he read, and a serious expression lined his face.

"Everything okay?" I asked, resting my hip against the counter opposite him.

He brought one hand up to his chin, his index finger resting across his lips. "Sorry, Cam. It's official."

He spun his laptop so I could view the screen. Under a news headline was a photo of me leaning against my Camaro with arms crossed and a wide smile plastered across my face. It was one that Tom had taken at the garage. I remembered the day clearly. We were heading to a classic car show, and I had the black SS looking as good as it ever had. I struggled to reconcile the beaming girl in the photo with the banged-up mess I was now. My eyes flew over the words.

Grave Concerns for Missing Philadelphia Woman

Police are appealing for help to find Cameron McKenzie, 27, who was last seen by neighbors at her home in North Philadelphia two days ago. Police were alerted to her disappearance when she failed to arrive at work on Friday morning. Her friends and co-workers are concerned for her wellbeing, stating that it is out of character for her to disappear without contacting them. If you have any information regarding her whereabouts or have noticed any suspicious activity, please contact the PPD.

Seeing that report made it all so real, so final. This was my life now. Everyone I knew, everything I'd worked for, everything I owned. Gone. I had nothing. How would I get through this?

Light-headedness overcame me as blood rushed from my face. My vision narrowed, going gray and fuzzy around the edges. A cold sweat broke out over my skin. It was as if all the air had been sucked out of the room.

One knee buckled, and I braced my hands on the counter.

Shep was there in a flash, supporting me around my shoulders before my legs gave out completely.

"Whoa, easy. I've got you."

And then I was in his arms, being carried to the living room. Shep sat on the sofa, keeping me on his lap with my head resting on his chest. "Take deep breaths. Slow ones, all right?" His large hand smoothed over my hair. "Don't allow it to overwhelm you. The fear will eat you up if you let it. Try to get through this one step at a time." The low rumble of his voice helped to calm me, and I knew his words to be true.

Being held by Shep, surrounded by his reassuring warmth, was the one thing anchoring me to reality. If he wasn't consoling me, I was sure I'd float away into nothingness. After all, I'd already vanished from the only world I'd ever known.

"My team trained so hard that we ran on instinct. In combat, muscle memory kicked in and I didn't need to tell my body what to do because we'd practiced it so many times. Sometimes I had bullets flying past my ears and mortars going off around us. Crazy shit when I look back on it now. But I didn't stop to think how close we were to death, because if I did, that fear would consume me and get me or one of my brothers killed. We all knew that the moment you stopped and thought too hard about what was going on around you, that was the moment you were most likely to meet your maker. We did what we had to do, one step at a time, so we'd come out alive at the other end."

I was unsure if Shep meant to distract me with his words or pull me back into myself, but sitting with him, listening to his voice and the steady cadence of his heart beating against my cheek centered me. He might not have much experience with women, but he sure had solid skills for dealing with traumatic situations.

One of his callused hands moved to my arm where he rubbed away the goose bumps pebbling my skin.

He went on. "What I'm getting at is, you're a fighter, too. Maybe not a battle-hardened soldier, although I've seen plenty of them more intimidated by me than you were. But when you thought your life was on the line, you never backed down from me. You were ready to fight tooth and nail if it came to it. So I know you can do this. Work through each day, each hour if you need to, before you decide how to tackle the next one, and we'll get you through this together."

I squeezed my lids shut as tears spilled down my cheeks. Where would I be without Shep helping me?

As my breathing evened out, his words sank in. Everything I was mentally dealing with was too much to process in this moment. I'd put the whole damn elephant on my plate and left the knife and fork in the drawer.

"Shep?" I hated how defeated my voice sounded.

"Yeah?"

I sniffled as my breath hitched. "This sucks."

"I know, darlin'." He rested his stubbly chin on top of my head.

"I think I hate Franky Russo."

He took a moment before responding. "Me too." From the harsh edge in his voice, it seemed like he wanted to say more, but held it in.

I snuggled into his chest, soaking up the warmth and comfort of his scent. He tightened his hold around me as I clung to his shirt.

After perhaps ten minutes I had my shit together again, but was content to stay put. When had I become so comfortable with Shep's touch? His arms were my only safe haven in all of this.

God help me, I didn't want him to let go.

He continued running his palm over my hair. "I'm done working for that asshole."

I pulled back to take in his expression. He looked pissed,

although I knew it wasn't directed at me. "You mean, this'll be your last contract?"

"For Franky, yeah. Didn't say I was retiring."

My disappointment was hard to hide, but I wasn't here to convert Shep from hitman to saint. Still, I couldn't help thinking this job was exacerbating his problems. I suspected his time in the military had left him with some level of PTSD, so why would he continue to throw himself into situations that risked his life and ended with blood on his hands?

I sighed. "You know, there are other things you could do."

"Like what? A mall cop? Or even worse, a real cop? And work in that corrupt system?" He scoffed. "No thanks."

"I'm betting weapons aren't the only things your hands are skilled with. I saw all those woodworking tools in your shed. You any good with them?"

Shep shrugged. "Not bad, I suppose. They were my dad's. He taught me how to use them. Made that coffee table, the book shelf over there, and the bear lamp."

He was being modest. The solid pieces of furniture with wrought iron accents were beautiful. But my favorite was the table lamp, the stand being carved from a single piece of wood in the shape of a black bear climbing a tree. It was a work of art.

"Shep, they're amazing. People would pay a lot of money for those."

He laughed. "Sure, I'll open a store in town. Could you imagine me playing salesman? Or maybe customers could come here and annoy me." He shook his head. "That's not me, Cam. I hate dealing with people, and I'm crap at it."

"You're not with me."

He grunted. "You might be the one exception to that rule."

I smiled and worked hard to keep it small. I liked his words far too much.

My heart ached for Shep. He believed he had no options in this world other than being a paid killer. Perhaps it was all he'd ever known, but I wished for a different life for him. It was strange how protective I'd become of him, too.

My gaze raked over his rugged, yet handsome features. The crease between his brows, soulful hazel eyes, a strong stubble-coated jaw, and his lips, oh God, those lips. They didn't belong on a man so capable of killing. They looked soft and inviting and... and I shouldn't be thinking about what they'd feel like pressed against mine.

My gaze dropped to his chest where I fiddled with a button. I had the absurd urge to release it and trail my fingers over the smooth, tan skin of his chest. "I'm sorry about your breakfast. It'll be cold by now."

"Nonsense, it's fine."

Shep stood us both up and held onto my shoulders, testing my stability. Taking my face in both hands, he tilted my chin up so he could look into my eyes. One thumb made slow, gentle circles over my cheek while he assessed me. I suppressed the small shiver that went through me at his touch. Satisfied that I wasn't about to collapse on him again, he took my hand and led me back to the kitchen.

From the breakfast bar, I watched him cook up another batch of pancakes. He covered them with maple syrup, set the plate in front of me, and made sure I finished every piece. He even prepared a fresh brew of coffee while digging into his stone-cold meal. My heart squeezed at his kindness.

"What's on the agenda for today?" I asked, now recovered after filling my belly.

"Thought I'd check the fences. The deer make a mess of them sometimes. With this much land, there's always a section somewhere that needs repairing. You up to tagging along?"

Would Shep chain me up if I stayed? I didn't think so. That was irrelevant because I wanted to go with him.

"Sure."

I didn't mention that I was more comforted in his presence

than on my own, or that flirting with him provided a delicious distraction from the shitstorm that was my life.

I DRESSED in what had become my usual outfit here. One of Shep's long shirts and a pair of boxers. His leather belt snug around my waist finished the ensemble. It was comfy, even if it looked silly. I pulled on a warm jacket as we headed out the door.

In the workshop, Shep loaded the bike with the various tools he'd need to repair the fence and, of course, his rifle.

I walked a casual loop around the quad, inspecting it. "Are these things hard to ride?" I squatted to check out the engine and suspension. The mechanic in me was curious to pull it all apart and put it back together.

"Not at all. You want to give it a go?"

"Really?" My smile was genuine. I loved all things fast and loud, but had never handled a bike before. This could be fun.

"Hop on up front. You're driving today." He pulled a set of keys from the top drawer of his toolbox, put his cap on, and gestured for me to get on the quad bike first.

Did that high-pitched squeal come from me? I clapped my hands and climbed on. Then I fought the urge to squeal again, but for a very different reason. Shep got on behind me. And if his closeness was anything to go by, he'd be monitoring my every move.

At least I'd be warm with his solid chest flush against my back and his long arms encircling me while we both gripped the handlebars. I wiggled in my seat to create some space, but there was none to be found. Shep's body went taut behind me and a strained groan rumbled through him.

Okay, maybe try not to wiggle.

He cleared his throat. "So, you need to turn the key. See that green light?" He pointed to the dash. "That means we're in neutral. Flick this switch to 'On' and then press that red button with your thumb."

I did as he said and the engine roared to life. He lowered his lips to my ear so I could hear him above the noise. His breath was warm on my cheek, and when his stubble tickled my lobe, a small shiver rippled through me.

Shep explained how to accelerate, brake, and shift gears. It sounded straightforward, but I was still a tad nervous.

"Here goes." I pressed the thumb throttle, and the bike crept forward. I applied it a little harder to increase speed. Ranger bounded along next to us while keeping pace.

We meandered along trails, Shep showing which way to go, but I was too focused on the track to take in the surroundings. We found the fence line and followed it, looking for damage.

"There's a spot up ahead we need to stop at. I noticed it last time I was up here," he said.

I eased on the brakes, and the bike came to a stop. Shep showed me how to shut it down.

"That was awesome." I pressed my palms to my cool cheeks and tried to smooth down my windblown hair.

"You did great." He hopped off first, wearing a proud grin.

"You're an excellent teacher." I returned his smile. He held out his big hand to help me off, and I took it without hesitating.

It was so serene in the forest. The earthy, woodsy scent was calming and the crisp air awakened the senses. Sunshine filtered through the foliage and when a light wind blew, leaves of every autumn hue glided to the ground. The only sounds were birds calling and Shep's movements as he worked. I was more isolated than I'd ever been in my life, and I loved it.

Ranger barked in the distance. Shep didn't appear concerned, so I assumed this was normal behavior for the pointer. A rustle of the nearby undergrowth sounded his return.

"Shep!" I yelped and shimmied up onto the bike to put some space between me and Ranger.

"What is it?" He was on his way to me in an instant.

I pointed at his dog. "There's something in his mouth." Something small, fluffy, and no longer alive. Ranger sat in front of me like he was offering a sacrifice. He seemed pretty satisfied with his kill if the intense wagging of his tail was anything to go by.

"It's only a rabbit." Shep adjusted his ball cap before patting Ranger on the head. "Good boy."

I wriggled back further. "Erm, why is he still sitting there staring at me with a corpse in his mouth?"

Shep tried to hold back a smile. It wasn't working. "My guess? He's waiting for you to tell him he's a good boy, otherwise he's going to be heartbroken."

It was worth a try. "Oh, okay. Good boy, Ranger." My gut roiled at the floppy bundle cradled in his jowls. He dropped his gift at my feet and returned to the bushes.

I hoped he wasn't hunting for another one.

I WANDERED to where Shep worked. "Is there anything I can help with?" I'd never repaired a fence before, but I was good with tools.

I tried not to stare at his delicious biceps and corded forearms as he twisted thick wire around an upright timber log. "Can you grab the cutters?" He nodded toward the tool bag on the back of the quad bike.

"Sure."

I did like he asked, and as I returned, I couldn't help but appreciate how capable he was with his hands. He knew what he was doing out here. The country boy with a fetish for guns, and the most lethal human I could ever imagine. And yet to me he wasn't frightening or cruel. Serious, yes, but also charming, kind, and thoughtful.

I handed him the wire cutters and our fingers brushed with the exchange. The small contact sent a tingle across my skin, the sensation foreign but not unwelcome. His eyes shot to mine for the briefest of moments, and heat pooled at my core.

I needed to stop this foolishness right now. Becoming friends and flirting with Shep? That was trouble enough. But craving anything more was sheer stupidity.

Why did he have to be so damned caring and sweet? No. I wouldn't fall for him. My life was plenty wretched without having my heart broken when I had to leave the country.

He glanced at me after trimming the wire. "You all right? You look like you've seen a ghost."

"It's nothing." I shook my head and wiped sweaty palms down my shirt. "I guess I was worrying about Justin and thinking about the move to Australia."

And shouldn't I be doing that instead of lusting after Shep? What the hell was wrong with me?

"You wanna talk about it?" he asked.

I'd rather distract myself by watching him work, but there was something I'd been meaning to ask. "What's going to happen to my house? At some stage, the authorities will assume I'm dead, right?"

He laid his tools on the ground and made up the short distance between us. "Unless you own it, I guess the bank will keep taking mortgage repayments from your account until there's nothing left, then they'll repossess it."

I frowned. "What about my belongings?"

"Not sure. They might put them into storage for a while. Perhaps auction it and put the money away in case you turn up."

I pinched the bridge of my nose. "What a mess. Years of hard work down the drain. I'll have to start from scratch."

"At least you'll be alive. Hey, listen to me." My gaze snapped to Shep's when he rested his hands on my shoulders and lowered himself to my eye level. "You'll be okay, Cam. You're still young. And you're smart, a hard worker. One day you'll look back on this as a blip in your life."

A nervous laugh escaped me. "A blip? It's a pretty serious blip, don't you think?"

"It is. But everything fades with time." He winced a little. "Sorry, I'm not very good at giving a pep talk."

A small smile formed on my lips. "You're not so bad."

"Come on," he said, and I hoped he might put his arm around me, but he didn't. "I'm finished here. Let's go to the next spot."

He retrieved his tools before securing them on the bike.

I hopped on up front and flashed Shep a wicked grin. "I'm driving, big guy. You scared?"

He got on behind me and put his hands around my waist, giving my belly a light squeeze. "Not at all."

At least that made one of us.

12

SHEP

The sun sat low in the sky by the time we returned to the cabin. Cam insisted that since I'd been the one working, I should take the first shower. She took her own soon after.

I already had a chicken roasting in the oven and half the potatoes peeled when she entered the living area. She wore gray boxers, her white tank, and a khaki button-down shirt of mine, which she'd knotted at the front. Sweet Jesus, how did she make my clothes look so good?

"Can I help?" she asked, snapping me from my thoughts.

"Sure. You wanna wash the beans and shuck the corn?"

She nodded before curling her loose hair behind her ears and getting to work.

We moved about each other in a comfortable silence as we prepared the food. It didn't take long with her help.

With the chicken almost ready and vegetables on the stove, I grabbed us two beers. We clinked bottles and both took swigs, our backs resting against the kitchen counter.

Cam gnawed on a fingernail. "Have you heard any news about Justin?"

"No."

"I guess that's good, right?"

I grunted and took another pull from my beer. Was it good news that Franky hadn't found that dipshit yet? I wasn't so sure. I didn't mean to be short with Cam, but the more I got to know her, the more frustrated I was that I wouldn't get to deliver Justin's punishment myself.

She sighed. "I know you don't think much of my brother, but Justin wasn't always such a screw-up. He had my back when we were kids." She sipped her beer, then stared at the bottle. "When Dad drank, he would get… angry. Justin bore the brunt of it, mostly. In fact, he made sure he did, so I wouldn't have to. And when he was old enough to leave home, he didn't. That house was hell for him, but he stayed to protect me until we could go together."

Hearing about their father's abuse cut me up. That someone could hurt a child, their own flesh and blood, made me see red. It didn't excuse Justin's treatment of his sister now, though.

"I understand your loyalty, Cam, but you shouldn't let it cloud your judgment." As I turned to check on the vegetables bubbling away on the stove, I bumped the handle of a pot, splashing boiling water on my hand.

I hissed.

"Are you all right?" Before I could answer, Cam grabbed my forearm, dragged me to the sink, and held my hand under cool running water.

"I'm fine. It's not that bad."

"Quit being stubborn. I've had enough burns from engines and exhaust pipes to know that they never seem like much at first."

The injury was minor, but I let her fuss since she seemed determined to do so.

I watched as she turned the tap off and inspected the burn,

her brow furrowed and lips pressed tight. Fingertips brushed across the reddened skin on the back of my hand.

Cam's touch moved beyond the burn to trace over the bumps and ridges of my knuckles. The contrast between our hands was glaring. Mine were big, scarred, and ugly. Hers were slender and graceful, even if the nails were short-trimmed and a little chewed. It might have been my imagination, but I thought they trembled. What was she doing? The contact felt electric. Did she feel this, too?

She avoided meeting my eyes, but I was desperate to peer into those pale green pools to see what I'd find. I turned her hands over and held them in mine, rubbing slow circles over her soft palms. She drew in a sharp breath, but her focus remained on where our hands were joined.

Dammit, Cam. Look at me.

I let go of one hand to hook my index finger under her chin and tilt her face upward. What I was about to do was a bad, bad idea, but I still couldn't stop myself.

Blood quickened through my veins. When Cam's eyes met mine, that was my undoing. All logical thought dissolved. I wanted her. Under me, on top of me. I could think of a thousand ways to make her come, and I was eager to try them all. Never realized I was so damn inventive. I needed to see the look on her face when she was at the edge and hear the sounds coming from her mouth the moment that release tore through her. I didn't deserve her, but that wasn't enough to stop me from wanting it.

Her eyes flickered. She took small, panting breaths. Her pupils dilated, and yet her feet shuffled as though preparing to run. The messages were conflicting. The only thing overriding my need to press my lips to Cam's this instant was the thought of scaring her or pushing her into something she wasn't ready for. Because as much as I wanted to taste her, I'd never take more than she was willing to give.

She retreated one small step. It could've been a mile.

When her hands pulled away from mine, I tried not to let my disappointment show. Cam was making the sensible decision, and a part of me was glad one of us had the willpower to shut this down before it went too far.

"I can't. I'm sorry," she said, and a pained expression crossed her face as she moved beyond my reach.

"You have nothing to be sorry about."

"I don't want to complicate things, you know?"

I nodded. "Listen, Cam. I'm not always good at sensing what people need, but know this. I'll be anything you want me to be. Someone to talk to, a shoulder to cry on, a distraction. Whatever you need, just say the word. Even if it's 'stay the hell away from me,' all right?"

She smiled through glistening eyes. "Stop being so damned sweet. I swear to God, you're ruining me for all other men."

I tried not to react to Cam's words, but thinking about her with another man was as fun as a swift kick to the balls.

"Not being sweet. I'm treating you the way you deserve."

She made up the small distance between us and put her arms around me, resting her head against my chest. I folded mine around her and soothed my hand along her spine. She exhaled a deep breath, and the tension left her body.

I angled my head low and breathed her in. "I'll be there for you until this thing is through. I promise."

She pulled back and lifted her gaze to mine. "For a guy that gets paid to murder people for a living, you're incredibly kind."

I smirked. "Hmm, thanks. I think. Don't tell anyone, though. Can't have you ruining my badass reputation."

"Your secret is safe with me." She placed one hand on my chest, right over my heart. I hoped she couldn't feel how hard it pounded. Instead of backing away like I should, I rested my hand over the top of hers.

Living with her was so much harder than I ever thought.

Those upturned eyes shifted to my mouth. "You hungry?" Cam sounded a little breathless.

I gnawed on my bottom lip and stared at hers. "Starving."

Were we even talking about food?

She blinked twice and gave a sharp shake of her head as if trying to clear it. I resisted the urge to keep hold of her hand when she took a step backwards.

"We should get the chicken out of the oven before it burns," she said.

Something was burning up, but it wasn't the food. I could use a bucket of cold water to pour over my head.

"You're right." I nodded.

We finished preparing the meal together. Cam seemed quieter than usual. Damn, I was screwing things up with her. She didn't need a fuck-buddy. She needed a protector and someone to support her through all the bullshit she was dealing with. Because this cat-and-mouse game with Franky? It wasn't a game at all. One wrong move and it could all turn to crap. I had to get my priorities right. And number one was looking after Cam, both mentally and physically.

I served up a plate for each of us while Cam popped the tops on two fresh beers. We moved to the table and sat opposite each other, same as the night before.

My eyes followed the lines of her slender neck as she drew long from the bottle. Damn. She even made drinking a beer look sexy as hell.

She took in the food on the table. "Looks delicious."

"It does. Do you like to cook?"

Cam shrugged. "I don't mind. Same as you, I guess, I learned out of necessity. Dad wasn't home much at dinner time, or ever."

"Was your mom never around?"

She poked at her food. "Not for long. She died when I was little."

"I'm sorry to hear that."

She shook her head, dismissing my pity. "It's okay. Mom left when I was a baby. From what I know now, sounds like she suffered from postpartum depression. She wasn't coping with two little ones, so she left. Walked out the door and never looked back." Cam picked at the beer label. "Dad said he tried to find her. I guess he thought she'd come home when she was ready. It wasn't the first time Mom had left him. Turns out she'd hitchhiked all the way to Seattle, got herself as far from us as possible without leaving the country. A few months after she left, the police contacted Dad and told him they'd found her body. She OD'd on painkillers. We never knew if she did it on purpose or not." She drew a ragged breath.

I didn't know what to say.

She rolled her lips together and swallowed hard. "Dad started drinking after that. At least, that's what Justin told me since I was too little to remember when it started. He blamed us for what happened to Mom. When he was drunk, he'd say all kinds of awful things about how her death was our fault." She took a long drink from her beer.

I scrubbed a hand down my face. "Fuck, Cam."

"What about your mom?" She eyed me with caution. "Has she passed too?"

I should've expected this, but I didn't want to get into it. "No, she's alive."

"Oh?" Her brows pinched. "I thought you said your dad raised you?"

"He did. Since I was seven." The silence lingered between us. Cam continued to stare as though waiting for something more. Her story was much worse than mine, yet here I was, clamming up over the prospect of talking about my childhood in any detail.

"We can change the subject if you like. I don't mean to hound you." She returned to her food, giving me an out, but after sharing her difficult history, it seemed wrong if I didn't reciprocate.

"No, it's fine." Yet my chest tightened as if Ranger sat on it. I put my cutlery down and leaned back in my chair. "My mom's kind, pretty, and far too good for my dad. She left his ass when I was six and had found another husband by the time I was seven." I took a long pull on my beer. It didn't take the edge off.

She winced. "Ouch. Sorry."

I spun the leather band around my wrist as I considered how to explain the situation. "Her replacement husband's a pompous dick. We never took to each other. Guess I was too much like my old man. Mom always said every time she looked at me, she'd see Dad staring back. And I think she wanted to forget about him and move on with her life. She didn't push me away, but when she had kids with the new husband, I felt like an outsider. She didn't argue when I told her I preferred to stay with Dad. Said it might be for the best since we were so similar." I chugged the last half of my beer. At this rate, I'd be reaching for the scotch again tonight. "Anyway, I don't blame her for leaving him. He wasn't a drunk or violent, but he could be a real asshole."

"She must've been in love with him at some point."

I snorted. "Love isn't a requirement for a shotgun wedding. Getting knocked up by my old man was the biggest mistake of her life. Yet another reason she resented him... and maybe me, too."

"Oh."

"I'll give her credit for sticking around as long as she did. With Dad being in the Army, we moved a lot. Social circles are tight on the bases. The guys make friends and the wives form relationships within that group. So, it was hard for Mom to meet new people because Dad was... well... about as sociable as me. And when he wasn't working, he'd take off hunting or hide away in the workshop to build stuff. Sound like anyone you know?"

One side of Cam's mouth lifted, but it dropped a moment later. "I can't imagine how lonely she must've felt."

I nodded. "Being with my old man sucked the life out of her. She was a different person with her new family. Bright, bubbly. It took me a long time to come to terms with it, but she made the right choice."

I wasn't sure if it was genetic or because he raised me, but I was my dad version 2.0. Us Shepherd men were suited to a solitary life so we didn't drag anyone down with our loner ways and ornery nature.

Plus, in my case, it would never be safe to be involved with a woman. Loved ones were targets, and it was better to have none than risk being vulnerable in that way. I accepted those conditions a long time ago.

13

SHEP

We packed away the leftover food and washed the dishes together. It was strange how well we'd adapted to sharing the same living space.

Afterwards, I sat at the breakfast bar with my laptop. Cam retired to the sofa with her book and Ranger curled up beside her. I reckoned they'd be out cold in five minutes.

I scanned news websites, searching for leads on Cam's disappearance. Nothing noteworthy, but there was a heartfelt article by a reporter who had interviewed her boss, Tom. Although distraught with worry, he wasn't giving up hope of finding her alive. Not wanting to upset Cam, I didn't show her.

I checked my email and sat up fast when I found one from Franky. There was no good reason he'd contact me.

It was an open catch or kill contract for Justin McKenzie. Underneath was a police mug shot of Cam's brother looking like a strung-out junkie. Now all of Frankie's shady contacts were on the job, and the mob boss was offering a pretty penny to have it done. To make things worse, it gave a suburb in Springfield, Illinois. Justin was screwed. He deserved the hit, but his death would devastate Cam, and *that* bothered me.

"That's Justin!" Cam sprang from the sofa and approached in a hurry.

Shit! The new information distracted me, and I hadn't realized she was paying attention.

When I tried to close the laptop, she intercepted.

"No! Please, Shep. I need to see this."

I groaned, but let her have her way. She'd bust my balls if I didn't.

One hand covered her mouth as she read the screen. "What's an open catch or kill contract?"

"Either do the hit, or bring the target to Franky. It's a free-for-all gig. Whoever's the first to complete it gets the cash."

"I thought you said Franky would want to find Justin and try to get his drugs and money back. Why doesn't he care about that anymore?"

"I'm guessing Franky's pissed and sick of looking for him. Now he's hell-bent on revenge. When Franky is angry, he becomes volatile."

Cam faced me. "Why didn't he ask you to do it?"

"Told Franky I needed a few weeks off and he must want this done fast."

"Look!" She pointed at the screen. "It says Justin's in Springfield. That's where Aunt Sarah lives. It can't be a coincidence,"

"You think he's staying with her?"

I shrugged. "At her house, perhaps. But Aunt Sarah hasn't lived there for months. She had a stroke a while back and is living in a rehabilitation facility while she recovers."

"Makes sense that he would've gone there, but it's a stupid move. If she's a relative, her address would be easy to find."

"She's not our aunt by blood. She was Mom's best friend. We spent a few summers with her when Dad was at his worst."

Franky must have been tipped off some other way, then.

Cam chewed her bottom lip. "What if I called Justin to tell him he's in danger and needs to get out of there?"

I considered it for a moment. It wasn't a bad idea. "That's possible. Does your aunt have a landline?"

"Yeah. I can't remember her number, but it's in the directory."

I located it, then pulled out a burner phone. "Let me do the talking. It's best if he's unaware you're alive and with me."

She nodded and steepled her fingers at her lips while I dialed.

An automated voice cut in before it even rang. "Line's disconnected."

She rubbed her forehead. "What about his cell?"

"There's no way he has it on him. Franky would've used it to pinpoint him already. Those things are a goddamn tracking beacon."

Cam's eyes darted between the screen and me. "How far are we from Illinois?"

I didn't like her train of thought.

"Nope, not gonna happen." I shook my head and gave her a stern look. "Someone recognizes you and it's over. And the area will be swarming with bounty hunters and hired killers."

"We have an advantage. They don't know exactly where he's hiding, and we do." She gripped my forearm hard and held my stare. "If we go now, we can help him."

"No. And get that idea out of your head."

Cam tore her hand from my arm. "Would you stop being so pig-headed and listen to reason?"

"Not changing my mind. There's no way in hell I'm letting you leave and that's final." We'd already discussed this. Why couldn't she see I was trying to keep her safe?

"I can't believe this." She snapped, unable to contain her simmering fury. "So, I'm back to being your prisoner? Will you chain me up again?"

"If I have to." I raised my tone to match hers. "Are you gonna try to leave?"

"That contract has sealed my brother's fate, and you expect me to accept that?" Her voice cracked as emotion overcame her.

Cam hurting like this tore me up. I hated fighting with her. My two least favorite people in the world were Franky Russo and Justin McKenzie. I wanted to kill them both.

What a goddamn mess. I took a few deep breaths and considered my options. They weren't great.

"There might be one way to help him, but it involves bringing in a third party. I don't like that because it increases the risk for us."

"Go on."

I angled my body toward her, my elbows resting on my knees. "There's this guy I served with. I think he'd be able to get Justin faster than the others."

Ben Landers was ex-Delta and had been an Operator in Team Zulu. As our intelligence tech guru—which is a sophisticated way of saying he's a damn good hacker—tracking down those who don't want to be found was what he did best.

"How?" Cam asked.

"Last I heard, he was living in rural Missouri, close to the Illinois border. I could ask him to do a catch and hold on your brother. We expedite your documents as much as possible. Once the wheels of your plane are off the ground and you're safe, I'll go get Justin and work on an extraction plan for him, too."

After getting Cam tangled up in his bullshit, I couldn't believe I was offering to save her brother's ass. But he meant a lot to her, and if this would ease her burden, then I'd do it.

"Do you trust this... what's his name?" she asked, sounding a little calmer.

Maintaining secrecy regarding the guys from my team was paramount, but I figured a first name wouldn't hurt. Besides, he used an alias since leaving Team Zulu.

"Ben. And I do. We've had each other's back plenty of times before."

"Won't it be dangerous for him? What if Franky finds out he's helping us?"

"Franky will be pissed if he catches wind of this. But trust me, Ben can take care of himself."

If he did his job right, Franky would never suspect his involvement. And Ben was good. *Really* good. The bigger issue was whether he could get to Justin in time. I didn't mention that to Cam because I needed her on board. I didn't want her plotting to run off on her own.

She paced the room. "What if Ben says no? What if he's on holiday overseas? There's too much uncertainty, Shep. The one thing I am certain of is a bunch of hired killers are on their way to murder my brother. If anything goes wrong with this plan, Justin's either dead, or hand delivered to Franky, which might be worse." She paused her pacing and faced me with glistening eyes. "Isn't there something else we can do for him?"

The urge to go to her was strong. I stood, but didn't approach since she was angry with me. "I'm sorry, Cam."

Showing her strength of character yet again, Cam blinked away unshed tears and pulled her shoulders back. "All right. Contact your guy." She sighed and took a step toward me. "I don't mean to sound ungrateful. I'm not, I promise. I'm scared because every move we make puts lives at risk."

I made up the distance between us and put my arms around her because I couldn't help myself. She collapsed into me. "I hate what this is doing to you."

Cam nodded, or perhaps nuzzled her face into my chest, I wasn't sure. But she shared her burden with me and that was as much as I hoped for.

"Come, sit." Taking her hand, I led her to the sofa. "Wait here."

When I returned from the kitchen with a heavy-handed

pour of whiskey, she gave a wan smile. "I guess I could use that. Thanks."

"No problem."

I grabbed a soft woolen blanket from the lower cupboard under the bookshelf and draped it over her legs. Cam snuggled against the arm of the sofa and sipped from the tumbler.

After collecting my laptop, I sat beside Cam, ready to get down to business. An email to Greg about speeding up the passport, and one to Ben with the offer for Justin. If I had Ben's number, I'd call him, but he changed it often to remain untraceable. Plus, he had some extreme encryption bullshit on his email, so it was both the safest and only option.

"It's done." I turned to find Cam fast asleep with the empty glass still cradled in her lap. Perhaps the whiskey had worked a little too well. I closed my laptop and placed it on the coffee table, then did the same with her tumbler.

This was the second time in as many nights she'd passed out on the sofa. Couldn't say I minded carrying her to bed.

When I scooped her up, she stirred and gazed at me through sleepy eyes.

"Did I drift off?" Her voice was raspy. The smell of whiskey tinged her breath.

"It's all right. I got you."

I lowered her to the edge of the bed and pulled the covers back.

"I'm so worried, Shep." Her chin trembled. "Someone might be trying to kill Justin this very minute. How can I lie here and sleep while that happens?"

I perched next to Cam and reached for her hand.

"We can't change anything right now, but I think we can help him. Franky's go-to assassins aren't in Illinois. They'll have to travel to get there. And who's to say Justin's even in that location anymore? Franky hasn't been able to find him, so maybe he's been on the move the whole time." I had to give her some hope. She was falling apart.

She sniffled and rubbed her nose. "I'm tired of being scared. I'm afraid for Justin and for me. And moving overseas and starting a new life feels so overwhelming. I can't see how everything is going to be all right."

I'd never helped a person through pain like this before, at least not someone I cared about. It tore me up.

"I wish I could tell you it will all be okay, but things will get worse before they get better." I ran my thumb across her cheek and wiped away a falling tear. "But I'm doing everything in my power to make your life sweet again. It'll take some time, though."

Cam nodded as her breath hitched. I put my arm around her shoulders and tucked her against me. I wasn't good with this stuff, but she needed me to comfort her somehow.

"Would you lie with me?" she asked. "To help me sleep, I mean. You don't have to."

I tightened my grip on her. "Of course."

"Thank you."

Cam stripped down to her tank top and boxers before folding herself under the covers. I flicked the light off, then removed my shirt and jeans and hopped under the blanket on the other side. I left a safe distance between us, not wanting to assume how much contact she might need. But she shimmied toward me, rested her head on my shoulder, and placed her hand on my chest. I tucked my arm around her and brought her closer. She wasn't seeking anything more than a warm body to hold for the night, and I could give her that.

And if I was honest with myself, I needed this too, because with everything happening so fast, the one thought dominating my mind was that I might have less than a week left with her. It wasn't enough.

I covered Cam's hand with my own. When I gave it a

squeeze, she returned the gesture and didn't let go. A short while later, she stilled, her breathing deep and steady.

It'd been a long time since I'd laid next to a woman. Couldn't recall it being this incredible. The intensity of this thing between us was hard to ignore. I hadn't expected her to see me beyond the killer I was, but I was grateful she did. And every time I made her smile, it was like a small piece of me was being put back together.

In the soft glow of the hallway light, she looked so peaceful. Not a hint of anguish or fear. I'd love to see the day when she looked untroubled for more than a few fleeting moments.

I wasn't ready to give her up. When she boarded that plane, it would hit me hard, like a goddamned wrecking ball to the gut.

The only thing worse than that was Franky getting hold of Cam, and the sickening thought of what he'd do to her was enough motivation to send her very far away.

14

CAMERON

Gentle light filtered through the window. The cool morning air didn't trouble me because I was cocooned in a toasty warm Shep blanket. With his chest at my back, one large arm held me against him, and a muscular thigh was wedged between mine. The early riser still slept. His slow, deep breaths tickled my ear on each exhale.

I must have rolled away from him during the night and he'd followed. Waking up in the security of his embrace and surrounded by his scent was heaven. I wished I wasn't so affected by the big guy, but it was hard not to be when he took such good care of me. The problem was, Shep had become an emotional crutch, and it was dangerous to rely on other people for anything. Soon, I'd be on my own, and his absence would feel like a phantom limb.

I studied Shep's tanned forearm and wondered how he'd react if I traced my fingertips over the thick veins there and continued walking them up his firm bicep and huge shoulders. What would he do if I turned to face him, ran my hands through his hair and hooked a leg over his hip, drawing him nearer? God, I wanted to find out. A tingling warmth blossomed low in my belly.

Foolish girl. Hadn't I convinced myself last night that it was a terrible idea to complicate things?

My reality came crashing down around me when I remembered the contract on Justin. A wave of nausea rolled through me. Every hour that passed brought him closer to danger. I needed to know if Ben would help us.

I wiggled to stir the slumbering beast draped over me. He groaned before adjusting his position and pulled me tighter against his chest.

Round one to the beast.

I cleared my throat and poked a finger into his forearm. That got a reaction. Shep froze, and every muscle in his body tensed.

He loosened his grip on me and shuffled back a few inches.

"Sorry. I didn't mean to smother you like that." His morning voice was extra raspy.

He sat up against the headboard, hair disheveled and cheeks flushed. He was cute when he woke, even more so when he was embarrassed.

"It's okay. You must've been doing something right, because I slept like the dead. I was sure I'd be awake all night."

He smirked. "You were out cold in under five minutes."

"Then I guess you have another superpower to add to your list." I flashed Shep a half smile, but it was all I could muster. I sat up next to him. "Do you think Ben would've replied by now?"

"I'll go check my email." He rolled off the bed, then padded down the hallway.

I headed to the bathroom to relieve my aching bladder. After washing my hands, I stared at my reflection in the mirror. For all the craziness going on, I didn't look too awful. My scratches and bruises were well on their way to healing, and there was a blush on my cheeks brought on by Shep's presence. Seemed the mountain lifestyle agreed with me, or maybe it was just him.

I used a comb to bring some order to my hair and styled it into a loose braid over my shoulder. When I opened the bathroom door, I found Shep slipping into a pair of jeans, his impressive chest still on display. I let my eyes roam over him. He caught me checking him out and grinned.

I leaned against the doorframe and folded my arms. "You know, shirts are overrated and completely optional in my opinion." I licked my lip and gave it a nibble. He looked delicious.

"I agree," he said, his eyes flickering between my face and breasts, unleashing a swarm of butterflies in my belly.

Shep zipped up his fly before putting on a white long sleeve T-shirt. Damn shame he wasn't putting the optional shirt policy to use.

"Last night, in here," he glanced at the bed, "it was... nice. If you need that again, even if it's only for comfort, I won't ask for more. I know that's not what you need right now." He scratched the short stubble on his cheek, looking nervous while I considered his words.

He was so handsome standing before me. Total alpha male, but with a compassionate side that melted me.

"Thanks. I know you'd never do that. Push me into something physically, I mean. I trust you."

His brows raised. "You do?"

Although I'd never said so, I thought my actions around him implied my trust. But it seemed like hearing those words meant a lot to him.

"With my life. Lucky, given the situation, right?"

He smiled and nodded.

I returned the smile and shook my head. "You really have no clue, do you?"

He chuckled. "Clearly, but about what in particular?"

I took a small step closer because he was like a magnet pulling me in. "About how amazing you are. I'm so lucky to have you helping me through all this."

"There are plenty of people who would've handled it much better than me."

I shrugged. "Perhaps. But if I had the chance to choose now, I'd still pick you." I stared up into hazel eyes that held no hint of humor as they roamed my face. "You're good and kind and thoughtful. Please try to remember that after I'm gone."

He sucked on his bottom lip and nodded. Either he didn't believe what I told him, or he disliked thinking about us parting as much as I did.

It hit me how much Shep gave expecting nothing in return. I wasn't used to having another person put my needs above their own. For some time now, I'd been the only one looking out for myself. I'd always tried to be strong and not dwell on the fact that something was missing from my life. Or someone.

I sighed. "So, lay it on me. What did Ben say?"

Shep's frown told me enough, but he gave me the bad news, anyway. "He hasn't replied yet. I'm sorry."

Not what I wanted to hear.

"Give him more time to come through, all right?" Shep nodded as though trying to convince himself as much as me. He was playing it cool, but I suspected he was more concerned than he let on.

I didn't know what to say. Most people couldn't go thirty minutes without checking their cell. How could I believe that Ben, a supposed tech guru, hadn't checked his email in over twelve hours? Something seemed off about that. He must've seen it. If he didn't want to help, he should let us know. But then again, this was a business deal. Shep wouldn't have told Ben about me or my personal connection to Justin.

Either way, I was convinced Ben wouldn't help. We were on

our own. No, *I* was on my own because Shep wouldn't do anything more for Justin. He'd told me that last night.

My world closed in around me. Justin's time was running out, and there was no one coming to help him. The thought made me nauseous.

"Get dressed," said Shep. "I'll make us coffee."

"I think I'll shower first." I swallowed down the bile rising in my throat.

"Sure." Shep gave me a tight-lipped smile and headed for the front of the house with Ranger on his heels.

Nausea churned in my gut on my way to the bathroom.

MY HANDS SHOOK as I turned the shower on. How had my morning gone from one of sheer bliss to one of terror as I considered how I was going to help my brother?

I stepped under the scorching water and tipped my head back. The spray stung like needles pricking my skin.

My hollow stomach continued to roil. I had to come up with an alternative plan fast. Justin didn't know his location was compromised. I had to warn him to leave town.

There was no way to call Justin. And contacting him via email or social media was useless if he didn't have a cell. I doubt I could crack into Shep's laptop, anyway.

The warning had to reach him in person. Someone had to find him before an assassin did.

Even if I could find one of Shep's burner phones without him noticing, there was no way I would risk using it to ask Tom or one of my friends to deliver a message to Justin. I could never endanger their lives like that.

It needed to be me.

Perhaps it was a death sentence to leave here, but could I live with the guilt of doing nothing? Could I spend the rest of my days knowing that I sat on my hands while dangerous people hunted my brother? I'd rather try and fail than do nothing at all.

I washed my hair and used Shep's razor to tidy myself. I didn't know when I'd next get the chance to shower.

It occurred to me that Shep, a complete stranger, had helped me, even though it was risky, and the consequences were fatal. I'd do the same for Justin because he was my blood. He was the only person who showed me love and protected me as a child. We were siblings, and you didn't give up on family when things got shitty. And despite all of Justin's shortcomings and mistakes, I still loved him.

How the hell was I going to get to him?

I had one edge over the descending hitmen. I knew where Justin was hiding. If I got to him in time, we'd move south fast until we crossed the border into Mexico. My friend, Abby, who lived in San Carlos, would provide us safe haven. I'd helped her through her own crisis two years ago when she'd needed to escape an abusive relationship. We could count on her.

I rinsed off, although I wished I could stay in the shower and hide from my problems.

Don't wimp out now. Do what needs to be done.

I didn't want to deceive Shep, and I dreaded the prospect of leaving him. My throat closed over thinking about how much this betrayal would hurt him. After everything he'd done for me, he didn't deserve to be treated this way.

My decision was bolstered by reminding myself that Shep forcing me to stay was total bullshit. It still pissed me off he'd given me no choice in how to deal with my problems.

I thought about the logistics of what I needed to do. It was a risk to go out in public, but I could remain disguised using sunglasses, hair dye and a pair of scissors. Most of America would assume I was already dead, so nobody in Illinois would look twice at a girl in a hoodie and suspect I was the missing woman from Philly.

To get off this mountain, I needed a solid escape plan. One that gave me a decent head start before Shep realized I'd gone.

An idea was forming. I didn't have time to waste. I thought I might actually throw up while I dried myself because shit was getting real. It was a long shot, but there was a chance I could pull this off.

After dressing for the day in my usual get-up of a cinched shirt and rolled-up boxers, I walked out to the living room. Shep stood in the kitchen pouring two steaming cups of black coffee. He flashed me a smile, which made the rock in my stomach ten times heavier.

I wasn't ready to say my silent goodbyes to Shep or Ranger. They meant so much to me, and I would miss them both. I'd never forget the generosity Shep had shown me, or that I'd be dead right now without his help. My nose stung, and I blinked to clear my blurry vision.

Pull yourself together, girl. Your brother needs you.

We drank our coffee sitting on the deck overlooking the mountains. A mist had rolled in overnight and covered the lower lands in a white fluffy blanket. I worked hard to steady the trembling cup in my hands and kept my eyes directed over the ranges. Eye contact with Shep was impossible because of what I was about to say.

"I might need you to get me some… supplies."

He angled his head toward me. "Sure, what do you need?"

"Tampons, mostly."

Shep's spine went rigid.

"Maybe some peanut M&M's and ice cream since you have zero PMS comfort food in your house." I glanced at him and rolled my eyes because seriously, who didn't have a single piece of candy in their pantry? He was neglecting an essential food group.

His gaze dropped to the steaming mug in his hand. "Right. Okay."

How to make a guy go from relaxed to uncomfortable in two seconds? Start discussing the menstrual cycle.

"I'm cramping, and my boobs are killing me. Sorry if that's too much information, but I'm going to need those things soon."

He cleared his throat and shifted in his seat. "It's no problem. I'll head into town this morning. Why don't you make a list of everything? Be as specific as you can because I won't know what I'm looking for."

"Thanks, you're the best."

And I was the worst. I clutched my stomach. Not because of period pains, but because my gut soured at the lie.

I wasn't sure how long Shep would be away for, but I guessed I'd have somewhere between one and two hours to get my things together, jump on the quad bike and book it out of here. I still didn't know where *here* was, but my plan was to find the nearest town and get on the first bus headed anywhere near Illinois.

We went inside and ate a light breakfast, although I wasn't hungry. I forced the food down knowing I'd need energy today, and also because I didn't want Shep becoming suspicious of my sudden loss of appetite. My nerves were getting the better of me. I needed to act natural.

I wrote up a list and added a few extra random items hoping to extend his shopping trip as much as possible.

"So, how far is the nearest town?" I asked with indifference, but this would be useful information.

He sat next to me on the sofa and tied the laces on his hiking boots. "It's about a twenty-minute drive down the mountain. Not far. Why?"

"No reason." I forced the smile and refocused on my book. I'd mastered the art of pretending to read.

When he made no move to leave, I glanced his way and found him staring at me. "What?" I asked.

"Nothing." He stood and headed for the back of the house.

A minute later, he returned, jangling as he walked.

Son of a bitch!

I cut him my absolute filthiest death stare and jumped from the sofa to face him.

"No! You will not put those on me, Elias Shepherd! You hear me?"

Crap, crap, crap!

This wasn't part of the plan. He hadn't brought out the cuffs since that first night. I thought we were past that.

"Yes, I am. Now settle down." He made calm-down hand gestures which had the opposite effect.

"Shep, come on. You know how much I hate being chained up. You must trust me by now, don't you?" Was I the sort to resort to dirty tactics? You bet.

"I do trust you. With everything except bolting from here as soon as I leave. After Franky's email last night, I'm sure it's on your mind."

He stalked toward me like a cowboy preparing to lasso a wild horse. The way he stared me down had me itching to run. It was a reflex action to him herding me. I moved to keep the sofa between us.

Shep paused and shook his head, chin angled low. "Cam," he warned, "Don't make this any harder than it needs to be. I don't like this either, but you know I've got no choice." He held the open cuff in one hand and the length of chain in the other.

I dodged left, then right, but he mirrored my every move. Ranger thought it was a super fun game and jumped at Shep's side trying to bite the chain. *Good boy.* There was my window.

While Shep brushed away Ranger's playful advances, I bolted down the hallway to the bedroom. Maybe I could lock the door and push the drawers in front of it. What would that achieve? Nothing but being a pain in his ass. But I was all for that because I was furious.

Halfway down the hall, a pair of viselike arms clamped around me. Shep hoisted me off the floor.

"Let me go, asshole!" My feet kicked the air as I writhed and growled, trying to get out of his hold.

"No! You know I have to do this. Quit your fighting!"

As pointless as it was, I continued attempting to escape his grip while he carted me back to the living room. He dumped me on the sofa with the cuff already around my left wrist. How the hell had he slipped that on without me noticing?

His nostrils flared. "Now, do you need me to get those things on your list, or am I staying here on babysitting duty?"

I bared my teeth like a feral woman. "I can't even look at you right now." I stabbed a finger toward the door as tears stung my eyes. "Get out!"

Shep had made things difficult for me, but I wasn't giving up. I'd find a way out of these chains and continue with my plans. Maybe it was for the best that we parted this way. It made my decision easier to swallow.

He looped the chain through the coffee table and back onto the empty cuff.

When Shep reached the front door, he opened it and paused, perhaps preparing to issue some final words of wisdom. I picked up *The Count of Monte Cristo* and pitched the paperback at his head. He was quick to dodge it, but the startled look on his face made the effort worthwhile. First time the damn book had been truly interesting.

He raised his hands in surrender. "Cam. I'm sorry. You know I'm keeping you here for your own safety. What do you want me to say?" He looked as goddamn miserable as me.

"Nothing. Don't hurry back!" I hadn't spoken to him with so much anger since he first brought me here. Even as I said the words, I regretted them.

He shook his head before calling for Ranger to follow, then closed the door behind them.

As Shep walked out of my life forever, the devastation that we'd spent our last moments together fighting hit me like a wrecking ball.

THE CRUNCH of tires over gravel signaled Shep's departure. The house fell into silence.

The sense of loss was more profound than I'd anticipated. If I allowed myself to think about it for another moment, it would swallow me up. I had to get moving.

I studied the cuff around my wrist and the chain linking me to the coffee table. My plans had turned to shit, but I wasn't giving up.

The coffee table was coming with me to the kitchen because I needed tools. I grabbed hold of the chain, dug my bare heels into the floor, and dragged it with all my strength. This thing was solid.

Heaving my way across the floor, I cringed as the table legs scraped along the hardwood boards, leaving scratches in its wake. Shep would kill me for this if he ever tracked me down.

My muscles ached, and the chain kept slipping through my clammy hands, but I made it to the kitchen. There, I rummaged through cupboards and drawers for something that might cut through the table. I held up a large saw-like knife that must be some kind of butchering tool. Perfect!

I dropped to the floor and hacked through the timber support bar the chain was looped through. The knife wasn't working as well as I'd hoped.

"Come on. Hurry!"

My lungs wheezed and hands cramped. Sweat dripped down my back, but I had to keep going. When I was almost through, I tossed the knife on the floor and kicked the timber until it snapped.

Thank God!

The wall clock showed Shep had been gone for fifteen minutes. I needed to get moving.

The cuffs and chain were still attached to my left wrist, and I didn't have time to cut it off. Guessed I had some chunky bling coming with me. I wound the chain around my forearm and threw on one of Shep's hooded jackets to conceal it.

In the bedroom, I grabbed a backpack and tossed in clothes and toiletries. I rifled through the chest of drawers and found a credit card for Ethan Sharp, whoever that was, and a Gerber multitool. No cash, though. The gun cabinet was locked, and it would use up too much precious time to break into it.

I slipped on my running shoes and a ball cap, tucking my braid underneath, then allowed myself one final look around the small cabin where my life had forever changed. A knot lodged in my throat as I closed the door behind me.

No more wallowing. You can feel sad about it later.

I jogged to the workshop. Shep had left it unlocked, which was lucky because I didn't want to destroy any more of his property.

I grabbed the keys from the tool cabinet and ran to the quad bike, throwing my leg over the seat. Taking a deep breath, I steeled myself.

I could do this. I *had* to do this.

With the push of a button, the bike started, and I drove through the barn doors.

Holy crap. This was happening.

I followed the driveway for perhaps a mile and stopped when I reached a letterbox and open gate. The gravel drive met with a narrow, sealed road. Opposite was a wooded forest with a dirt track running parallel to the main road. That would be the best path to follow. As soon as it intersected a track heading further into the woods, I'd travel in that direction to stay hidden from traffic. Namely, the truck of one large, lethal killing machine who'd go ballistic if he found me out here.

I had one decision remaining. Did I go left or right? I chose left, which led downhill. Shep said the town was a twenty-minute drive *down* the mountain, so I assumed this was the right way to go. I crossed the road with care.

This was it. I'd left the safety of the cabin and was on the run from Shep and from the rest of the world. I couldn't afford to be identified. Any mistakes would mean I'd fail to help Justin and risked drawing the attention of Franky Russo.

15

CAMERON

The fog lifted as the mid-morning sun warmed the air. I'd lost all sense of time in my heightened state of panic. Had I been riding along this track for one hour? Two? Was I going the right direction? I navigated using the slope of the mountain and the sun in the east. The last thing I wanted was to ride in circles.

I hoped I had enough gas. In my hurry to leave, I hadn't thought to check if the bike needed refueling.

It was too late to turn back. Shep might already have returned home and discovered I'd gone. He could be searching for me right now. My heart rate soared thinking of him hunting me down, mostly because I didn't want my plans thwarted, but also because facing his reaction petrified me.

At the crest of a hill, I slowed. *Yes!* A small town sprawled in the distance. If I kept up my pace, I might be there in thirty minutes.

And there was that goddamn sinking in my gut again. Something inside me telling me this was wrong, that I should turn back and return to Shep. He'd be pissed with me, but also relieved. It wasn't too late to choose that path and make things right between us again.

And I wanted that so badly, but I couldn't let guilt and my growing feelings for Shep sway me from my task. I was safe, and Justin was in imminent danger. There was no choice to make.

With a steadying breath, I pushed on. The trail descended and remained well hidden from the road. At some point, I'd have to abandon the quad bike in the woods and walk the rest of the way. Although that would eat into precious time, I didn't want to attract unwanted attention by riding through the streets.

I came around a bend and slammed on the brakes.

No!

Blocking the track was Shep's black truck and one pissed-off hulk of a man leaning against the tailgate. He was menacing with huge arms crossed over his broad chest, chin angled low, and a murderous look in his eyes.

My breath caught in my throat. I was in the deepest level of shit possible. There was nowhere for me to go, nowhere to hide.

I'd failed Justin and Shep. And as I hung my head, averting my gaze from the man struggling to contain his anger before me, my world crumbled. It hit me hard in that moment how much I valued Shep. Both as someone who'd helped me through this disaster and as a person I cherished. And deceiving him like this? It was a shitty thing to do.

He strode toward me, jaw clenched. I held his intense stare despite every bone in my body screaming for me to look away.

Leaning over the bike, he shut it off and removed the keys.

"Get in the truck." His gravelly voice was clipped. He returned to the pickup without waiting to see if I'd followed. I closed my eyes and let my shoulders slump. What choice did I have?

With heavy legs, I made my way to the pickup and climbed

into the passenger side. Ranger sat silent on the back seat, alert and aware of the palpable tension filling the cab. My hands shook in my lap as I stared out the window and waited for the explosion of anger.

"Buckle up, Cameron," was all Shep said as he started the engine.

Cameron? I guessed I deserved that, but it still felt like a glass of cold water tossed in my face.

I expected yelling, swearing, growling, but not this silent drive home. Shep stared straight ahead, eyes on the road, hands white knuckling the steering wheel.

When we reached the cabin, Shep parked the truck in the workshop. He collected a bunch of brown paper bags from the rear and slammed the door. He took the stairs two at a time before heading through the front door. Ranger followed close behind. Even the pointer seemed pissed with me. I drew in a shuddering breath before following them.

Inside the cabin, I found Shep crouched, running one hand along the scratch marks I'd made on the floor. My mouth went dry. All hell was about to unleash.

"You fucked up my floor?" His stare glazed over as he inspected the damage.

If he heard my pained moan, he didn't acknowledge it.

He moved to the coffee table that lay abandoned in the kitchen and clicked his tongue at the hacked-up mess before him.

"You ruined my table?"

The one he'd made with his own hands. I didn't know what to say. He couldn't even look at me. I assumed I wouldn't be around to see his reaction to my escape, and now that I was witnessing the hurt in his eyes, it was worse than I could have imagined.

He picked up the knife and ran his finger along the dull

blade. “And my knife?” Walking to the pantry, he tossed it into the metal trash can.

I flinched at the jarring clang it made when it hit the bottom.

When Shep turned to face me, the pained look in his eyes almost brought me to my knees.

“What the fuck, Cam?” he yelled, nostrils flaring.

My heartbeat pounded double-time. I hated what I’d done to him, but this situation wasn’t all my fault. I was angry with him, too.

“What was I supposed to do?” I snapped. “I can’t sit around while a bunch of assassins go after Justin!”

He jabbed his index finger in my direction. “We had a deal. You were meant to sit tight while Ben got your brother.”

“No, *you* made the deal!” I yelled, stabbing a finger right back at him. The chain and cuffs jangled at my wrist. “I couldn’t stand to wait around any longer. And there was no point arguing my case because you made it clear last night you weren’t willing to consider any other alternatives.” I shook my head. “You forced me into this.”

Shep jerked backwards, the insult hitting true. “Everything I’ve done has been to protect you, since you’re unwilling to do it for yourself.”

I threw my hands up in the air. “Are we back to that bullshit? Because last I checked, this is *my* life.” I took slow steps toward him, my anger surging. “You keep me holed up here and take away my freedom to choose how to deal with my problems. You say it’s dangerous, and I get that, but I’m a grown adult, and it’s my life to risk. My choice to make.” My chest heaved as I struggled to contain my frustration. “You’re such a goddamn hypocrite. You put yourself in danger to help me, even when I was no one to you. Yet you won’t let me do the same for my brother. My last remaining family. My flesh and blood!”

In full bossy, overprotective mode, Shep folded his arms and widened his stance. "Because you never would've made it to him without Franky finding out you're still alive."

"You don't know that." I shook my head. "I might not have the skills you do, but I'm not helpless, and I'm not a fool."

"It was a suicide mission. And have you forgotten that there are consequences for me if Franky finds out I didn't kill you? There'll be a contract on me too."

Shame swept through me because he was right. "I… I hadn't thought about that."

I'd been so caught up in my desperation to help Justin that I'd overlooked the risk to Shep. Oh God. How could I have been so thoughtless? If anything had happened to him because of what I'd done, I didn't know how I could live with that.

He raked a hand through his hair and glanced away before returning his gaze to mine. "Look, I can handle Franky and his men if they come after me, but it will be tough to do that and keep you safe at the same time."

The thought of him defending himself against the Mob while still trying to protect my troublesome ass sent a fresh wave of guilt through me. He must wish he'd never set eyes on my contract.

Shep rested his hands on his hips and stared me down. "And you put yourself at risk for nothing. Ben called while I was on my way to town. Accepted the offer. He's already located your brother and is working on an extraction plan."

The overwhelming relief at hearing those words almost made my legs buckle. "He is?"

He said no more, he didn't need to. The working of his jaw told me how pissed he was. Shep had been right about Ben. That made my escape attempt look stupid, but I still stood by my decision. I couldn't have known Ben was going to accept the offer, not when he'd taken so long to do so.

"When we'd heard nothing from him this morning, I

thought...” I swallowed with difficulty. “I thought we were on our own. You said you didn’t know if he’d accept your offer. The contract was live. The clock was already ticking. How long was I supposed to wait for Ben to respond? One day? Two? Justin might be dead by then.”

“You could’ve had a little faith in me.”

“Yes, but I was scared. You don’t understand how hard it was deciding to leave. I never wanted things to go like this.” Tears blurred in my eyes. I took a step toward him.

He held up one hand. “I don’t want to hear it. And don’t you cry on me now, acting like you’re sorry for what you’ve done.” His hazel eyes narrowed. “I trusted you, and you played me. You were damn convincing about it, too. And I’m not only talking about sending me to town on a fool’s errand. I know you’ve been working on me to drop my guard since you got here.” His bitter laugh cut me to my core. “I can’t believe I fell for it. You asking me all those personal questions, pretending like you wanted to know me, even letting me sleep with you last night. The entire time making me think we were... that you really...” He pinched the bridge of his nose. “I’m such a fool.”

With arms outstretched, I moved toward him. “No, it’s not like that. I swear!”

“Don’t! I can’t do this with you right now.” He stormed to the back of the house.

“Shep, wait!” I called after him, but he didn’t stop. Instead, he went to his bedroom and slammed the door with enough force that the entire cabin shook.

I remained there, deciding he needed time to cool off but desperate to tell him how wrong he was. It hurt that he thought I was capable of that, but what did I expect? Of course, he’d think I was an untrustworthy bitch after the stunt I pulled.

I removed the cap and jacket, tossing them on the dining table before slumping into a chair. Leaning forward, I covered my face with my hands. What had I done? My heart ached with how much I'd hurt Shep. I'd ruined this thing between us and wanted to make it right again. Would I have enough time before I got on that plane? I could spend my entire life regretting this day. What a mess.

I eyed the shopping bags on the table. There were a lot of them, but my list hadn't been long. Curiosity got the better of me, so I snooped. I sighed and closed my eyes. All of it was for me. A warm jacket, hiking boots, thermals, socks, sweaters, jeans, t-shirts, even underwear. He'd done a good job of choosing casual clothes that suited me and would fit.

More bags were filled with puzzles, board games, and an adult coloring book with markers. Activities for me to pass the time when Shep was busy, and things we could do together.

There were a bunch of candy bars and six tubs of semi-melted ice cream in different flavors as though he was unsure which ones I'd like and didn't want to disappoint me. I pressed a hand to my aching chest.

Other bags contained a range of books, magazines, hairbrushes, soaps, lotions, and the tampons I'd asked for.

When I checked the last bag and found a large shoe box, I drew in a sharp breath. I recognized the label. These must have cost a fortune. I opened the lid and one hand flew to my mouth. Cowboy boots. Similar to my favorite ones that I wore every day back home except much better quality. The smell of tan leather filled my nose as I ran my fingers over the intricate aqua stitching in the shape of wings up the side of each boot. They were incredible.

I rubbed my eyes so hard I saw stars, the damn chain and cuffs still dangling from my wrist. The sourness in my stomach intensified. How the hell could I fix this?

Water pipes groaned when the shower came on. I laid on the sofa and curled into a ball. Ranger jumped up next to me and I drew him closer, needing his comfort more than ever.

16

CAMERON

Shep entered the living room wearing faded blue jeans and a black T-shirt, his still-wet hair combed back and his face clean shaven. I almost groaned at how gorgeous he looked.

Now he hated me and was so far out of my reach I wasn't sure I'd ever be able to bring him back.

Without making eye contact, he shifted the coffee table back to its original position and sat on it. I had the urge to lean toward him and inhale his soapy scent. Didn't think he'd appreciate that.

He pulled the handcuff keys from his pocket. "Here, let's get these off you." It surprised me to find no anger in his tone.

Shep removed the cuffs and chain. When his gaze met mine, a fresh wave of melancholy hit me. He looked like a broken man. The light that had shone from his eyes these last few days was gone, replaced with a coldness I hadn't seen in them since I first arrived. Even though Shep sat right in front of me, I missed him because this wasn't the same man I'd woken up next to this morning.

I shook my head. "Please, let me explain. I never wanted to hurt—"

"Wait." Shep held up a hand. "I've been thinking, and there are some things I need to say. You know I'm not great with this sort of thing, so hear me out for a minute."

I nodded, nervous as hell at what he might be about to tell me.

He hesitated with his words and instead focused on twisting the leather band at his wrist. Then his crestfallen eyes came to mine. "I don't regret deceiving Franky and bringing you here. But you're right. I shouldn't have chained you up and held you against your will." He rolled his shoulders and gazed out the window as if those mountains held answers. "Too many years living the way I have, it's fucked with my head. Sometimes I don't even know what's right or wrong anymore. Those lines are so blurred that I won't ever be... normal again."

God, I hated seeing him struggle with this.

His focus returned to me. "What I'm trying to say is, you should have had a choice to stay or not, and I'm sorry I never gave that to you." Shep's throat bobbed. "When Ben has your brother, I'll send you to him. I'll get you a car, cash, whatever you need to give you the best chance possible. I don't think it's a good move for you to leave here, but I'm giving you the choice to decide where you go and how you do it. The choice I should have given you at the start of all this."

I stared at him in stunned silence. That wasn't what I expected him to say. Perhaps more accusations about my behavior, or him renewing his stance on keeping me here, but not my freedom and the means to do whatever I wanted.

"Thank you." It couldn't have been easy for him to arrive at that decision, not after the way I'd treated him.

"So, take some time to think about it and let me know what you need."

He stood to leave, so I grabbed his hand. "Wait. I already know what I need. I don't have to think about it."

He resisted, but I held on tight and pulled him back to sitting.

"There's only one thing." I squeezed hard. "I need *you*."

Shep clicked his tongue. "Cam, don't do this."

"You've said your piece, now it's my turn."

I took his exasperated sigh as my cue to continue.

"You're wrong about me. I haven't been playing you. Except for what I did today, my words and actions have been genuine the whole time."

He held my stare, but seemed unconvinced. I expected that, so I drew a deep breath because it was time to come clean. No more holding back. If I had any hope of salvaging things between us, I needed to be honest. With Shep and with myself.

"I can't describe the whirlwind of emotions I've struggled with since you brought me here. Fearing for my life, learning about my hit contract and worrying about Justin non-stop has been really hard. The weight on my shoulders should have broken me ten times over. But it hasn't... because of you. And even though my whole world is falling apart around me, there are moments shining through where I'm... happy." An incredulous laugh escaped me. "That shouldn't be possible. I should be a non-functioning ball of fear and anxiety."

I licked my dry lips. "Being here hasn't gone at all like I thought. I didn't expect your generosity, and I sure as hell never imagined I'd enjoy your company so much. I think maybe you're surprised by how well we get along, too."

A slight shrug was the only acknowledgment I received.

"I like it here. The quiet, the space. I adore Ranger." The pointer, still on the couch beside me, lifted his head at hearing his name, so I scratched his neck.

I gazed deep into Shep's eyes. "And then there's you." My throat tightened as I considered what this man meant to me. "I never dreamed of finding someone like you among all of this. You're important to me, and not only because you saved my life.

I'm talking about the complete package. You think you're a bad person. You're not. Yes, you've done things that are messed up. And I know you've been living in a dark place, but I see who you are beyond that. I see the real you, Shep. A man who is considerate and kind and so damn sweet sometimes it makes my heart melt. When I'm with you I feel safe and cherished, and I can't remember the last time I experienced that, or if I ever have." My voice quavered. "You make me stronger and you give me hope that I'll get through the toughest time of my life."

Shep adjusted his position, shifting his body closer to mine. I did the same because I ached to touch him. Our knees bumped, and I stretched my hands out to grip his thighs.

"I haven't been tricking you. The only person I've been fooling is me. Pretending that my attraction to you is nothing more than a distraction from what's been going on. Telling myself that it's better if I don't get close to you because I'm terrified of having my heart broken when I leave. Refusing to acknowledge that you're the best damn thing to come into my life." I hoped like hell he saw the truth in my words. "I care about you so much. And this thing going on between us, I don't even know what to call it, but it means a lot to me. *You* mean a lot to me."

Did I have a crush on Shep? No, it was much more than that. I couldn't define it, but I'd always have a place for him in my heart, that much I was sure of.

His brow knitted. "You're serious?"

"Completely." My palms clutched his jaw. "I don't need time to think my plans over. I don't want to go anywhere. I just want to be with you."

Then I kissed him. I had only meant to touch lips before releasing him and assessing his reaction, but his warm mouth felt so incredible that I couldn't pull away. And besides, he wasn't pushing me away either. His lips parted when I deepened the kiss. The groan that came from him lit a fuse inside me. I wanted more from him. So much more.

Oh hell, I wanted *everything*.

Large hands cupped the back of my head while drawing me nearer. At that, I launched myself at Shep, throwing my arms around him and straddling his lap. He caught me and didn't miss a beat, returning my kiss with as much fervor as I dealt out.

We couldn't get at each other fast enough. There were too many clothes, too many barriers between our bodies. I wanted them gone, stat.

"Your bed," I panted between kisses.

He didn't answer as he carried me to the back of the house, never once taking his lips from mine. I clung to him, arms around his neck, thighs around his waist while he supported my ass with his hands. His grip on me was firm, squeezing and pulling me ever closer.

In the hallway, he pressed my back against the wall, releasing my mouth only to run his scorching lips down my neck, nipping and sucking as he went. I turned my face skyward as goose bumps spread across my body. Goddamn, I wanted him. Needed him.

Shep paused to rest his forehead against mine.

"Why have we stopped?" I gasped when he ground himself against me.

"I have to know this is what you really want before I get you naked on that bed." His breaths came rapidly, his voice rough and strained. "Do not misunderstand me. I need to be inside you more than I need my next breath, but you should tell me to stand down right now if you're not sure about this."

His lips returned to my neck while he waited for my answer.

I gripped his hair as I fought to catch my breath. "If you even think about stopping, I'll have to hurt you."

"Thank fuck for that," he mumbled against the sensitive skin behind my ear.

And we were off again. It was my turn to lay claim to his neck now, and when I breathed him in, oh my God, he smelled divine. Soap, pine, and Shep's intoxicating scent. I couldn't get enough of it.

He took long strides toward the bedroom. When we got there, he tossed me onto the bed and wasted no time pulling my shirt over my head and the boxers down my legs, leaving me bare before him. He towered over me, gazing at my body like he was a starving man and I was his next meal.

"So beautiful." Shep crawled up the bed to meet me.

My skin tingled where he placed a chaste kiss on the inside of my ankle before wrapping it around his hips. I dug my heel into the firm muscles of his lower back and dragged him closer. My heart stuttered when that elicited a smile from him. A short time ago, that seemed impossible.

I flashed him a sly grin in return before yanking his shirt over his head. When my eager fingers fumbled with his fly, he helped by shucking off his jeans, boxers going with them. Good to know he was as impatient as me.

His lips crashed to mine with urgency. Heat pooled low in my belly with his body pressed against me, his hard length between us.

I wanted to touch Shep everywhere, run my lips over every inch of golden skin, explore every muscle and scar on his body. I wasn't sure how many days I had left to memorize everything about him. Even if I had weeks, months or years, it still wouldn't be enough.

I pulled him closer and kissed him harder. His lips were soft but full, and they fit to mine perfectly. I could spend hours devouring them, never coming up for air. It was sweet relief not holding back anymore. To show him how much I wanted him was gratifying.

I reached between us and his whole body tensed above me when I took him in my grip. Damn, he was hot, thick, and hard as smooth, sculpted marble. Before I had the chance to do anything more, he groaned, grabbed my wrist, and pinned it above my head.

I pouted. "That's not fair."

"It's been a while between dances. If you're gonna enjoy this like I want you to, keep that hand up there."

How long had it been since Shep was with a woman? If he wanted to slow things down so this would last longer, I was on board with that. Well, I'd try, but I couldn't make any promises.

I did as he asked, and he rewarded me with searing kisses down my neck and collarbone. My free hand clutched his hair when his mouth found my breast. While one large palm squeezed gently, his tongue swirled over my hardened nipple. Dear lord, his touch ignited me.

Fingertips skated over my hypersensitive skin and wherever he touched, his lips followed. It surprised me he wasn't rushing this. In my experience, most guys wanted to sprint right to the finish line. If Shep wanted to take his time and get me all worked up, I was one lucky girl.

He moved further south, kissing a trail past my navel, hip bone, and along the inside of my thigh. My fingers dug into the sheets as every nerve ending sparked to life.

Shep smoothed a hand all the way down my leg until he gripped my calf and propped it over his shoulder. He stared between my thighs, and his warm breath fanned across delicate flesh.

"Christ, you're gorgeous." His voice was heavy with need.

A flash of insecurity hit me at what he was about to do. "Wait."

He paused and gave me his full attention. "You want me to stop?"

I had to give him extra credit for not sounding annoyed or

frustrated. If anything, he seemed concerned about my wellbeing.

"It's just... I know some guys don't like to do that." I didn't want Shep doing something to please me if he didn't enjoy it.

A flicker of confusion crossed his face. "Maybe selfish dumbasses who don't know what they're doing." I watched him moisten his lips before he added, "Lately, I can't get the thought of tasting you out of my head."

Oh, boy. His words had me burning up. "Really?"

"Mmm hmm. You all right with where this is heading?" He ran a finger along my seam.

My eyes rolled back. "God, yes."

I was a goner.

Shep's gaze followed his finger as it stroked through my wetness before he pressed a scarred hand flat on my chest and eased me back down onto the bed. My heart pounded with nervousness, excitement, and anticipation.

He brought his mouth to where his finger had been and traced his heated tongue over me. Blinding pleasure overwhelmed my senses, and any lingering shyness vanished. My hips bucked off the bed and the leg wrapped around his shoulder squeezed tight. The sensation was intense. I guessed it had been a while for me, too. Or maybe it was because Shep turned me on like no one else.

When he gripped my thigh to hold me in place, I knew I was in trouble. Except it was the most delicious trouble I could ever imagine, and he was only getting started. This was pure, heavenly torture. Any minute now, I'd be making enough noise to scare away all wildlife within a ten-mile radius.

He kept at me, tasting and teasing, making me quake with every pass of his tongue until he had me in a frenzy. Sweet Jesus, that man's mouth was sinful.

But it was when he concentrated his efforts on my most sensitive spot and pushed one long finger inside me that I came apart. The orgasm that ripped through me was cataclysmic. I couldn't stop the moan that escaped me, even if I'd wanted to.

As I came down, my entire body pulsed like a slow-beating tribal drum. There must be fingernail marks on his shoulders from how hard I gripped them, but the only thing I could look at was Shep's face as he gazed at me with hooded eyes.

Yeah, he'd done good, and now all I could think about was getting my mouth around him.

"Get your ass up here," I panted. "It's my turn to play."

"Yes, ma'am." He kissed a scorching path back to my mouth.

I clutched his face between my palms. "You are insanely good at that."

A small smile played across his lips. "I'm glad you think so because I plan on waking you up like that every day you're here. That all right?"

"You might legit kill me with orgasms, but that sounds like a good way to go." I latched onto his full bottom lip with my teeth because there was something about Shep that drove me to behave like an insatiable animal. My need for him was spiraling out of control.

My hands couldn't decide which part of him they wanted to touch next. Every inch of him looked inviting. His broad shoulders, those fine, fine biceps, his ass. Having unrestricted access to all the parts I'd been fantasizing about made me dizzy.

I wanted him on his back so I could explore, but when I tried to roll him, he held me in place by pressing himself against me and letting me know he was still as hard as he'd been earlier.

Wicked, wicked man.

He rubbed the tip of his nose along mine. "You can play later. Right now, I really need to be inside you."

Shep's words sent my pulse into overdrive. He didn't have to convince me any further, but when he kissed me and stroked his length across my entrance, my craving for him was absolute.

I wrapped my legs around his waist and dragged him toward me.

He jerked back and his entire body went rigid before he closed his eyes. "Wait."

"What's wrong?"

"I don't have any protection. I never thought this could happen between us. And you're not on the pill."

I breathed a sigh of relief and smiled. "It's all good, I'm covered."

He tilted his head in question.

"I swear, you won't knock me up."

"You're sure?"

Shep must be clueless about all the methods of female contraception available, and I wasn't about to enlighten him right now. "Yes! Don't stop!" I didn't mean to snap at him, but there was only so much this girl could take.

He came back to me, his lips finding a new, less hurried pace against mine. Then he pushed inside me, inch by glorious inch, giving my body the chance to adjust to his size. My jaw dropped at the ecstasy consuming me. I kept my eyes open and held his gaze.

He stilled above me once he was all the way in. "You okay?" he asked.

Perhaps he mistook my silence for discomfort, but the reality was, I struggled to grasp how much Shep meant to me after such a short time. Those emotions were genuine and not misplaced. I couldn't use the L-word, because it would be crazy to speak of so soon, wouldn't it? Whatever this was, it was real, and it was precious, and I wanted it more than anything.

I smiled and told him the truth. "Never better."

I'd been waiting my entire life for something as powerful as this, never believing I'd ever find it, and certainly not with a hitman. With my family dramas and proven track record of terrible boyfriends, I'd given up hope of meeting someone like Shep.

If only I could keep him.

No, I wouldn't dwell on that. Not when the man I hungered for was in bed with me and rocking my world.

I moved my hips to meet his, to draw him even nearer, and so he understood I was one hundred percent ready.

"Gonna move now, darlin'. You feel so good I can't hold back any longer." He whispered the words against my lips before kissing them gently.

It was the last gentle thing he did.

Shep hitched one of my thighs higher and made good on his words. I tossed my head back on the pillow and gasped because, damn, that was curl-your-toes good.

His lids closed for a moment as though needing to compose himself, and when he opened them, there was enough intensity there to intimidate someone who didn't know and trust him the way I did. His expression was one of a man trying to hold himself back, but desperate to give in to his desires. I wished he would, even if I had agreed to his earlier request to take things slow. Seeing Shep come undone above me was something I ached to witness.

"Fucking hell, Cam." He shook his head as if he couldn't believe how good this was.

Sex had never been this way for me before. I didn't know it could be so... emotionally charged. Was it because we'd argued earlier, and this was makeup sex? I didn't think so. It was more than that. It was meaningful, beautiful. And Shep had opened my eyes to how unbelievable it could be.

With each commanding stroke, a slow heat built inside me. I ran my hands over the expanse of Shep's chest, marveling at how darn sexy he was with his flexing muscles, disheveled hair and a light sheen of sweat glistening on his skin. I decided I very much liked this wild, unkempt version of my well-ordered man. I liked it even more that I was responsible for transforming him into this incredible beast.

And yet I sensed he still held something back. That wouldn't do. I had to have more. "I need you, Shep. All of you. *Everything.*"

His mouth met mine. "You have me. I'm yours."

And then he gave in and let himself lose control. His movements became more frantic, his breathing rapid. Each of us clung to the other with firm hands, our bodies coming together in a way that made my belly tighten and my heartbeat skyrocket.

He was close now, as was I. His pace took on a new urgency, working me in just the right way. That was all I needed to tip me over the edge. Wave after blissful wave crashed through me as I tightened around him. Moments later, I watched in awe as he found his own release. He held himself above me, chest heaving and a reverent look in his eyes.

Sheer sublime perfection.

He collapsed over me, but took most of his weight on his elbows. I brushed aside the hair sticking to his brow and planted a firm kiss on his mouth. I was lucky to have Shep, for however long that may be.

My troubles hadn't gone away, but I set them aside to enjoy this moment with the man I adored.

17

SHEP

If Cam's body hadn't been clenching around me with her release, I might have thought I was dreaming. But this was happening. And she was as real as could be, complete with hot, flushed skin, heaving chest, and a glint in her eye that told me she'd enjoyed that as much as I had.

I couldn't have asked for anything more.

I gazed down at her with amazement and tried to catch my breath. "Woman, what have you done to me?"

"Not enough. Come here." Cam reached behind my head and pulled me in for another kiss.

Nope, wouldn't tire of these lips anytime soon. Or her lower ones. The taste of her drove me wild.

Delicate fingers ran down my neck and across my shoulders. I'd be trying for round two if she kept that up. Damn, I hoped this wasn't a one-off thing for her. A pity fuck for the stunt she pulled earlier. We had plenty to discuss.

"Stay here, darlin'. I need to look after you. Then we'll talk some more."

Reluctantly, I removed myself from her and the bed, then went to the bathroom to grab a warm, damp cloth. When I returned, Cam lay on her side, one arm propped under her head and a lazy smile on her face. It filled me with a ridiculous amount of pride that I'd put it there.

Rolling her onto her back, I used the cloth to clean between her thighs using light strokes. I hadn't been gentle with her earlier, yet Cam had welcomed it. Hell, she'd demanded more.

She sat up on her elbows to watch me take care of her, a half smile on her lips. "No guy's ever done *that* for me before."

I grunted. Cam deserved better than those douchebag ex-boyfriends, and she deserved better than me.

I tossed the cloth on the side table and pulled the covers over both of us to make sure she was warm.

I laid on my side with my hand resting on the smooth, flat skin of her belly. "You let me come inside you. You sure that was all right?" Complicating her life with an unplanned pregnancy wasn't something I wanted to send her overseas with.

"It's fine. I've been getting the contraceptive shot for a while now. It keeps my cycle pain free. It's good for another couple of months at least." She winced. "You might have figured this out already, but my period isn't arriving soon like I told you. The shots pretty much stop them for me."

"Yeah, that was a clever move on your part. You were acting weird before I left. Thought it was PMS mood swings or something, but I couldn't be sure. That's why I chained you up. I felt like an asshole for cuffing you. I almost didn't."

Cam gnawed on her bottom lip. "I'm sorry for manipulating you like that."

"I was a fool to leave you. I figured since you were restrained and I had the truck, there was no way you'd try to get the chain off and escape on foot. The damn quad slipped my mind."

It was also a stupid mistake to leave the shed unlocked. I should've at least hidden the keys, but our fight had distracted me.

Flopping onto my back, I scrubbed my face and tried not to

think about how close I'd come to losing her today. I hadn't experienced fear like that in a long time. True *clench your bleeding heart in your fist* kind of fear. Gotta say, not a fan.

It was as though my sanity depended on Cam's safety and happiness. What was up with that? She had me vulnerable in a way I'd never been before. If she suffered, it drove me to make things better for her. Not only that, I wanted Cam to have a life full of every beautiful thing she deserved.

A messed-up hitman wasn't one of those things.

Cam rolled over and propped herself up on my chest so we were face to face. I didn't miss the fact that her breasts were pressed against me. Maintaining eye contact might be difficult.

"I'm sorry I stressed you out like that." She tilted her head. "It's weird, you know. This whole situation my brother has got us into is a nightmare, but if he wasn't such a screw-up, I'd never have met you. And I'm glad that I did."

"That was a hell of an apology." I pulled the rest of her body on top of mine so she was laying flush against me. Her wild hair hung loosely around her face and draped over my chest.

I traced my fingers from temple to jaw. She was so damn beautiful. That she'd let me touch her, be inside of her, blew my mind. Even if Cam didn't have to leave the country, someone like me didn't get to keep a woman like her. My old man was evidence of that. And besides, she'd had enough assholes in her life. She didn't need one that came with as much baggage as I did. Not to mention that it would never be safe to bring her into the seedy world I lived in. I couldn't protect her from that twenty-four seven.

I don't know why I tortured myself thinking about it. Whatever the outcome of the next week, it wouldn't end with us staying together.

"So, what happens now?" Cam asked. "With us, I mean?"

And this was why I was an asshole. I should be able to control myself with her because I was supposed to be a goddamn professional. But I didn't have the willpower to shut it down because I'd never wanted anything the way I wanted Cam. Yeah, I gave her what we both craved, but now things were even more complicated, and there was nothing I could do to fix that.

I tucked a wayward lock behind her ear. "As far as I see it, we've got two options. One, we try to pretend this didn't happen and go back to the way things were when we woke up this morning. Or two, we make the most of the time we have left by spending a lot more of it in this bed. I'm firmly voting for option two. Choice is yours, though."

"I like option two as well." She dropped her forehead to my chest to conceal her shy smile. I don't know why that embarrassed her. I was one hundred percent onboard with getting familiar with every inch of her.

I trailed my hands down to her ass and pulled her against me. "Excellent decision." I glanced at her swollen lips before kissing them.

I couldn't believe she wanted that, too. Deep down, I thought she'd come to her senses and realize it was a mistake. Maybe she still would.

"It's going to make things harder when I have to leave. At least for me it will." She pressed her lips to my chest, then looked up at me through shining eyes. "I don't care how complicated things are, I'd still choose to have this time with you."

I guessed we were both fools, then. From the moment I decided to help Cam, I knew I was playing with fire. Didn't expect it to be a flame thrower.

Getting to have her, knowing how good it could be, brought us even closer. Giving Cam up would be bittersweet. She needed to get out of here to be safe, but she'd leave a gaping hole when she got on that plane. This place wouldn't be the same without her.

And dammit, it made me see red that she had to do any of this. Fucking Franky and his revenge-seeking ego. He was the vilest kind of asshole. It didn't help that he had a bunch of cops in his back pocket, and the rest were too scared to go against him for fear of retribution. Franky's direct competition—the other gangs or wannabe mafioso families—were too weak to take on the Wolf Street crew. Somewhere along the line, they'd become so powerful there was no one to stand in their way.

Or was there? Cam would never ask for this, but maybe there was something more I could do.

"What if there was a way you could stay? What if I could make it like none of this ever happened?"

"What are you talking about?" She pushed herself a few inches from my chest and stiffened. "What about Franky? The Mafia? My hit contract?"

"Has anyone ever told you, you ask a lot of questions?"

"You're not the first." She pinched my ear lobe. "Stop trying to change the subject."

I stroked my hand along the smooth skin of her back. "Franky's upset me a lot. I'm thinking he should stop upsetting people—permanently."

Cam's brow creased. "Sweet Jesus, you're talking about killing him?"

"The guy's a menace. It needs to be done. Once you're in Australia and safe, Franky's dead."

Cam groaned as she rolled off the bed, grabbed my shirt from the floor, and slipped it over her head. "No, Shep. I don't want you to put yourself in danger because of me."

I sat up with the sheets bunched around my waist. "Think about it, Cam. If he's dead, all your problems go away."

I wanted that for her so badly. The same way I craved peace and solitude, Cam wished for her simple life back. I wouldn't have told her any of these plans, but if her ticket to Australia was return instead of one-way, it might give her some hope that everything would turn out all right. It would make this whole situation less stressful for her. Although, judging by her narrowed eyes and hands jammed against her hips, I could be mistaken.

"No, all my problems won't go away." She paced the room. "When a Philly scumbag gets killed, it's most often by you. So, they're going to know or at least suspect it's you that did it. Then every single one of them will be after you, and I am *not* okay with that." Cam paused her pacing to glare at me. "What happens then? How are you going to prevent a war with the entire Wolf Street Mob?"

She wouldn't like this part. "I wasn't planning on preventing it. Franky will be the first to go. Others will follow."

She rubbed her eyes. "Holy hell. You're talking about killing them all?" When her hands dropped to her side, she let out an exasperated sigh. "You don't have to solve every problem with violence. I don't want that for you anymore, and I don't want to be the cause of it. What if something happens to you?"

I had to lie because I didn't want Cam worrying about me, but taking on the Wolf Street Mafia solo might not be my brightest idea. The odds were against me because of the sheer numbers Franky had at his disposal. I still thought it was worth the risk, that *she* was worth it.

"Nothing's going to happen to me. I'll be fine. This is the only way to deal with Franky. I can't just call him up and ask him to back off. He'll never stand down." I reached for her hand. "I want you to have your life back. Your brother would be safe, you'd be able to see your friends again, you wouldn't have to lose your house or your car."

She sat beside me without letting go of my hand. "I don't like the way you're talking, Shep. It's scaring me. You versus the entire Wolf Street Mafia? And anybody else they pull in for support? Are you tracking how crazy this plan sounds?"

I soothed my free hand along Cam's arm. "Would it make

you feel any better if I told you it might not be the craziest thing I've done?"

She blinked a bunch of times. "No, it doesn't. Do I even want to know what you're referring to?"

"Probably not."

She paused and held my stare. "Wait, is this something to do with the Army?"

"Sort of."

"I knew it." She stabbed a finger at my arm. "You never gave me the full story, did you? What are you, Shep? Because it's obvious to me you weren't some ordinary soldier."

I took a deep breath and nodded. Time to confess. "Started out as infantry, then went to Ranger school and served in Iraq with the 75th. Worked alongside Special Forces there. They impressed me so much I decided I'd try for the Q Course. Passed that, then spent most of my time deployed in Afghanistan."

Cam's eyes bugged out. "You were Special Forces? What, like a SEAL or something?"

I snorted. "Those showy sons of bitches get all the glory. No, not a SEAL, a Green Beret. SEALs go about flashing their trident tatts and telling their hero stories, but we do our business without all the fanfare. Quiet professionals. We were involved in unconventional warfare, working with the local forces and villagers to hunt down the Taliban hiding in the mountains. We'd spend months deep in enemy territory. Long deployments, a lot of frustration, and a lot of death."

I was hesitant to admit any more. But I trusted Cam, and I didn't think her knowing about my time serving with Team Zulu would place her in any further danger. She was already up to her eyeballs in it.

"One day, a guy from the CIA approached me. Had me do a heap of practical skills and psych tests. Said they were putting together an elite team made up of operators from different units. The group was so secretive we didn't have an official name. We called ourselves Team Zulu. As in, we were the last guys you wanted tracking you down. A select few knew of our existence and gave us our missions."

"Wait, what?" She shook her head. "Now you're telling me you're some kind of CIA spy?"

"No, not a spy." I shrugged. "Just part of a team of operators who got shit done that no one else could. Most of the unit is still together, but a few of us have quit."

"Your friend, Ben. Was he one of them?"

"Yeah, he was our intelligence and tech specialist."

"What was your specialty?"

A slow grin spread across my face. "I was the weapons guy."

Cam rolled her eyes and smirked. "Should've guessed."

There were twelve in Team Zulu and we were all elite operators, multi-disciplined with specialties to boot. On our own we were lethal. As a group, we were unstoppable.

Apart from Ben Landers, we also had the best sniper on the planet, an explosives specialist, a medic, a kick ass tactician, an engineer and a couple of guys who could somehow fly anything with wings or a rotor.

"Right. So, you're telling me you were part of a coordinated bunch of the baddest baddasses in the country."

I pursed my lips. "Something like that."

I let Cam take a moment to process it all.

Her hand went to her forehead. "Wow, I didn't expect our pillow talk going in this direction." She sighed. "So, you believe you can take Franky out? You're not bluffing, are you?"

"I understand how groups like the Mafia work. I'll cut the head off the snake, watch his minions scatter and deal with them if need be. But once they see the body count rising, they'll realize that it's better to leave me in peace. Most of them are cowards, overgrown schoolyard bullies. And anyone who wants to avenge the death of Franky Russo is welcome to try. They'll get no mercy from me."

"Do you think anyone from your team will help? Ben already is." There was hope in her voice, but I'd thought this scenario through.

"Of the guys who are no longer in active service, yeah, they'd help if I asked them. But I can't do that, Cam. I won't get them involved in this."

"Why not? Are you worried about them getting hurt?"

"It is dangerous, but that's not why. Our jobs were always on foreign soil. We'd slip in, complete the mission, and be back home before anyone knew what we'd done. But doing something this high profile in our own backyard is risky. If any of my brothers got caught, I'd be condemning them to one of two fates: death row, or fleeing the country and living a life on the run."

She recoiled. "And what if you get caught?"

"Wasn't planning on sticking around to find out. Might dig out my fake German passport. Or maybe the French one. I haven't decided." I smiled.

Cam pulled her hand from my grip. "So that's what you're proposing? Trading your life for mine? Everything you have here, you'd give it all up for me?"

"I would. It's the right thing to do. For the first time in my life, I could make a difference for something that matters." I traced my thumb along her clenched jaw. "Get you home where you belong and delete Franky Russo from the world."

"Just hold up a second." She curled her hair behind her ears. "First, there's no way I'm comfortable with you putting yourself at risk like this. As impressive as your skills may be, what you're proposing is still crazy. Think about what you'd be giving up if you got caught. This place, which is your sanity. And what about Ranger? Does he go on the run with you?"

We both looked to the dog bed on the floor where Ranger

slept, his paws and lips twitching in a dream. I'm not sure when he followed us in here, or how much of our bed activities he witnessed, but he didn't seem too traumatized.

She was right, though. There was no way he could tag along if I left the States in a hurry.

"And second," she continued, "what's wrong with the original plan? You know, the one you spent so much time thinking through and demanded I go along with?" Cam gave me a pointed look.

"It's not enough anymore." I shrugged. "I don't know. Everything's different now."

"What?" she chuckled. "Because we just had mind-blowing sex?"

I smirked. "Thrilled to hear you say that, but it's not because of what just happened in this room. I mean everything is different since you got here. I didn't expect to get so protective of you. And I didn't expect things between us to be so..." I rubbed the back of my neck. "I don't even know what I'm saying."

A small smile lit Cam's face as she moved closer. "I appreciate what you're offering, but you shouldn't start a war over this. Yeah, I'm nervous about making a new life in Australia, but there are worse places in the world to go, and I'm tougher than I look. Justin will join me, and after a bit of time, we'll be fine. I'm not willing to risk your life so I can have my old one back." She placed her hands on either side of my neck. "Please, Shep, you don't need to do this to be a hero. You already are."

Her expression was so troubled, it stirred something inside me. I wanted to give back what they took from her. Eventually, she'd see it for the gift it was. Cam's sudden acceptance of moving to Australia was only because she worried about me. All along, she'd resisted the plan to start over in another country. I didn't like her making compromises for me.

I hauled her onto my lap, and she wrapped her arms

around my neck. With my nose in her hair, I breathed her in. I'd do anything to bring peace to her life again. Why couldn't we find a solution that allowed us both to be happy? It sucked that we had to choose from two fucked-up endings.

I pressed my brow to hers. "Is that really what you want? Tell me the truth."

Cam pulled back to look me in the eye, but kept her hands on my shoulders. Her answer took so long I thought perhaps she was thinking up an alternative plan. A foolish part of me wanted her to ask me to come to Australia. Hearing her say those words would mean she was in this as deep as me. More proof that I enjoyed tormenting myself.

Maybe she knew not to ask and save us both from the pain of me turning her down. Even on another continent and away from the Mob, I'd still be a messed-up asshole. A handbrake to her living the full and happy life she deserved. She couldn't have that with a cranky-ass recluse. No, I wouldn't make the same mistakes as my old man because I never wanted to see the day Cam lost her spark because of me.

She nodded. "Yes, one hundred percent. We stick with the original plan. It's a good, solid plan."

I huffed a breath. "It doesn't seem very fair that you should have to leave your home and run from one psychopathic Italian."

"Fuck fair, Shep. Life isn't fair. It never has been and that trend is continuing. Listen to me." She gripped my shoulders hard and stared me down. "Your life matters. I don't want to think about you being killed, or on death row, or on the run just so I can have my stuff back. Please don't do anything crazy after I'm gone. Promise me?"

I thought about Ranger and what we had here in the mountains. My life wasn't all sunshine and rainbows, but I was content living on the land. Going on the run, it would be hard to find peace again. Leaving Ranger behind would suck.

I didn't want to admit it to myself, but this woman had some power over me. Her negotiation skills were decent, but when it came down to it, I struggled to say no to anything Cam asked for.

I ran a hand through her hair. "All right, we stick with the original plan, for now."

A look of relief washed over her. "Good, thank you."

"But if things change with Franky and you're at risk from him, the new plan is the fallback."

"You're a decent man, Elias Shepherd." With a small smile on her lips, she leaned in and kissed me.

When she pulled away, I forced a grave expression. "Darlin', we got another serious problem we need to do something about."

Cam tensed. "Oh God. What else?"

I sucked on my bottom lip. "Love the way you look in my shirt, but you're wearing too many clothes." I shifted her so she straddled me. She giggled as I lifted the shirt over her head.

Goddamn, the sight of her naked was something to worship.

I grabbed her ass and ground my hardening length against her. "Your choice. Stay as you are, or let me decide how to make you come."

Her eyes widened before her smile turned mischievous. "I'm not sure how much I can move. My legs are still a little wobbly."

"Good." I grinned. "Plan on keeping you that way."

I flipped her onto her back so fast she squealed. Brushing her hair aside, I went right for her neck. Her scent there drove me crazy. I grazed my teeth across her skin and she let out a moan. Yeah, I needed to hear more of that.

A low growl rumbled from my chest. I kept acting like a Neanderthal around Cam, all instinct and little logic. Already I wanted to plunge deep inside her, to have her cling to me and forget about anything outside this room. But I had enough sense to hold back and make this good for her.

Our mouths met, and it reminded me why I should take my time. Every part of her warranted my attention.

Sex with Cam was like nothing I'd experienced before. It was the comfort of coming home and an adrenaline rush all at once. Our bodies moved like they were meant to be together, not awkward like it could be with a new partner. And yet, being with her set me on fire and brought me to life.

Long ago, the battlefield beat my emotions into submission. Nothing rattled me, nothing got me worked up. But this week with Cam had awoken something in me.

I pulled back from our kiss to look her in the eyes. "Almost lost you today." The thought of what might've happened to her away from my protection sent a chill through me.

She brought a hand to my cheek. "I'm here, Shep. I'm with you, and I'm safe."

I turned my head and kissed her palm. "I know. It's gonna take a while to sink in."

What I wouldn't do for this woman.

I ran my hand down the length of her body, taking the time to explore every soft bump and curve along the way, then stopped at the apex of her thighs. She moaned as my fingers explored, finding her slick and hot. When I moved my thumb a little higher, she inhaled a sharp breath and her hips jumped.

That was all the encouragement I needed.

One of her hands clutched the bedsheets while the other dug its nails into my bicep. I continued to work her, stroking and circling, all the while kissing her and watching her beautiful face to discover what things she liked most.

Her moans grew louder and her movements more frenzied until she cried out. It was a magnificent thing to watch her come.

This I could do for her. Use my hands, mouth, and cock to

make her body sing with pleasure. Which was lucky because I didn't do flowers and romance, and I sure as hell was no wordsmith. It was hard for me to explain how I felt about her. It was intense and had come on fast.

I needed her right now. Before Cam had even come down, I pushed all the way inside her in one hard stroke. Beyond incredible.

Her head flung back onto the pillow. "Yes," she moaned, her voice husky.

My control faltered at her words, but I willed myself to refocus so I could appreciate this moment. I brought my mouth to hers while driving in even deeper.

This is what I craved. Being so far inside her I couldn't tell where my body ended and hers began. And still, it wasn't enough.

I thrust in harder, needing more and became hyper-aware of every sweet sensation. Her panting breaths against my lips, her smooth, heated skin pressed against mine, and her inner muscles already tightening around me. I catalogued all of it because in the pit of my stomach I knew I had to make the most of our remaining time.

As I continued to move in her, the dark thoughts fell from my mind because being with Cam was so damn perfect. This right here was better therapy than some shrink asking me what I felt about shit. She made me want to do better, be better. For so long, I'd been numb to the world around me. Then this beautiful, strong-willed woman crashed into my life and changed everything, and I wished I never had to let her go. I wanted to tell her these things, but it was unwise to put those words out there with where we were heading. Besides, I was useless at verbalizing that stuff, so I did my best to show Cam how much she meant to me.

And judging by the way she shuddered and cried out in my arms, I showed her two more times.

18

CAMERON

The scalding bathwater soothed my tired muscles. If I laid here with my eyes closed for much longer, I risked drifting to sleep.

When footsteps approached from the hallway, I opened one eye and tilted my head toward the door. My pulse quickened when Shep entered the room with a knowing smile on his face.

Perhaps I wasn't sleepy after all.

"Thought you might be hungry." He placed a sandwich on the small table next to the bath.

"Thanks." I grinned, then sank lower.

A girl could get used to this treatment. I needed to remember that I wasn't that girl.

Shep sat on the edge of the tub, letting his gaze roam over my submerged body.

His eyes returned to mine. "Good news. Ben's picked up Justin. Your brother is safe."

I gasped. "He is?" I closed my lids and let that information soak in. When I opened them, I reached for Shep's hand and squeezed. "Thank you."

He nodded as if saving my brother's life was no big deal.

"Stay here awhile. I'm gonna take the truck and go get the quad. Won't be long."

He leaned down and pressed his lips to mine. Before he could pull away, I brought my dripping wet hand to his neck and held him to me, deepening the kiss. It sent a fresh spark of electricity through me.

I let him go and when he righted himself, he looked as though he were contemplating jumping in the bath with me or tossing me over his shoulder and hauling me to the bedroom. Both were great ideas.

I flashed him an innocent grin. "Bike, babe. Remember?"

He dragged a hand through his hair and chuckled. "Ah, right. I'm on it."

"And Shep?"

"Yeah?"

"Hurry back." I ran my hand down my neck, over one breast and between my legs. His eyes blazed as they followed the movement. I was a cruel woman.

He'd never leave the house if I carried on like this so, I stopped teasing and blew him a kiss.

Shep shot me a meaningful look before heading for the door. "We're finishing this when I get home."

I was so up for that.

~

WITH AN OVERSIZED FLUFFY white towel wrapped around my body, I rummaged through shopping bags looking for something to wear. I rarely bought clothes for myself, so Shep's gift was a real treat. I settled on a pair of light blue skinny jeans and a white V-neck T-shirt. And because I could, I slipped on the gorgeous tan leather cowboy boots. I also threw on an olive-green knitted sweater because it was cool this afternoon, even though Shep had stoked the fire before leaving.

God, what a day. It had started out troubled, but ended up incredible when Shep and I took things to another level.

Did I want that? Absolutely.

Was it a terrible idea? Maybe.

My feelings for him grew stronger every day. I wished I didn't have to give him up, but I could never ask Shep to leave everything he had here and move overseas. It was obvious he loved this place. These mountains and Ranger were his therapy.

Plus, if all things went to plan, Justin would live with me in Australia. I'd have to keep a close eye on him to make sure he stayed clean and out of trouble. I laughed at the mental image of Shep, my brother, and me sharing a house. That could never happen. Justin's life would be in more danger than it was now.

Rolling thunder echoed in the distance. I glanced at the dark clouds gathering in the east. I hoped Shep and Ranger made it home before the bad weather hit. But I couldn't think of anything better than a stormy night spent tangled up in bed with my attentive man. In fact, if we never had to leave his room for the next week, I was fine with that. My belly tumbled thinking about it.

After preparing a batch of coffee, I left it to brew for a few minutes.

When the sound of tires on gravel signaled Shep's return, I smiled and reached for a second mug.

The hair at the back of my neck stood on end. The engine noise was wrong. That wasn't the low V8 rumble of Shep's truck.

The cup slipped from my grip in my haste to spin around.

Smash!

My boots crunched over shards of porcelain on my way to the window. I staggered back from the sheer curtains when a black sedan came into view.

"Holy shit," I whispered.

The car stopped at the front of the cabin. The two men inside it didn't look like cops. I didn't like the alternative any better. Shep said this place was a secret and he never had visitors.

This was bad.

Seriously fucking bad.

The older one, a stocky guy in his mid-forties, stepped out of the car with an air of cockiness about him. He took in his surrounds as if he owned the place while stroking his dark beard. As he removed his suit jacket, twin pistols in a leather shoulder holster were exposed giving me the impression he was eager to display the firepower he wielded.

The younger guy's eyes darted around the property, his face set in a grim expression. One hand scraped back and forth over his short-cropped dark hair while the other fidgeted over a bulge at his hip, his black leather jacket concealing what must be a pistol.

My heart hammered in my chest. I covered my mouth to hold in a whimper. With no weapon, no phone, and nowhere to hide, I was a sitting duck.

Shep, I need you.

The older one lit a cigarette, then leaned against the car casual as can be. "Lopez, go knock on the door." His voice carried a thick Philly accent.

Lopez shifted his weight between his feet, his head whipping back and forth between the older guy and the house. "What?" He choked out a nervous laugh. "Jesus, Pauly, he would've heard us pull up. The workshop's open, there's no car inside. He's not home. We should leave."

Pauly sneered. "Why are you so scared of him? He sneaks around killing assholes, probably shoots them in the back. Anyone can do that." He took a drag on his cigarette before blowing the smoke skyward. "You're right, he's not home. But the boss said look around, so that's what we'll do." He pushed away from the car, then swaggered for the stairs.

Lopez stayed put, his caramel skin turning pale. "I think that's a bad idea."

Pauly ignored the comment.

Lightning flashed, and I startled when booming thunder rattled the windows. My heart pounded even faster.

Lopez glanced at the darkening sky and mouthed what appeared to be a string of obscenities, or perhaps a prayer. He lifted the collar of his jacket around his neck and tucked his chin to his chest as though he noticed a sudden drop in temperature, then jogged to catch up with his offsider.

Pauly flicked his cigarette onto the gravel drive. "Quit being such a pussy."

I had to get out of here.

With trembling fingers, I locked the front door before creeping to the utility room at the back of the house. It was the only other exit.

I flinched when the timber stairs out front creaked. Moments later, the door handle rattled.

Hurry, hurry!

My skin prickled as I snuck out the back door and closed it behind me, the small click of the latch making me wince. Every tiny sound I made was amplified in my ears.

I moved around the back of the house and crept under the deck near the wood pile. My heart threatened to punch right through my chest.

One of them tried to kick the door in. Wood groaned and hinges rattled. Again, they kicked, then again, with success on the third attempt judging by the almighty crash of the heavy door.

I peeked between gaps in the decking. They were inside the cabin. Time to get going.

On shaking legs, I bolted for the cover of the workshop.

From there, I made a beeline for the woods and kept running, too scared to check if they'd noticed me.

The pulse throbbing at my temple was almost as loud as the crunch of dry leaves underfoot. I wished there were traffic noises or anything that might disguise my hurried steps.

I ducked behind a large tree and took a moment to catch my breath. Slowly, I peered around the trunk. I was well hidden, but still close enough to peek glimpses of the house.

I could hide here, wait until they'd finished snooping, then return when it was safe. One thing was certain. If I ran too far away and Shep returned, he'd see the busted down door and think someone had taken me. Then he'd lose his ever-loving mind and go on a killing spree, so I needed to remain close.

The men spent a few minutes inside before returning to the front deck. Pauly stood with hands on hips, scanning the tree line. His gaze passed right over my hiding spot.

I froze.

They couldn't see me; I was sure of it. Lopez looked to the trees while holding his weapon at the ready. Something spooked him.

They walked down the stairs and entered the workshop only to emerge empty handed a short time later.

Lopez skulked to the far side of the clearing while Pauly headed for the tree line, only a hundred feet from my hiding spot.

I ducked back behind the trunk, the rough bark digging into my spine. I tried to slow my breathing and calm my nerves.

Maybe I should have gotten further away when I had the chance. I wished I'd had time to bring a weapon with me. I wished I wasn't glued to the spot listening to Pauly's footsteps grow louder. But most of all, I wished Shep was here. He'd know what to do.

"Shep's lady friend," Pauly drawled. "You can come out now.

We know you're around here somewhere. We only want a little chat. Not gonna hurt you."

Holy hell. I hadn't been thinking straight. My new things were on the dining table, the fire was lit, hot coffee sat on the counter. Of course they knew someone was home. At least they seemed unaware it was me, the woman they'd paid to have murdered.

"We're pals of Shep's," Pauly continued. "Work colleagues, you could say. We only want to pass on a message."

I crouched low and risked another glance. On the far side of the clearing, Lopez looked twitchy. He clenched his weapon and stared into the woods as if a lion might leap out and pounce on him. Pauly also had his pistol drawn. The sinister grin on his brutish face told me the son of a bitch was enjoying this.

"Don't make us come looking for you. We might get angry if we have to track you down." Pauly bent to inspect something on the gravel. "We know you're on your own."

Please don't find my footprints.

He stood and used hand gestures to call Lopez over.

Twigs snapped and leaves crunched as their footfalls grew louder. If I stayed here, they'd find me. If I moved, I had a chance of escaping. It had to be soon because they were coming this way. Frozen in fear, I wasn't even sure I could will my muscles to move.

Bright lightning was quickly followed by deafening thunder. I almost jumped out of my skin, but instead flung into action hoping the echoing boom might disguise my frantic steps. I ran downhill toward the river setting a cracking pace.

"There she is!" shouted Pauly.

I sprinted faster. Franky's men crashed through the woods, giving chase.

Their shouting grew more distant. I was thankful for my nightly runs as I fled over the forest floor.

Low branches whipped my face and arms as I raced past. If I made it to the river with enough of a lead, the noise from the fast-flowing water should conceal my sounds. I'd change direction from there, find a new hiding spot, and sit tight. It was a vast forest. It could take them hours to track me down. And that would buy me time for Shep to return and figure out what had happened. It could be my only shot.

The sound of rapids grew louder. *Almost there.*

A gunshot fired and splinters exploded on a tree next to me. A scream erupted from my lungs. I ducked for cover but kept moving. I had to.

Bursting through foliage, I stumbled on an embankment. As I slid down the steep slope, my hands grazed against rocks. At last, I'd reached the river.

Go faster.

I sped along the rocky shore. My energy flagged as the adrenaline ran dry. I sucked in cold air, my lungs burning, and pushed onward. A little further and I could find a hiding spot and rest.

Movement flashed before me. Lopez sprang through the trees.

I cried out as I skidded and fell on my ass.

Lopez already had his weapon aimed at me, his face ruddy and chest heaving. "Don't you"—he bent over, gasping, but kept his pistol aimed at me—"Don't you fuckin' move."

It was over. They'd kill me out here once they realized who I was. I held back stinging tears. Misty white clouds formed on each ragged exhale.

Pauly emerged a moment later, flushed and out of breath. He wheezed as he lumbered for me. His mouth twisted in a cruel grin.

As he advanced, I crawled backward along the pebbled shore. My grazed hands stung as they met with cold water. My jeans and boots were soaked through.

He combed his fingers through his receding hair, trying to bring it into line. “Well, well. What have we got here? Your face has been all over the news. Aren’t you supposed to be dead?” Pauly laughed. Lopez didn’t appear amused. He still looked nervous as hell.

I shivered, my teeth chattering so hard my jaw ached. I didn’t want them to see me scared. The slimy bastard in front of me would get off on it.

“Holy shit.” Pauly continued. “Shep is in a whole heap of trouble. I guess Franky was right to send us up here to snoop around. He won’t believe what we found.”

I stood, shoulders back and spine straight. They wouldn’t have the satisfaction of witnessing my fear. Instead, I channeled my terror into anger.

These men, these monsters, wanted me dead. Their boss had turned Shep and my lives upside down, and I was so sick of being afraid. If flight was no longer an option, I’d fight these assholes until my dying breath.

Pauly holstered his pistol and sauntered toward me, hands on hips. His tongue traced the side of his mouth. My stomach churned as he approached.

“Now what are we gonna do with you?” Pauly tilted his head, the look of a predator assessing its trapped prey. “Since you’re supposed to be six-feet under, we could have some fun out here, the three of us, and then finish the job that Shep was paid a lot of money to do.” He raised a hand to his bearded chin. “Or we could take you back to our boss. Leave a little message here for Shep.” He reached for my hair. I flinched as he picked up a lock and rubbed it between his fingers. “An ear, a toe? Tell him to come collect you. Would be much easier than tracking him down. And sweetheart, I know he’s gonna come for a pretty thing like you. I bet he’s already been doing a lot of coming for you. Am I right?” He laughed at his vile joke.

Slimy creep.

More thunder rumbled overhead, and the first drops of rain were like ice on my skin.

I wanted to tell this douchebag what I really thought of him, and to explain that if anything happened to me, Shep would hunt them down and end them.

It went against all my instincts, but I held my tongue. Aggravating Pauly wasn't clever because I absolutely did not want to have *fun* with him out here before meeting my end. If the alternative was being taken to Franky Russo, then at least I'd stay alive a little longer. There was always the possibility of escaping on the journey there. First, I had to bluff my way out of the current situation.

I worked against the dryness in my mouth to get my voice to work. "I have information. For Franky Russo."

"Oh yeah? What kind of information?"

I shook my head. "Take me to your boss. I'll only tell him." I tried to take a step back, but Pauly grabbed me around the waist and pulled me against him.

"You know, I could make you tell me. I would enjoy that. A lot." I cringed at the feel of his arousal pressing into my belly.

Sick bastard.

The rain fell heavier. Fat drops soaked my clothes and plastered Pauly's hair to his forehead.

"Get your hands off of me," I growled and aimed him with a death stare.

"Or what?" His dark stare traveled to my chest. I wanted to gouge his eyeballs out of their sockets.

"If you hurt me, Shep will come for you."

"Is that so?" A cruel smile emerged on his face. "I'm not scared of him. No, sweetheart, the only man I fear is Franky Russo. Your boyfriend should too, because he's gonna be meeting him real soon, and I can't wait to see how that plays out."

"I don't think you want Shep in the same room as your boss. It won't end well for him." I shoved against his chest to break his hold, but his hands tightened around me.

"You wanna know what I think?" His eyes widened with excitement, sending a shiver of repulsion rippling through me. "I think your mouth should be doing something other than talking."

It didn't matter if I gave him any information or not, he wasn't going to let me leave these woods unscathed.

Pauly loosened his belt buckle.

Not a chance, asshole.

I grabbed him by the shoulders and rammed my knee into his balls. He unleashed a strangled moan before doubling over, eyes bulging. I let loose a feral snarl and slammed his face with my elbow. The sickening crunch of bone and cartilage released a gush of blood. He staggered back. One hand clutched his nuts, the other his nose.

I'd thrown everything at him, yet he still stood.

Pauly bared his teeth and charged. I dodged, but he caught my sweater and hauled me to him. His hands clamped around my throat. A choked sound escaped me. I couldn't breathe, couldn't scream. My fingernails clawed his face and shredded his wrists, but he didn't let go.

"You stupid bitch. You're dead!" Pauly yelled. The pouring rain streaked blood down his lips and chin.

Seconds felt like minutes. The rage in his eyes would be the last thing I'd ever see. My vision closed in and flickered. My heavy arms weakened.

There was a flash of movement before we were thrown sideways. Pauly's hands tore from my throat as we slammed into the shallow riverbed. I coughed and sputtered, sucking in desperate lungfuls. Dizziness lingered, but I had to move. On hands and knees, I crawled through the icy water.

My spinning head filled with strange noises. Hysterical shouting. A savage animal growling.

Ranger!

The pointer's long white fangs clamped around Pauly's forearm. The vicious snarling intensified as Ranger thrashed, tearing flesh.

Pauly shrieked like a dying animal as he writhed on his back. He tried to shove Ranger away with his free hand. "Shoot it! Kill it!" he yelled.

Ranger didn't let go.

Lopez panicked. The aim of his weapon darted as he tried to find a clear shot, but Ranger was all over Pauly.

A shot rang out and I ducked. When I glanced up, Ranger lay motionless in the shallows. Blood leaked from a wound in his chest.

"No!" I screamed.

Lopez stared at the scene in disbelief. His discharged weapon shook in his trembling hands. A moment later he came to his senses and searched the trees where Ranger had emerged.

Where are you, Shep? Hurry.

The heavy rain eased. Pauly staggered to his feet and clutched his forearm. His shredded, crimson-stained shirt exposed a bloody gash where Ranger's teeth had cut to the bone. Blood trickled down the fingers of his mauled arm, which hung limp at his side.

Pauly lurched for me, gasping and grimacing in pain. He withdrew a pistol and cocked it. He wasted no time aiming it at my head.

I squeezed my lids shut.

BANG!

I flinched, but opened my eyes in time to see Pauly thrown backward into the water.

A moment later, another shot rang out, sending Lopez to the ground.

The gunshots echoed off the mountains. Both men lay motionless. Bloodstained water flowed around Pauly's skull, his stare wide and unblinking.

"Shep!" I yelled. My breath hitched as a sob left my throat.

I ran to Ranger, tore my sweater over my head and pressed it firm against the bullet wound on his chest. There was so much blood.

Feet pounding over pebbles brought my eyes up. Shep bolted toward us along the river's edge, rifle slung over his shoulder. "Are there any others?" he called out as he approached.

I stood and shook my head.

When he reached us, he threw his arms around me and squeezed the air from my lungs. He held me at arm's length, checking for injury. "Did they hurt you?" He ducked to my eye level. I'd never seen him look so alarmed.

"I'm fine. We have to help Ranger."

I wasn't fine. Not at all. But I had to keep my shit together. I shrugged Shep off and pulled him to the ground so he could check Ranger's injuries.

He removed my sweater from the wound, but replaced it right away.

He shook his head. "He's alive, but I think the bullet has punctured his lung. We have to get him to the vet. Can you walk? Run?"

I nodded. "Let's go." I was an exhausted wreck and freezing cold from being soaked through, but I'd find a way.

Shep scooped Ranger up and headed the way he'd come. I stayed close on his heels as he set a fast pace.

We reached his truck in a matter of minutes. It was parked in the driveway close to the entrance to his property. How Shep and Ranger knew we were at the river was a mystery. Perhaps Ranger tracked my scent.

He laid Ranger on the rear seat with his wounded side facing down, muttering something about gravity helping to stop his lung from collapsing.

I sat in the back with Ranger. Each of his shallow breaths made a thick, gurgling sound. I ran my hand over his smooth roan coat and kissed the top of his head while whispering words of love, encouragement, and gratitude as we sped to town.

"Shep, they were Franky's men." I hadn't taken the time to contemplate what that meant. Hadn't even expected to live through what just happened.

"I know who they were." His eyes connected with mine through the rear vision mirror. "Pauly is one of Franky's most trusted. It won't take long for their absence to be noted."

How did this all go so wrong so fast?

"How did they know where to find you? I thought you said no one knew about this place?"

"Franky's crew doesn't have the skills to find me here, but Ben does." He flicked his eyes to mine in the mirror. They looked murderous. "I think he's screwed me over."

My stomach dropped and a pained cry escaped me. Ben had Justin. If he'd betrayed Shep, what did that mean for my brother?

"Did they seem surprised you were here?" he asked, perhaps to distract me from where my thoughts had headed.

"They were looking for you. They didn't realize who I was until we reached the river and they got a close look at me."

"That's good. Means Franky still doesn't know about you. But he must be suspicious to send his guys up here. It was a risk on his part. He wouldn't have expected them to receive a warm welcome. And when they don't report back, he'll assume the worst."

The muscles along Shep's forearms bunched as he gripped the steering wheel. I didn't need to see his face to know how concerned he was.

We might have won this battle, but there was a war coming our way.

19

SHEP

The tires struggled to hold traction as we sped down the mountain. I knew every twist and turn, so I pushed my truck to its limits, even though the roads were wet.

The all-too-familiar metallic tang of blood hung thick inside the car. Each of Ranger's labored breaths spurred me on. I was thankful he was still breathing. I'd seen a soldier die with a similar injury, and it was a horrible way to go.

My only solace was that Cam comforted him in the backseat. If he could hear her quiet words, he'd try to rally. I think he cared about her as much as I did, and he sure as hell had stepped up when she needed him.

"How much further?" asked Cam.

"Five minutes. Maybe less."

Her pale green eyes met mine in the rear vision mirror. "Go faster!"

That wasn't what I wanted to hear because if we went any quicker around this hairpin, we'd all be going over a five-hundred-foot drop off.

He'd saved her life today. I wasn't sure how, but I was grateful for it.

When we'd turned off the road and onto the driveway to the house, the distinct sound of gunfire surprised me. It wasn't the pitch of a rifle, which you might sometimes hear if people were hunting nearby. It was the sound of a pistol. Ranger jumped right through my rolled-down window and bolted toward the river. I grabbed my rifle and went after him. He'd bought me precious time to get close enough to line those fuckers up.

I'd almost lost Cam for the second goddamn time today. I struggled to think about it without crushing the steering wheel in my grip.

My girl was holding herself together for Ranger, even though her pale face suggested she was in some level of shock. She was a strong woman. Stronger than I gave her credit for when I first laid eyes on her.

We pulled into the parking lot outside the vet.

"Hurry, Shep. His breathing is shallow." Cam's voice was thick with emotion.

I jumped out and scooped Ranger from the back seat. "Stay here. Keep out of sight. Grab my jacket from up front."

She nodded and did as I asked. She needed warmth to prevent the shock from getting worse, plus her clothes were soaked through.

I pushed through the clinic door and found Debbie, the town's vet for the last twenty something years, seeing off a client.

She tensed when she saw us. "Ethan? What the hell happened?" She rounded the counter and rushed us into a consultation room, calling me by the alias name I used in town.

"Bullet wound. Hunting accident." I laid his limp body on the table.

She peeled Cam's sweater away to look at the injury and used her stethoscope to listen to his chest.

"Bring him through to the surgery." Her stern voice echoed through the room.

She charged to the back of the clinic, her short, stout frame taking two steps for every one of mine.

Debbie issued rapid-fire orders to a vet tech, who moved with haste to assemble what they needed.

I laid Ranger on the stainless-steel table. My heart jammed in my throat as I stepped back to give them space to work.

Debbie tied her hair back. "I've got it from here, Ethan. Why don't you wait out front?"

I nodded and backed out of the room, hating that I was powerless to help Ranger.

I paced in the waiting room for twenty minutes before slumping into a chair. The wait was killing me. My knee bounced like a jackhammer as I stared at the door leading to the surgery.

Other clients shot me furtive glances, but thankfully none engaged in conversation. The fact that I was soaking wet and covered in blood probably helped. Or perhaps they could tell I had murder on my mind. I scrubbed my hands over my face and groaned.

It hit me extra hard how much this damn dog meant to me. When I'd picked Ranger out at the shelter four years ago, he was a day from getting the big green needle. He didn't deserve it then, and I wasn't ready to let him go now. His name, scrawled on a whiteboard hanging on the door of his cage, had been a beacon. That and the sad goddamn look in his eyes. We were a perfect match.

The 75th Ranger Regiment I once belonged to had a creed. *Rangers Lead the Way*. And somehow my boy had done that. He'd taken me straight to Cam and led the fight by taking down Pauly. He deserved a Medal of Honor.

Debbie pushed through the surgery doors. I stood and braced myself to receive the news.

"Come through," she said, and ushered me into the consultation room. "One tough dog you've got there, Ethan," she said, stripping the surgical mask from her face and resting her hands on her wide hips. "He's not out of the woods yet, but he's stabilized for now."

I bowed my head in relief. "He's a stubborn beast like his old man. Can I see him?"

"Of course."

I followed Debbie to the surgery where Ranger lay sedated. A machine beeped. The repetitive sound of his steady heartbeat comforted me. Ranger's wound was bandaged with clean white gauze. It seemed like a miracle he no longer leaked blood.

"Even if his recovery goes well, he'll still need to stay with us for a week, maybe more," Debbie said.

I nodded, but didn't mention that it was for the best. I needed to get Cam somewhere safe and couldn't be nursing an injured Ranger back to health. But it sucked leaving him here, not knowing when I'd be able to return.

Debbie left the room to give us privacy. I crouched next to my boy and ran my hands over his head and neck.

I kept my voice low. "You trying to upstage me, huh? Saving my girl out from under me?" I swallowed against the lump in my throat. *Hold it together, man.* "You did, you know? You saved her life. Don't go getting all cocky about it. You're still a goddamn pain in my ass. But I promise we'll go hunting again once all this is over. Just get yourself better." I pressed my forehead to his. "Love you, boy. Hang in there." I stood and moved back. I couldn't stay in here any longer.

As I turned to leave, Debbie appeared at the door.

I cleared my throat. "I have some urgent... business to deal with. I'll be gone for a few days, but I'll call and check in on him when I can."

She nodded. "I'll look after your boy."

I made for the door.

"Ethan?"

I spun and caught the bullet Debbie tossed to me.

"Thought you might want to keep that." She folded her arms. "You and I both know that didn't come from a rifle. This was no hunting accident."

Should've expected a country girl like Debbie would know her ammo.

I glanced at the bullet, rolling it between my thumb and forefinger, then met her eyes.

"I know how much Ranger means to you, so I hope you'll make sure whoever's responsible for this is held accountable."

"Yeah. I'm on it." I nodded and headed for the door.

I FOUND Cam curled up in the rear seat, arms wrapped around her knees while rocking back and forth. Her vacant stare broke when I opened the door.

I didn't keep her waiting for the news she'd be desperate to hear. "He's alive. Stable for now, but he should pull through."

One hand flew to her mouth as she let out a relieved sob. "Thank God!"

I sat next to her and flipped the jacket hood down to get a better look. Soaked through, eyes red and puffy, blood everywhere, although I was pretty sure none of it was hers. Disturbing, striped bruises marred her slender neck.

I clicked my tongue. "Darlin'." I skimmed my fingertips over the purple marks and tried not to let Cam see the anger raging inside me. I'd never found pleasure in killing, but I wished I could have taken more time to end Pauly and Lopez. Make them pay for what they did to her, and to Ranger.

She cupped my cheek, bringing my eyes back to hers. "I'm okay."

Her reassurance settled me enough to remember to breathe. I leaned into her open palm, then kissed the inside of her wrist. "I don't like leaving Ranger like this."

"Me either. But he's tough. He'll be all right, Shep, I know it."

We both had to believe that, because abandoning him at the vet felt so wrong, but we had to move.

Cam rallied fast for someone who'd gone through hell, perhaps already sensing the urgency of our situation before I explained it to her.

"We're leaving town right now, aren't we?" she asked, determination in her eyes. She was with me no matter what lay before us.

"It's not safe for us here anymore. We might have a few hours lead time on them, but Franky will know what's gone down soon and I'll be at the top of his hit list. He won't stop now until it's over."

"Over?"

"Until one of us is dead."

She let out a whimper and gripped my forearms so hard her short nails dug in.

I held her by the shoulders and stared straight into her eyes. "Until *he* is dead, Cam. I'd stay here and stand my ground, but I won't risk you. We stick with our plan and get you out of the country as a priority. Once the wheels of your plane are up, I'm going after that son of a bitch."

This whole situation was royally fucked. My well-laid plans had to be scrapped with new ones being made on the fly. This wasn't how I liked to operate, especially not with Cam in tow.

Her body shook in my hands. "Shep, please, no."

"There are no other options now." My teeth ground together.

"Come with me to Australia. Forget about Franky. And we'll get Ranger somehow when he's recovered. Don't stay here and risk everything."

"I won't turn my back on this. I know it deep in my bones. This is the right thing to do. Franky needs to be taken out. I'm not running from that asshole."

She wouldn't like my answer, but the images of Pauly hands around Cam's throat and Ranger lying motionless on the riverbank were burned into my brain. My bloodstained shirt and the purple bruises on Cam's neck were a constant reminder of what Franky had set into motion. No way would I let him get away with this. He needed to be stopped.

She pressed her forehead to my shoulder and sobbed.

I folded my arms around her. "Shh, don't cry. This is a good thing. He won't be able to hurt anyone anymore."

Cam gripped my shirt as more tears fell, and I sensed she'd accepted there would be no changing my mind. I was the only one who could end this.

"What will happen to you?" she asked.

"Not sure. I'll take it one step at a time, adapt as I need to, and find some way out of this mess." I might not have my brothers backing me up, but I wasn't useless on my own.

She kissed me hard, then rested her forehead against mine.

"Promise me you'll be all right. *Promise me*!" she demanded, clutching my face in her hands.

"I promise."

With the hell Cam had been through, I had to lie, even though I hated it. On top of everything else she had going on in her head, I didn't want her worrying about me. But I was in no position to make promises like that.

Franky would throw everything he had at me, and I would do the same to him because we both knew the score.

Kill or be killed.

20

SHEP

The quad needed offloading from my truck since it made us identifiable. Rather than waste time taking it to the cabin, I dropped it at my mechanic's workshop on our way out of town. I also changed the license plates with a fake set in case Ben had given Franky that info, too.

We left town with only the bloodstained shirts on our backs, my wallet, a Glock, and a hunting rifle with fuck all ammo. I was ill prepared and under armed. For Cam's sake, I kept a brave face, but I needed weapons. A lot of them and fast. My fingers twitched with the lack of firepower.

Cam remained silent in the passenger seat as we twisted our way through rural lands and small towns. She gnawed on a thumbnail and gazed out the window, although I was certain she saw little of it.

We hadn't discussed what happened by the river. More than most, I understood how replaying those situations in your head caused anxiety. It concerned me she'd seen me kill two men right in front of her. Yeah, it was justified, but for someone unused to seeing things like that, it probably freaked her out.

What did Cam think of me now? She knew what I was, but

that differed from witnessing it. It wouldn't surprise me if she wanted to put some distance between us. I'd be lying if I said that didn't worry me.

She faced me with red-rimmed eyes. "Are you sure it was Ben that ratted you out to Franky?"

"Not certain, but it seems the most likely scenario. The systems I have in place to protect my identity and location are advanced, but an intelligent person with elite skills could decode all the clues if they wanted to. And for Ben, finding the unfindable is what he does best." I glanced between her and the road.

Ben was a brother, same as all the guys from Team Zulu. We trusted each other with our lives. I thought what we had was solid, and it cut deep that he'd sold me out. Why would he double cross me like that?

"What do you think Ben will do with Justin?" With shaking hands, Cam picked at dirt and blood under her fingernails.

"I don't know. All bets are off at this point. Ben's not a hitman, so I don't think he'll kill him. If I had to guess, I'd say he'll deliver him to Franky."

She slumped in her seat and rubbed her eyes.

I gripped the steering wheel hard. I hadn't mentioned it to Cam yet, but after Franky, I'd be tracking down Ben Landers. He owed me answers, and if I didn't like them, he'd follow Franky to hell.

Before crossing the state line, I pulled into the strip mall of a medium-sized town. I left Cam in the truck while I bought clothes, food, burner phones, weapons, and ammunition. We both changed out of our bloodstained threads and into new jeans and shirts.

Then we were straight back on the road, heading south. My plan was to get to Miami where Cam's documents would soon be ready. Right after that, she'd be on a plane out of the country.

It was almost dark outside. Later, we'd need to stop and rest for the night. It had been one hell of a day and we were both exhausted, but I wanted to put more miles between us and whoever Franky sent our way.

I worried about Cam. She barely spoke, drank, or ate. Even the candy bar I offered her went untouched.

What was I supposed to say? That everything would be all right? I wouldn't feed her that crap. At the very least, her brother was a probable casualty. I had no more tricks up my sleeve to help him.

I'd let her down. I shouldn't have left her alone and unprotected in the cabin. That mistake almost got her killed. The guilt from it burned like acid in my gut, eating me up from the inside. If I'd lost her... I couldn't even think about it.

Instead, I focused on the job ahead of me. I kept a constant eye out for tails or any suspicious activity. Franky's power spread far and wide, and he'd have all his resources trying to locate us.

Somewhere in North Carolina, I used the burner to call the vet and check on Ranger. Debbie told me his vital signs were strong, and he'd passed the most dangerous stage. She would stay with him at the clinic tonight to monitor his condition. I conveyed my gratitude, which didn't seem like enough.

I gave Debbie the contact details of my friend, Kane Daniels, in case she couldn't reach me. Kane was an ex-Navy SEAL, and we'd formed a close bond while on Team Zulu. Even though he lived in San Diego, I knew he'd step up and look after Ranger if anything happened to me.

Late in the evening, we crossed into South Carolina and pulled into a motel for the night. Exhausted and filthy, we both needed a shower and a place to rest our heads. The room was clean and functional, and being at the back of the motel allowed us to remain unseen from the road.

Stopping was risky, but it was more important that I

remained well rested and clear headed. Mistakes happened when you were tired.

Cam opened cupboards until she found a mini bar. Selecting a mini bottle of vodka, she downed it in a few sips.

She screwed her face up. "Ugh, that's disgusting." Her voice was raspy, no doubt a combination of the strong liquor and the damage to her larynx. Those purple bruises darkened by the hour.

Tossing the empty bottle in the trash, she reached for bourbon next and tipped it down her throat. She coughed and wiped her mouth with the back of her hand.

I had to give her a distraction from this mess. "Why don't you take the first shower?"

Cam nodded and moved to the bathroom on unsteady feet. Moments later, the water started up.

Her face appeared at the doorframe.

"Shep?"

"Yeah?"

"The shower's a decent size. Will you come in with me?" There was doubt in her voice, perhaps worried I'd say no. Not likely.

"Sure."

I followed her into the steamy bathroom. She shucked off her jeans and T-shirt, tossing them on the counter before stepping under the scorching spray. I did the same.

I pulled her close. The devastation and exhaustion in her eyes dampened any lustful thoughts. I needed to take care of her. Nothing else mattered.

"You holding up?" I asked.

Cam's heavy-lidded eyes met mine, and she nodded with little conviction. I supposed it was a stupid question. How the hell could she be all right after almost being murdered?

We were filthy, so I took the time to lather up and rinse both of our bodies. Cam was content to let me wash her hair and clean the dirt and dried blood from under her fingernails.

I held her face in my hands and traced my thumb over her cheek. Guilt ate at me. I couldn't let it sit between us any longer. "I'm sorry I let you down today."

She gazed up at me, her thick wet lashes clumped together. "You didn't let me down, Shep. You saved me. And you couldn't have known those assholes were going to show up."

I shook my head. "I convinced you to trust Ben. That was poor judgment on my part."

"You were trying to do your best with the hand we've been dealt." Cam shrugged and dropped her eyes to my chest. "We don't know anything about Justin. I'm not giving up hope yet."

I didn't share her optimism about her brother's fate, but now wasn't the time to discuss that.

I hooked a knuckle under her chin and tilted her face up to mine. "You watched me kill two men today. I don't regret it or feel even a little bad." I held her eyes, relieved to find no fear in them.

She placed one palm over my heart. "I know you, Shep. The *real* you. Seeing what you did hasn't changed how I feel about you at all." Her throat bobbed and her jaw set firm. "And I'm glad you killed them. You did what you had to do, and I'm only alive right now because they're dead."

Cam blinked long and slow, too exhausted to hold her lids open. I supported her around the waist when she swayed on unsteady legs.

"I got you." I turned the tap off and assisted her out of the shower. After helping her dry and dress, I carried her to the bed. She objected by giving my chest a light slap, but still let me fuss over her and tuck her under the covers.

After changing into boxers, I double checked that the windows and door were secure and placed my loaded Glock on the side table. I flicked the lamp off, then climbed into bed behind Cam. I held her close and drew my first full breath since hell was unleashed upon my world by the river.

I'd killed Pauly. No regrets about it, but that act alone was enough to instigate a Mafia vendetta against me. Pauly was high ranking in the Wolf Street Mob and had been by Franky's side from the beginning. They might even be related. There was no backing out now.

Cam tightened her grip on my forearm and snuggled against me. What she'd been through today was enough to bring a seasoned soldier to his knees, but she hadn't fallen apart. At least, not yet. Perhaps she was too exhausted to process anything, or she was holding it together until she felt safe enough to let go.

"What happens tomorrow?" she asked, her voice low and scratchy. Her throat must ache.

"Hit the road again. Keep heading south for Miami. It'll be a long day of driving, but we can make it there by evening. Set up a meet with my guy to get your passport sorted, then pick up your documents a day or two after." I kissed the nape of her neck and breathed her in.

"And then I'm on my way to Australia." Cam said like it left a foul taste in her mouth.

"Yeah. Where you'll be safe and won't have to watch your back anymore." I gave her a squeeze. "You've seen first-hand who we're dealing with. Now you understand why you need to get the hell out of here until it's over."

She loosened her grip on my arm and rolled to face me. The small amount of light in the room reflected off her glistening eyes. "I get it. Trust me, I'm more than happy to be thousands of miles away from Franky Russo. But the thought of leaving you behind to deal with those monsters..." Her forehead dropped to my chest, and she took a shuddering breath. "How am I supposed to function when I'll be going out of my mind worrying about you?"

I smoothed my hand over Cam's hair and kissed her forehead. "You will, because that's what I need you to do. It'll make my job easier if I know you're safe." I cupped my hands around her face. "I knew what I was getting into, Cam. From the moment I decided to take you, I knew there might be consequences for my actions. I've always been ready to accept them. And once I deal with these assholes, you'll be free to come home."

I didn't give voice to the alternative. That if anything happened to me and Franky somehow stayed breathing, she should continue on in Australia, never to return home.

"I'll send word to you whenever I can. But I can't risk them finding you, so it won't be often."

She nodded and sniffled.

I pressed my lips to Cam's. "I've got this, darlin'. If they thought I was dangerous before, they've got no idea what I'm capable of now I've got something worth fighting for."

I didn't plan to make a spectacle out of this. Their deaths would be swift. No warning. No witnesses. No evidence that I'd ever been there. Those still breathing would know who was responsible and that they were next. Their fear would eat them alive before I sent them to burn in hell.

"Now come here and close your eyes. Get some rest." I tucked her close to me, her head resting on my shoulder, and our arms and legs twined together. I waited for her to drift off to sleep before I allowed myself to do the same.

21

SHEP

I woke early the next morning and untangled myself from Cam's limbs, careful not to wake her. I checked out the front window and found no obvious signs of unwanted company. The parking lot contained the same few vehicles from the night before.

My phone chimed. Cam stirred as I checked the screen, expecting it to be a data usage reminder because no one messaged me on a burner.

> Leave your cell in the motel and get out of there ASAP. Watch your 6.

I growled and resisted the urge to crush the burner in my hand. Destroying it wouldn't help any, but if I left it in the room, it could act as a decoy and buy us some time.

The message came from a blocked number, but it must be Ben. How the hell had he tracked a burner? And what was he playing at? Giving Franky intel to track me, then helping me like this? Had he remembered his loyalties, or was this part of another plan to fuck me over since the first attempt had failed?

Whatever his reasons for sending that message, we had to leave fast.

Cam sat up all sleepy eyed and messy haired. “What is it?”

I tossed the cell under the bed. “Get dressed and grab your shit, darlin’. We gotta move. Right now.” I shrugged on a pair of jeans, already mentally cataloguing everything I needed to do to get us out of here alive.

My girl sprang into action, a flurry of movement as she did what I asked.

“What’s going on?” Her voice wavered as she scurried around the room, shoving things into a duffle bag.

I pulled on my boots, shirt, and jacket, then armed my body with as many loaded weapons as possible. “I think I just received a message from Ben warning us to get the hell out of Dodge. Sounds like Franky has our location.”

“What? Are they here?” She froze, hand outstretched for her jeans, and her wide unblinking eyes fixed on the door as if someone might bust it down at any moment. Who knew, maybe they would?

“Don’t clam up on me now.” I moved her boots next to where Cam was making like a statue. “You’ve got a fine ass, but dragging you out of here with nothing covering it will draw attention. Jeans, shoes. Let’s hustle.”

She blinked and resumed her task, although her face was pale and her eyes had a glazed-over look about them.

“Is it a trick?” she asked. “Why would he help us now?”

I dumped my bag by the door and took another peek beyond the curtains. No change out there. “Don’t know, and it doesn’t matter at this point. They know we’re here. We have to leave.”

Clothes on and bags packed, we were ready to go. But first, I had to check that the coast was clear.

“Stay here. I need to do a quick trip to the truck.”

She wrung her fingers and nodded as I headed to the door

with the loaded Glock in my hand, safety flicked off. I didn't tell Cam that I was setting myself as bait. If anyone was already here and watching us, I needed to draw them out while keeping her safe inside.

A shootout with these dipshits would be problematic, but it didn't scare me. Franky's thugs were nothing more than overgrown bullies with guns. Their weapons intimidated most, but the mafioso lacked the skills and accuracy I'd gained from years of combat experience.

I let my instincts kick in as I made my way to the car, opening the driver and rear doors to provide additional cover. I checked the perimeter once more before starting the engine and heading back to collect Cam.

"All clear. I'll take the bags. I want you to stay close behind me, get in the driver's side, then shimmy across to the passenger seat." That way, I could see the street while keeping Cam protected.

She stood at the end of the bed, her feet shifting in place.

I leaned down and pressed my lips to hers. "I won't let anything happen to you, darlin'. I got this."

"I know." She nodded and kissed me again.

I threw my bag over my shoulder, carried Cam's in one hand, and kept my pistol concealed at my side in the other. The dawn sun sat below the reddening horizon, so I hoped the other motel guests wouldn't be awake to notice our hasty departure. I didn't want to draw attention with an unconcealed weapon, what with Cam's missing person status fresh in people's minds, but I wasn't prepared to walk out there without having it at the ready.

I remained vigilant as we made our way to the truck. She got in and I followed once she was in her seat and buckled up.

With no sign of Franky's men, we exited the parking lot and hit the road.

Cam turned to me. "Maybe we should drive for a while,

then find somewhere safe to hole up. Now that we've ditched the cell, they shouldn't be able to track us, right?"

It wasn't a silly suggestion. We could drive right into a trap if they got ahead of us, because it didn't take a rocket scientist to figure out we were headed south.

"I think it's best if we keep moving. We stay in one place for too long and they somehow find us, that'll give them time to gather resources and have us surrounded." I glanced at her. "And that puts the odds in their favor."

I understood Cam's apprehension to stay on the road, but it was a risk we had to take. We had a solid day of driving ahead of us. If everything went to plan, we'd arrive at our destination by the end of the day.

~

MIAMI WAS WITHIN OUR REACH. We'd made decent progress, even though we stayed off the interstate on our way south. On the outskirts of Orlando, we shed our excess layers and drove with the windows down, enjoying the warm, humid air.

The last thing I wanted was for the cops to pull us over and recognize Cam, so I observed all the road rules and stuck to the speed limit, even though my foot itched to press harder.

I kept an eye out for tails. None so far. And the longer we drove without incident, the more relaxed Cam's body language became. Except now, she wriggled in her seat, looking uncomfortable.

"You okay?" I asked.

"Yeah, I need to pee, though." She crossed her legs. "No more coffee today."

I shot her a grin and turned down a dirt track leading to a wooded area since there weren't any rest stops nearby. There'd be no amenities, but there also wouldn't be anyone to ID Cam.

We both exited the car. I leaned against the door while Cam

headed for the privacy of the trees. She had a cheeky grin on her face as she returned.

"What's so funny?" I asked.

"I was just thinking it's a lot nicer riding up front than being zip tied and laid out in the back."

When she reached me, her hands went to my chest and she rose on tiptoes. I met her halfway for a firm kiss. Cam's fingers raked through my hair and I groaned into her mouth. She tasted so sweet.

I grabbed her ass and pulled her against me. "So, you don't want me to tie you up and throw you on the back seat for old times' sake?"

She slapped me on the bicep and wiggled out of my grip. "Maybe later, handsome. We've got the Mafia to outrun."

I straightened and tracked her swaying hips around the hood, her thick wavy hair bouncing with the movement. "Really?" I asked.

She glanced over her shoulder and winked before getting in the truck.

"Goddamn." Where had this woman been all my life?

We drove along the bumpy track and onto the highway. Since the punishing afternoon sun shone through my window, I grabbed my hat from the dash.

Cam sat with her elbow propped on the windowsill, a small smile on her face as she watched me. "Did I ever tell you how cute you look in that ball cap?"

I glanced between her and the road. "Cute?" I laughed. "I don't think anyone's called me that since I was four years old."

Cam's gaze shifted beyond my shoulder before her eyes widened in terror. Her hands shot up to protect her face. I didn't have time to react as a vehicle slammed into the side of the truck, sending us spinning out of control. The tires screeched. I tried to correct our direction, but we careened off the road, hit an embankment, and flipped.

Airbags burst free as we rolled again and again. Glass shattered and flew around the cab. My pickup came to a halt when it smashed into a tree and, by some miracle, landed the right way up.

My ears rang, and my vision was patchy. White powder from the airbags floated in the cab, making me cough. Cam didn't make a sound. She was unconscious. Her chin rested on her chest. Only the seatbelt kept her limp body upright. I leaned across and checked her pulse. It was strong, but she was out cold with a bloody gash on the side of her forehead.

I'd let my girl down in the worst possible way because that collision was no accident.

They'd found us.

I reached for my Glock.

A pistol cocked by my window. "Don't move, asshole."

22

CAMERON

A hammer pounded inside my skull. My entire body ached. I was tired. Bone weary tired. I tried to lift my heavy lids because the incessant churning in my gut told me something was very wrong.

Oh, my God.

The crash!

My eyes snapped open and a sharp pain lanced through my temple. As my blurry vision adjusted, the ache subsided to tolerable thumping.

The last thing I remembered was a black sedan ramming Shep's truck. It hadn't even attempted to brake or swerve.

Franky had caught us.

I guessed that went some way to explaining why I sat opposite a balding, middle-aged man in a private jet. He stared daggers at me over the rim of his whiskey tumbler. Shouldn't I be the one pissed about this situation?

The anger in his eyes made me squirm in the large leather seat. *Dammit!* My wrists were tied to the armrests. I willed my galloping heart to calm down. My gaze darted between the restraints and Baldy. His lips twisted into a menacing grin. If he was anything like Pauly, this would be an airplane ride I'd sooner forget.

Whatever happened between the crash and now was a total blank. How long had I been unconscious? And where was Shep? Was he still alive? My breathing came in short, shallow pants.

Stop it!

I couldn't let panic take over. Not when I needed my wits about me.

A deep voice boomed from the back of the plane. "Hey Lou, you got any more of that sedative? The big fucker's coming around."

Shep was alive. Thank God! Knowing that allowed me to reel in some of my anxiety.

The man across from me, Lou, rested his drink on the table between us and stood. He removed a vial from his pants pocket, then headed down the aisle. Stuck in my seat, I craned my neck to follow his movements. In the back row sat Shep, eyes closed, his head bobbing as he tried to gain control. Next to him was a brawny, caramel-skinned man who reminded me of The Rock.

No sign of Justin on board, not that I expected to see him. I clung to a glimmer of hope that Franky didn't have him, even though that seemed like a fool's wish.

When he returned to his seat, Lou resumed glaring at me. I stared out the window to avoid his gaze. We were above the clouds and the setting sun sat low in the sky. There was only one place we'd be heading. Back to Philly. Back to where it all began.

The ache at the side of my head made me think I'd taken a decent bump in the crash. The skin there felt tight and crusty, probably dried blood.

"You gonna need any of this?" Lou's voice drew my attention. He held up the half-empty vial and shook it. "Nah. Little thing like you won't give us any trouble, will you?" He smirked before taking a sip of his drink.

No trouble? Like hell.

To pass the time, I imagined all the ways I could be a pain in his ass. Stabbing him in the eye with the pen in his pocket. Slamming his caveman forehead onto the table between us. Pitching the whiskey tumbler at his smug face. Nope. No trouble at all.

I shifted in my seat, uncomfortable under Lou's scowling stare.

He pointed at me with the hand holding the whiskey. "You and that son of a bitch" —he gestured toward Shep— "killed my cousin and a friend of mine."

I sat up straight and glared right back at him. "Given they tried to kill me first, I'd say they had it coming."

He took a slow sip, his eyes never leaving mine. "I'm gonna enjoy seeing what the boss does with you two. Might even let me help." He arched one brow. "Wouldn't that be fun?"

A shiver rippled through me. I didn't want to meet Franky, but being tied to the chair and with Shep unconscious, I couldn't see a way of getting out of it. I'd keep trying, though.

If Lou wanted to talk, I had questions. "How did you find us?" I really wanted to know if my brother was in the hands of a double-crosser.

"Why should I tell you?"

"I'll be dead before the day is through, so what does it matter?"

"I guess it doesn't." He let out a disturbing chuckle. "This is a kicker. Shep's buddy ratted him out. Made it easy for us."

"Ben? A new friend of yours, is he?"

"Hardly. He cut a deal. We have someone he wants. He has skills we need." Lou snorted and shook his head. "The things these clowns will do for a woman. Pussy-whipped fools." He took another sip.

It sounded like Franky had Ben backed into a corner. It didn't excuse what he'd done to us, but perhaps I could understand his choices. Shep and I had made our share of questionable ones lately.

I still didn't know how Ben had tracked Shep's truck. Traffic cameras, perhaps?

Done with me for now, Lou pulled out his cell and began scrolling. The airplane started its descent. My ears ached and popped as we moved through a patch of clouds. The small jet lurched and Lou's drink splashed onto the crotch of his gray suit pants. He grumbled and dabbed the stain with a napkin.

I glanced out the window and tried to hide my smirk because it looked like he'd pissed himself.

"What the fuck are you grinning at?"

"Nothing. I'm sure your mom always packs you a spare pair of pants in case you have an accident."

His expression turned murderous as he stood, but heavy turbulence jostled him about and flung him into his seat. The captain's voice came over the intercom, requesting everyone to fasten their seatbelts while we landed.

Lou remained calm as he pointed a chunky finger in my direction, even though his hard, unblinking eyes told me he was anything but. "You're in a world of shit."

I glanced at my bound wrists, shrugged, then stared at him like the lowlife bully he was. "Didn't need to buy a vowel to figure that out."

The brave face I put on was mostly bluster, but I refused to cower to these men. They were like a circling pack of wolves. One sniff of fear and they'd go in for the kill.

The airplane touched down and taxied to a remote hangar where two black sedans waited. The Rock's evil twin emerged from the back row to open the aircraft door and unfold the stairs. The whirring jet engines shut down, and the aircraft became silent enough to hear the ringing in my ears.

Lou rose from his seat. "I'm taking you to the boss. Any more smartass comments along the way, and you'll regret it. This is the one and only warning you're getting from me. Understand?"

I swallowed hard and nodded. Fear gnawed at me again. As much as I tried to be strong, I wasn't ready to meet Franky Russo.

~

IN SOUTH PHILLY, our sedan drove along Wolf Street before turning down a narrow laneway. It stopped at the back entrance to a plain red brick building much like the others in this area. Two burly bouncers guarded the entry.

Lou didn't wait for the driver to open our door. He yanked me out of the car by my arm and hustled me up a set of concrete stairs. I struggled not to trip over my feet. The dank alley reeked of sewer rot and trash. Seemed I'd gotten used to the fresh mountain air, and the once familiar smells of the city now added to my nausea.

"Would you stop pulling so damn hard?" I tried twisting out of his grip, which only hurt more.

The asshole attached to my arm didn't acknowledge me. The bouncers shared a laugh as we passed. For all I knew, a woman being dragged inside against her will happened every day around here.

As we moved down a dimly lit corridor, the beat of electronic music grew louder and pulsated through my body. Or was that my pounding heartbeat? The hallway opened into a large room with several near-naked women grinding against poles. Cigar smoke hung thick in the air along with the ripe scent of stale alcohol. As we neared the elevated platform, the vacant eyes of the scrawny, miserable women seemed oblivious to the ogling patrons. I'd seen that glassed-over look on Justin before. Those strippers were as high as clouds.

Other women escorted men to curtained-off rooms. The sticky floor made me cringe. *Gross*. It was all kinds of wrong in here, and soon I'd meet the owner of this classy joint. My gut roiled and my heart rate ratcheted.

I don't want to do this.

Lou led me past a long bar where a pretty waitress approached carrying a tray of drinks. She was different from the other girls. Set against ivory blemish-free skin, her long dark brown hair was thick and lustrous. The tiny black shorts and low-cut cami she wore showed off a curvy yet toned figure, and she had an alertness in her big brown eyes that the other women lacked. The way she balanced the drinks tray with both hands made me think she was new to her job. How long would it be before she ended up like the rest of them?

As we passed, I mouthed the words, *help me, please!* I don't know why I thought to appeal to her. Perhaps it was the sympathetic look she'd given me, or that she seemed as out of place in this club as I felt.

She slowed, and her eyes flared as they flickered between Lou and me.

"Get back to work," Lou growled when he noticed her attention on us.

The tray wobbled in her hands before she righted it. She sneered at Lou as if he were a persistent glob of gum stuck to her shoe. It made me wonder what the women here endured with creeps like him lording over them.

Lou pushed me in front of him and up a set of open steel stairs. The upper floor had a row of offices and a balcony that overlooked the club floor. My nerves ramped up when he stopped at a closed door.

This was it. I was about to meet the man who wanted me dead.

23

CAMERON

Lou's meaty fist thumped on the door. "Got the McKenzie woman, boss."

"Bring her in," came a man's voice from inside.

Lou opened the door and shoved me through.

My gaze shot to the man sitting with impeccable posture behind a solid wood desk. Franky Russo. Even out of the pizza commercial costume, he still looked nothing like a mob boss. At least not like any I'd seen in movies.

With neatly combed salt-and-pepper hair, thin, wire-framed spectacles, and hands clasped together on the desk before him, Franky looked more like a middle-aged accountant than a mobster. A gray knit vest sat over his crisp white shirt, and aside from a crooked nose that was too long for his face, his features were unremarkable. Although taller and broader in real life, he didn't give off an immediate sense of danger. Yet Shep's warnings rang in my ears. To underestimate this man would be a huge mistake.

I took in my surroundings. This room had a totally different vibe from the rest of the club. Decorated with dark hardwood floors and gray walls, the space resembled something from a stately mansion. Franky's immaculate mahogany desk was either rarely used, or he was anal about keeping it clutter free. Probably the latter. Three things sat upon it: a landline phone, an antique mantle clock, and a delicate bonsai in a black ceramic pot.

Unlike the stench of stale beer and cigar smoke on the lower level, the only odor in this room was the lingering scent of furniture polish. On one side of the office were built-in cabinets filled with books. The opposite wall had several TVs streaming direct feeds from the club's security cameras. No sign of Shep on any of them.

Franky gestured to a black leather tub chair. "Have a seat, Ms. McKenzie." He didn't even sound like the guy from the commercials. Where had the Philly accent gone? His articulate voice made me wonder if he'd been educated at an elite school, or was this businesslike manner a learned skill? Either way, his cool tone and expressionless face sent a shiver through me.

I remembered what Shep told me about the mob boss. That he wore many masks depending on the situation. Very few ever saw the *real* Franky, and if you did, you might not live to tell anyone about it. Which Franky did I talk to now?

Lowering myself into the chair, I willed my lungs to slow down so I didn't hyperventilate. If I had any hope of negotiating, I needed to compose myself. I was here, after all, and not dead. Yet.

"This isn't my preferred place to meet, but given the confronting nature of our business today, I'm forced to conduct it here."

Unsettled by Franky's assessing stare, I instead glanced at the cabinets where a single framed photo, the only personal touch in the office, sat among the stacked tomes. Beside it was a pair of worn white boxing gloves. I squinted at the photo of a young muscle-bound boxer bleeding from a cut above his puffy eye and holding a huge, gold title belt above his head. Wait... was that—

"Yes, that's me," said Franky, answering my unspoken question.

My gaze returned to the mob boss. "You were a boxer?"

"I like to think I still am. Once a fighter, always a fighter. There is no changing who we are at our core." Franky shifted his hands from the desk to place them in his lap. "I was the youngest boxer to take the Pennsylvania cruiserweight title. I can still remember the sound of Mad Dog Malone's jaw breaking when I knocked him out in the third round. The blow put him in hospital for a month, left him with ongoing seizures, and ended his career."

A chill swept through me at Franky's callous retelling of something so brutal. He didn't seem remorseful. Hell, he didn't even seem proud of his actions like I assumed someone as vile as Franky might. Rather, he didn't seem to feel anything at all, and that was scarier than the alternatives.

I held Franky's stare. His eyes were the deepest shade of blue I'd ever seen. So dark they were almost black.

"Where's Shep?" I asked, working hard to smooth the quaver in my voice.

He gestured to the video screens. "See for yourself."

One TV showed two huge bouncers, the men we'd passed at the back entrance, hauling a barely conscious Shep into view and dumping him onto a chair in the middle of a room. Two buckets sat to one side.

I covered my mouth, and a pained cry slipped from my throat.

The one sporting a flame-red crewcut cuffed Shep's hands behind his back and roped his ankles to the chair legs. His head lolled from side to side as he tried to gain control of his body. What the hell were they going to do to him? I had a sickening idea I already knew the answer. The urge to heave up the meager contents of my gut was unbearable.

"Your brother is more resilient and foolish than I gave him credit for. He still refuses to answer questions despite our... persuasive methods." Franky interrupted my troubling thoughts, only to supply me with fresh ones.

He confirmed my fears. They had Justin. What had they done to him? "Is he alive?"

"Yes. For now." Franky adjusted his glasses. "Although I'm unsure I have any further use for him since he's being rather unhelpful."

My skin prickled. Why hadn't Justin given Franky what he wanted from the get-go so we didn't all have to suffer?

Franky angled his head toward the screen where Shep sat motionless. "Now, we find out how informative Mr. Shepherd can be."

"Please don't hurt him!" I blurted. "Shep was only trying to help me." Perhaps begging for his life would make no difference, but I also couldn't stop myself.

"I paid a lot of money to have you killed, Ms. McKenzie. I don't appreciate being made a fool of, and that disrespect cannot go unchecked." The slight flaring of Franky's nostrils spoke volumes. "And since I'm fully aware how expensive Mr. Shepherd's services are, I find it curious that you could afford his protection. Your brother steals from me and suddenly you're able to pay for such things. How do you explain that?"

All right. I could see how this looked bad, even if Franky had the wrong idea.

"I didn't pay Shep a dime. He helped me because it was the right thing to do."

"You expect me to believe that Mr. Shepherd showed you mercy? That he is a good citizen? Have you any idea how many people he's killed in this city?" He shook his head. "No. A cold-blooded hitman like him would not have helped you out of the kindness of his murderous black heart."

"You know nothing of his heart," I spoke through gritted teeth.

The mob boss regarded me for an uncomfortable moment.

"You care for him?" Franky's head tilted and his penetrating gaze reminded me of a lion assessing its prey in utter stillness right before it pounced. "And you believe he cares for you?"

I remained silent, not wanting to give away any more than I already had, but also unable to deny my feelings for Shep.

"This makes things very interesting." The glimmer of excitement in Franky's eyes made me shudder. "Well. Let's find out how much Mr. Shepherd means to you, shall we?" He picked up the desk phone and pressed a button. The redhead henchman on the TV screen answered the wall-mounted handset. "You may begin," said Franky.

"Wait. Please don't!" I glanced at the screen where Shep sat with his eyes closed and chin resting upon his chest. The redhead bouncer approached and tossed a bucket of water over his head. Shep woke with a start, sitting bolt upright.

My fingernails dug into the armrests as I rushed to lean forward in my seat.

Red and Shep shared words, their silent conversation only lasting a minute before Shep looked him in the eyes and smirked. The muscle-bound ginger wound his arm back and punched him in the stomach, then his face. Stuck in the chair, there was nothing Shep could do but take the hits. I cringed and shut my eyes. When I opened them again, Red stood over Shep. Blood leaked down the side of my man's mouth and his chest heaved with...*what the? Goddammit, Shep!* Was he laughing? Sweet Jesus, he was antagonizing them.

"Stop this! I told you, he doesn't know anything!" I shifted in my seat, desperate to help Shep.

Franky observed me with mild interest. "This stops when

you tell me what I want to know. Where are my drugs and money?"

Red took two more powerful swings at Shep. This time he winced in pain and spat blood on the floor.

My pulse roared in my ears. "I don't know. I swear I'm telling you the truth. I had no part in this. Make him stop!"

It was all I could do not to leap from my chair, grab Franky by the collar and slap his infuriating, emotionless face. Every fiber of my being wanted to throttle him until he called off the beating.

I squeezed my lids shut as Shep took more hits.

Think, Cam! I had to stop this. Except I had nothing to bargain with. Only Justin knew where Franky's goods were. Only he could end this.

"Let me see my brother. I'll talk some sense into him and find out what you want to know."

It was the only way to salvage this disaster. I couldn't understand why Justin still held out. I hoped he had the drugs and cash hidden somewhere safe. If he'd offloaded them already, or blown it all, we had no hope. And there were no guarantees with Franky. He might get his goods back and still kill us all for sport.

"Shep doesn't deserve this. He was only trying to help me. He didn't go against your orders out of spite or to humiliate you. If I get your property back, will you please let him go?"

I had little leverage for dealing with Franky, but whatever I had I would use to free Shep.

"You would plead for the life of a murderer?"

"For him, absolutely."

Franky stood, straightening his vest before pressing a button on the remote and sending the screens black. "If you get me what I want, I will consider your request."

I didn't believe him. Franky had to know that once freed, Shep would kill him as soon as he had the chance. But right now, I was buying time to figure out how to get the three of us out of here alive.

Franky stalked around the desk and stopped in front of me. He grabbed the back of my head, yanking me to my feet by my hair. I cried out in pain and tried to pull away, but his grip held firm. "Understand this, Ms. McKenzie," he snarled, his mouth close to my ear. "You get what I want, or I'll have you begging me to put a bullet in your skull. And I'll enjoy every minute."

He tossed me back into the chair. I reached for the burning pain at my scalp, panting. My heart hammered in my chest. If Justin couldn't come up with something useful, all three of us were dead.

From what Shep had told me, Franky wasn't bluffing. But I didn't want to give him the satisfaction of seeing me cry, so I held back the tears and stared him down.

"Let me talk to Justin." I swallowed against the dryness in my throat. "I promise, I'll find out what you want to know. But if you kill any of us, I swear to God you'll never get your stuff back."

He smoothed a hand down the front of his vest and straightened his cuffs, the picture of calm composure once more. "That almost sounded like a threat. You better hope your brother comes through, or else you're all leaving here in trash bags."

Goosebumps rose on my flesh. All this talk about our impending deaths was more than I could handle.

"Take her next door. If she gives you any problems, put her in her place." Franky didn't spare me a parting glance as he moved to his collection of books.

"Sure, boss," Lou said from behind me. I'd almost forgotten he was there. He yanked me up by my forearm to haul me out.

THE ROOM next door was smaller than Franky's office and bland in comparison. The only furnishings were a sofa against one wall, and two steel chairs bolted to the floor in the center of the room. There were no windows to ventilate the stench of disinfectant, and I wondered if the last person held in here had been leaking blood or piss.

Probably both.

Lou pushed me into a chair.

I hissed as he clamped cuffs around my wrists and looped a chain through the back support. "Ouch! Dammit, they don't need to be so tight!"

"Yeah." He shrugged. "But I like it that way, so deal with it."

"Asshole!" I spat the word with venom.

I saw the slap coming before it hit, but I had no way to brace myself. The firm clout to the side of my face would have sent me falling to the floor if Lou hadn't cuffed me to the chair. My ears rang and cheek throbbed.

"I've wanted to do that since you woke up on the plane." He leaned down to my eye level, his hands braced on the seat on either side of my thighs. "So, go on. Give me another reason to make you hurt."

I stretched my jaw and licked the corner of my mouth, tasting blood. The effect was instant—I saw red.

I straightened my posture and lifted my chin. "If Shep and I get out of this alive, I'm going to tell him all about you. And then he'll come for you. You know that, right?" My cool tone belied the anxiety simmering beneath. I wanted this bully to have a taste of fear. If he had any clue what Shep was capable of, he'd feel it.

"You think your psycho boyfriend is ever seeing daylight again?" His menacing stare unnerved me. "He's being beaten to within an inch of his life as we speak. Only reason he's not dead already is because Franky will want this to take a long time." He rose so his hulking frame loomed over me. "Might go down there and have some fun, too. Come back up here with his blood on my knuckles. Show you what it looks like. Make you taste it. What do you think of that?"

That they were still hurting Shep felt like a knife to my gut. Franky had turned off the camera feed, but he hadn't given the order for the beating to stop. Shep was the strongest person I knew, but how much more could he take?

My heart ached, and I'd never been more desperate or helpless in my life.

24

CAMERON

How long were they going to leave me in here? The cuffs chafed my wrists and my shoulders ached from being unable to change position. Plus, my butt was sore. The steel chair offered little comfort all round. It seemed petty to wallow over something so trivial. It was nothing compared to what Shep must be going through.

Was he all right? Were they still beating him? Every minute stuck here pushed me closer to the brink of hysteria.

I stared daggers at Lou who relaxed on the sofa, cell in hand, watching episodes of my favorite TV series. He was late to catch on to its awesomeness; the baby dragons hadn't even hatched yet.

I let out an annoyed sigh. "You know he gets beheaded, right?"

Jerkface curled his lip.

A few minutes passed and judging by the intensity of Lou's focus, the show had his full attention. I listened in, welcoming the distraction, then decided to mess with him some more.

"He's dead too. And her actually." I clicked my tongue. "Nasty way to go."

"Shut up."

"I could save you the hassle and tell you how it all ends."

Lou rose from the sofa, nostrils flaring. "I said, shut up, bitch!" He took two steps toward me, then paused when the door opened with Franky leading the way.

I couldn't believe my eyes when another man ushered my brother into the room. "Justin!" My handcuffs jangled as I tried to stand, but they held me in place.

When he saw me, my brother clutched his already messy brown hair. "Cammy! No!" He lunged for me, although didn't get far. The tall man who'd led him in held a firm grip on his biceps.

My gut twisted. Justin looked awful, even for his usually scruffy self. Tweaker skinny, unwashed spiky hair, and several days' growth covering his jaw. Add to that the severe beating he'd taken, and he could be mistaken for a homeless person who'd been in a one-sided bar fight. His face was a brutal patchwork of purple bruises and red cuts. The swelling of his left eye distorted his features, and he stood hunched with one hand at his chest as though his ribs pained him. His entire body trembled. If it wasn't fear causing it, the forced detox would.

Why had Justin stolen from the Mob and gone on the run? And now they'd caught him and beaten him to a pulp, he still hadn't given Franky what he wanted. None of it made sense.

Justin's battered face twisted in anguish. "I'm so sorry. Dammit, they hurt you, too."

"I'm all right. Just cuts and bruises." My injuries were mild compared to his.

I glanced at the man holding Justin back. He wore a gray T-shirt stretched tight across his powerfully built torso, and black cargo pants that hinted at muscular legs underneath. And the way he held himself reminded me of a certain bossy hitman I knew.

Apart from his wavy dark hair, this guy's look screamed military, and I wondered if this was Ben, the double-crossing asshole himself. When his bright blue eyes landed on me, they contained something like sympathy or regret. Good. He should be ashamed of what he'd done to us.

"Please, let her go," Justin begged. "She's got nothing to do with this."

Franky's eyes bored into mine. "Your sister has something to say."

I wished we could have this conversation in private. There was so much I needed to ask Justin, and even more I wanted to tell him about what had happened over the last week. Instead, I rolled my lips and got straight to the point.

"Listen to me, Justin. This is important. It's over. Franky has us, and there's only one thing we can do to fix this. The stuff you stole, do you still have it?"

Justin glanced between Franky and me. "Well, it's complicated."

My jaw clenched and my hands curled into fists behind my back. "Do you have it or not?"

"They're gonna kill me as soon as I tell them."

He might be right. Would I condemn my brother to a death sentence if he did what I asked? Still, I had to try something, and I hoped this would buy us more time because I doubted Franky would murder Justin before he'd located his goods in case he was lying about the location.

"And what do you think happens to me if you stay quiet?" I asked.

Justin's eyes squeezed shut as he bowed his head.

I continued. "You have to trust me. This is our only chance."

His gaze moved from Franky to Lou and then returned to me. "I never meant for you to get dragged into this." His throat bobbed as he nodded. "Helen. It's in Helen. The drugs, the money. All of it."

My car. Of all the stupid-ass places to hide Mafia contraband, he picked my baby. The one thing he knew never to mess with.

Unwilling to face my fury, Justin's gaze shifted to the floor.

"Are you kidding me?" My voice cracked.

"Who's Helen?" asked Franky.

"Not *who, what*. Helen's my car."

"I'm sorry, Cammy." Justin found the courage to meet my stare, but I didn't want to hear his apologies. Now wasn't the time. And maybe there never would be a time if Franky killed us all once he had what he needed.

This felt more painful than the slap Lou had given me. This betrayal was a hefty thump to the gut with a baseball bat.

"I can't believe this. Why, Justin? Why would you steal that stuff?"

"For you!" His one good eye widened, pleading. "You've bailed me out of debt so many times, I had to find a way to pay you back. I'm your big brother. I'm supposed to be looking after you. But I fucked up." He hung his head and sobbed, his chest heaving with every breath, something I hadn't seen him do since he was a kid. He grimaced and clutched his ribs.

"Yeah, you did." I trembled with rage as I glared at my brother. "Because of you, we're probably all gonna die in this sleaze-infested shithole." It hurt like hell that our last moments together could be like this.

"I prefer the term gentleman's club," said Franky. "And I suggest you tell me right now where to find your car."

"She's in the garage of my house, and Justin is about to tell you *exactly* where in my car you can find your stuff, so you don't have to tear her apart to get it. Right, Justin?" I cut my brother a hard stare, daring him to cause us any more trouble.

He shifted on his feet, still reluctant to confess. I narrowed my eyes when he didn't speak up right away.

He cleared his throat. "It's taped to the underside of the driver's seat."

I turned to Franky. "There, you got what you—"

"And under the passenger seat." My brother cut in. "And under the carpet in the trunk." He scratched the back of his head. "And maybe a little in the glove compartment. And the center console, too."

How much had he taken? Heat rose within me as my blood simmered. "Aren't you creative? Did you think to shove any up your ass while you were at it?" I leveled Justin with a murderous look. His shoulders slumped.

If I weren't cuffed to the chair, I'd lunge for my stupid-ass brother. Instead, I gritted my teeth and did my best to protect my Camaro from any further defilement. "The keys to Helen are in my kitchen, top drawer. I don't care if you bust down the door of my house to get in, but there's no need to be reckless and break a window on my car."

Justin winced. "Actually... Helen's not at your place."

"What?" My glare snapped to him. "Where is she?"

"In Illinois." He shrugged. "I needed a ride to Aunt Sarah's, and the gear was already loaded in your car, so it seemed like the best option."

"I don't believe this. If there's even a single scratch on her, I'm going to kill you." Even if I had to join the queue behind Franky and Shep.

Franky clicked his fingers. "Lou, have Nicky get the car. Tell him to bring it here and park it underground so you can search it. Tally what's there and report back to me."

"Sure, boss." Lou punched some numbers into his cell and stood outside the room with it against his ear.

Franky turned to the man guarding my brother. "Mr. Lewis, you and I have business to discuss. Take the junkie to my office."

Ben, or whoever the hell he was, nodded and led Justin out with Franky close behind.

My brother shot me a parting look filled with grief. "I'm sorry, Cammy. I love you."

I was so damn furious with Justin, but I hated he was hurting, too. For years, his drug addiction clouded his judgment and led him to desperation more times than I could count. For all his stupid decisions, I still loved him. I wished I'd thought to tell him that before he left the room.

A few minutes later, Lou returned to the sofa like nothing out of the ordinary had happened. As for me, my life had spiraled out of control.

Following a tap at the door, the pretty waitress we'd passed at the bar entered the room with a drink on a tray. Long straight hair covered her cleavage as though the low-cut uniform made her uncomfortable.

Her eyes flashed over me before landing on my minder. "Hey Lou," she said in a sweet voice, her full pink lips forming a shy smile. "Nicky said you're stuck in here babysitting and could use a drink. I brought you the blue label. It's your favorite, right?"

Lou grunted and leered at her before taking the tumbler without a thank you. I guessed he was a rude asshole to everyone, not only his prisoners. As the waitress left the room, I could've sworn she winked at me.

Lou didn't take long to finish the liquor. Soon after, he made himself comfortable on the sofa by stretching his legs out, then opened his mouth wide for a lengthy yawn.

I watched him with interest because something was up with that waitress and the drink she'd brought him. Or was it that my foolish imagination hoped a miracle might be about to occur?

Lou sat up with effort. His droopy lidded eyes glanced around the room before they settled on me.

"What's happening?" he slurred and took a long, slow blink. With hands braced on his knees, he swayed where he sat. When he tried to stand, he fell back onto the sofa.

She'd drugged the bastard!

I stared at him wide-eyed and prayed he didn't make it out of the room or have the sense to call for help.

He groaned as he struggled to sit forward again, but instead of rising, he slumped to his side, lights out.

"Yes!" I squealed. Except, fat lot of good it did me being stuck in the chair. What was I supposed to do now?

A light knock preceded the waitress's return. She entered and closed the door.

"Thank God," she whispered and hurried to Lou.

Going through his pockets, she fished out a small silver key. Her warm brown eyes lit up as she flashed me a wicked smile. "Bingo."

"Who are you?" I asked, while she made quick work of unlocking my cuffs. I stood and rubbed my aching wrists.

"Sage. I'm here to help you, Cameron." She untucked some clothes from the back of her shorts. "Quick, put these on. It's a spare uniform. It should provide a good cover for you."

"How do you know my name?" With shaking hands, I shucked off my boots and jeans.

"Brandon told me."

"Who's Brandon?"

Sage handed me the shorts and sighed. "Honestly, I'm beginning to wonder if I have any idea who he is at all. But he's helping us all get out of here."

"Are you an undercover cop or something?" Moving fast, I shimmied into the little black hot pants which barely covered my ass.

"Nope. But we share a common enemy. I hate these assholes as much as you."

"Thank you for doing this." Although my words didn't seem like enough. Sage was putting her life on the line for me.

"Happy to help. I know what these sons of bitches are capable of." She patted Lou's sides, then tried to roll him over. "Help me shift him so we can get his weapon."

I pulled on my boots then helped her roll Lou to the side, but once we had the momentum going, he tumbled right off the sofa and on to the floor. His head hit the ground hard with a solid thud.

Sage's eyes met mine, and she gave a nonchalant shrug. "He's such a douchebag, I don't even feel a little bad about that." She leaned down and pulled a pistol from Lou's leather holster.

Her nose wrinkled in revulsion as she eyed him. She took one step back, wound up, and kicked him square in the balls with her shiny black pumps. His body convulsed once, but he didn't wake. "That's for grabbing my tits, you filthy sleazebag." She jerked her chin at the unconscious lump on the floor. "You want a turn? Don't worry, he's taken enough tranquilizer to bring down an elephant."

"You're sure?"

"Pretty sure. And when else will you have a golden opportunity like this?"

Touché. I lined him up and delivered another hefty kick to his crotch. With any luck, we'd prevented Lou from fathering mini versions of himself.

"Here, take this." She held the gun out to me. "Do you know how to use it?"

"Better run me through it." I ripped off my bloodstained T-shirt and pulled on the black cami, tugging it down in a futile attempt to cover my belly button.

Sage's hands moved fast as she checked the weapon was loaded. Wow, she really knew her way around a pistol.

"No bullets." She groaned, slamming the magazine back in. "At least we've still got this." She withdrew the handcuff key from her pocket and dropped it into my open palm.

I closed my fingers around it, struggling to figure out how we were all getting out of here.

She swept her shiny brunette tresses over her shoulders. "I've got good news and bad news. The bad news is, the boss doesn't drink, so he's still in play. He's in his office with the door closed, although he could leave at any moment, so we have to hurry." She reached for my hands and held them tight. "We need to get your man out of the basement. He's on his own down there, but he's in a bad way."

A whimper came from my throat.

"Listen to me," Sage said. "There's good news, too."

I nodded because I sure as hell could use some of that.

"The security cameras in here and in the basement are playing on a loop. If you can get to the basement and free Shep, no one will know. That key will work on his cuffs."

I squeezed it in my palm before placing it in my pocket for safekeeping.

"And you're not on your own," she added. "If you need help on your way out, Brandon and I have you covered."

We had help. Good. But I had no clue who Sage and this Brandon guy were, or why they were helping us. It didn't matter. A thrill shot through me because we had a real chance of getting out of this place alive.

Then my heart faltered.

"My brother. Franky has him."

She gave me a look filled with pity. "I saw him come in. Look, I can't make any promises, but I'll do my best to help him. You focus on getting your man free. We need him."

They needed him?

Sage fluffed my hair, bringing it around my face to conceal

some of my wounds. Blood matted my dark blond waves in places. I hoped the low lighting in the club made it less obvious.

She gripped me by the shoulders. "Right, follow me. When we reach the basement door, it's showtime. Good luck. Stay safe."

I blinked fast, not sure I was ready for this, but determined as hell to do what I had to. "You too."

Sage opened the door and checked both directions. She angled her head for me to follow.

My heart pounded in my chest as I tried to act casual on our way to the stairs. With sweaty palms, I clung to the balustrade, taking each step with care because my legs were numb from adrenaline.

I took in the room below. The scene had changed little since I'd arrived. The patrons were either focused on the women on stage or engaged in conversations at their booths. But as we reached the bottom of the stairs, one man charged for us.

He pulled up in front of Sage. "What do I gotta do to get a drink around here?" he said with hands on hips.

Sage didn't miss a beat. "Sorry, Tony. Angelo asked me to show the new girl around. I'll bring you your usual in a minute. On the house."

That seemed to appease the rude jerk because he returned to a booth near the stage without giving us another look. I exhaled in relief.

We headed across the room and down a dark hallway. Sage stopped at a closed door and kept her back to it. She looked both ways as she scanned the length of the corridor.

"All clear. This is it. See you on the flip side, Cameron."

Our eyes met for the briefest of moments before I slipped through the door and shut it. The sounds of the club muted behind me.

The enclosed concrete staircase before me was narrow and illuminated with fluorescent lights. I couldn't see Shep from here. I'd need to descend further.

Was anyone else down there? The ginger thug, perhaps? I took the first few steps with caution, and hearing no sounds below, descended a few more. The temperature dropped the lower I went. The musty odor of mold made my nose scrunch.

Halfway down, the room came into view. I spotted Shep, still motionless and cuffed to the chair. I flew down the last of the stairs.

"Shep!" He didn't respond as I hurried to him, but his chest rose and fell with slow, deep breaths. Thank God he was alive! Although blood leaked from a split lip and a nasty gash along his cheekbone. Bruises in various states of swelling mottled the rest of his face. My poor man.

I put my hands to his cheeks, being careful with his injuries. "Please, wake up." Tears prickled my eyes.

Hell no! What if I couldn't rouse him?

I shook him by the shoulders and spoke louder this time. "Shep, I need you!"

He groaned and his head bobbed, but he was far from conscious.

I noticed one empty and one full water bucket next to his seat. Red used one to wake him earlier.

I gnawed my lip as I struggled to lift the heavy load over my shoulder. When I dumped the water over Shep's head, his eyes shot open. His whole body tensed, muscles straining and chest heaving, as if preparing to fight. I jerked back from the wild man before me.

But then he shook his head. "Cam?" His blinking gaze raked over me as though he didn't trust what he saw.

A strangled sound came from my throat as I launched myself at him and threw my arms around his neck. I laugh-cried as I clung to him, but we didn't have time for a happy reunion yet.

The cold shower had washed the blood from his injuries, so he looked a little better. I pulled myself from him, my front soaked through.

With a smile, I took the handcuff key from my pocket, held it up, and wiggled my brows. "I'm breaking you out, baby."

His eyes darted over my face. "What? How? Are you all right? Did they hurt you?"

"I'm fine. Let's get you out of these cuffs." I fiddled the key into the barrel of the lock with shaking hands. The moment the cuff swung open, Shep reached for me and brought my mouth to his in a brief but firm kiss. I savored the warmth of his lips, even though I tasted his blood on them. He rested his forehead against mine, needing a deep breath to gain his composure.

He pulled back, his palms still cupping my jaw. "How did you get down here? And with that key?"

"We've got help. Sage, a waitress, and some guy, Brandon." I worked fast to remove the other cuff.

He blinked, then glanced down. When his eyes cut back to mine, he lifted a brow. "Ben is here?"

"Yeah. The asshole brought Justin to Franky. Sage said she'd try to get him out though." Was it too much to ask for two miracles in one day? Getting both Shep and my brother out of here alive?

One side of his mouth twitched up. "It's him. Ben's helping us. Brandon is his alias. The woman must be with him."

"For real?" I might have to temporarily revoke his asshole status. At least until he helped get us out of here.

"Yeah, and with him we have a shot. Let's get moving." He groaned as he bent over to untie the rope at one ankle. I helped with the other.

The basement door opened and loud music filtered through before it shut again.

Shep and I froze, wide eyes glued to each other. Voices came from above, one with a cold, emotionless tone I recognized.

My blood turned to ice.

Franky was here.

25

SHEP

Son of a bitch.

I held in a growl as the footsteps drew nearer.

My mind worked overtime to come up with a plan, except I had little to work with. I didn't have time to undo all these damned knots around my ankles. Every injury in my body pounded with my pulse.

Cam rushed to help me with the ropes. The terror in her eyes told me she knew who was coming down those stairs.

I pulled her closer and put my lips to her ear. "There's no time. The pillar over there," I whispered and pointed to a concrete support column on the far side of the room. "Get behind it and stay there. No matter what, all right?"

She made a small noise but nodded and ran to hide. Thankfully, she didn't argue with me because I couldn't have these assholes getting their hands on her again.

Judging by the casual steps approaching, I guessed Franky didn't know Cam was free and wandering around his club. And even though I had a serious beef with Landers, at least he'd remembered his allegiances before it was too late.

I worked to calm my breathing. Franky would say his piece

now, and then he'd finish me. Whether we made it out of here alive hinged on this moment.

One, two, three sets of shoes came into view as they descended the stairs. Just enough time for me to put my hands behind my back, rest my chin on my chest, and stare at the floor. The picture of a subdued prisoner.

Franky came to stand in the middle of the room ten feet in front of me. I raised my head slowly so it appeared heavy on my neck, which wasn't hard to fake. I felt pretty rough.

Two enforcers, the huge guy who'd dragged me off the airplane, and the redhead who'd laid into me earlier, took up positions at the wall behind Franky, flanking him.

No one suspected Cam's presence in the room. And if they noticed I looked like a drowned rat, they didn't mention it.

The mob boss wore an impassive expression that I wanted to drill into the ground.

"Mr. Shepherd." Franky clasped his hands behind his back. "It's been some time since we were face to face. You're looking significantly more... haggard than our last meeting."

"What, this?" I licked the side of my mouth where blood still leaked. "I've taken worse beatings from the guys on my team when we were fucking around. Your crew are pussies." I scowled at the ginger jerk on the left.

A muscle in Franky's jaw twitched. "You have nothing to gain by being disrespectful. Not after the trouble you've caused me."

I shook my head and leveled him with a hard stare. "You shouldn't have sent your men to my home."

"*You* should have done what you were paid to do." Franky raised his voice, a rare display of emotion from the unfeeling bastard.

"You're taking things too far, Franky. Hit contracts on innocent women? What next? Children? You're barely human anymore."

"I will do whatever it takes to keep order among my organization. My methods may seem brutal, yet it's because of my ruthlessness that I control this city and everyone in it. I even had your own friend track you down. How did it feel to be betrayed by an ally?"

Landers. It would be hard not to kill him on sight if I ever made it out of this basement.

I shrugged and spat a little blood on the floor at Franky's feet. "People only do what you want because you threaten to destroy something they love or you pay them off, not because they respect you. Your empire is built on fear and manipulation." I laughed and leaned back in the seat acting casual and insolent as fuck. "You're gonna lose it all. One day soon when you're dead, those of us who know what you truly are will celebrate. Good riddance to Franky Russo. The biggest piece of shit this city ever produced."

Franky's nostrils flared as he eyed the red stain on the floor, his hands clenched into fists at his side. When his eyes came back to mine, simmering with anger, I knew I'd hit my target. I needed all of Franky's masks to be stripped away. I needed the raw beast before me. The one whose wrath and vengeance led him to commit unspeakable acts.

He sneered. "When we spoke on the phone last week, you never mentioned how lovely Ms. McKenzie is. A rare natural beauty. Not long ago she begged me to spare your miserable life. On her knees, right before me." Franky adjusted his crotch. "She was so… convincing that I was almost tempted to give her what she asked."

Cam had said she was fine, but would she let on if she wasn't? And why was she wearing those clothes? The too-tight cami exposing plenty of skin and a scrap of material for shorts? My biggest fear for Cam had always been the abuse she'd suffer if Franky caught her.

My limbs trembled with rage. That Franky or his guys

would put their filthy hands on her made me want to charge like a raging bull and tear them limb from limb.

My teeth clenched and chest heaved with every fury-filled breath I drew. A roar threatened to burst from my lungs. I'd been trained for torture and interrogation, but it didn't make this any easier to endure. What small sense I had left told me to focus and stick with the plan. It took all of my strength to keep my hands glued behind my back, because Franky still hadn't done what I needed him to do.

But he'd discovered my weakness. Cam was the one thing that could bring me to my knees. I snarled like a rabid wolf and hoped Franky read my death stare as the promise it was.

The asshole grinned and arched one dark brow. "Aha, there you are. The feral animal has broken free from the semi-civilized facade. I see you now."

"And I see you too, Franky."

"What were you two doing up in the mountains? Playing house together? Did you think you could pretend you're normal and not a cold-blooded killer?" He shook his head. "No, Mr. Shepherd. Men like us don't get to have a piece of that life. You might have convinced Ms. McKenzie you're something better than you are, but you'll never change. I know what I am. A soulless monster, rotten to the core. And you are, too. I'm doing the world a favor by killing you."

I dug my fingernails into my palms. I wasn't the same as Franky, but he was right about one thing. Cam deserved a better life than the one I could give her. It was a sucker punch having this son of a bitch remind me of that.

I glanced at the thugs leaning against the back wall. With arms folded and smug faces, the only thing they lacked was popcorn.

"Let's finish this, shall we?" Franky removed his glasses and handed them to the redhead. "I learned at an early age that mercy will get you killed. When my father allowed a betrayal to be punished with banishment, instead of death, it cost him his life, and that of my brother. That is why you and the McKenzie siblings must die. There will be no mercy from me except this. After you take your last breath, I will end Ms. McKenzie's life quickly. Unfortunately for you, Mr. Shepherd, your demise will be much slower." He rolled up his shirt sleeves and took a step toward me. "I misjudged you. I thought you were loyal to me." His hand went into his pocket and he pulled out a set of brass knuckles.

I expected something like this from Franky. And since this thing between us was personal, it didn't surprise me he wanted to finish me himself. In fact, I counted on it.

He pushed the knuckle dusters over his fingers. Another step. "But once a dog bites its owner and tastes blood, it must be put down." He wriggled his fingers, making final adjustments. Those calculating, cold eyes told me he would enjoy this.

Face twisting into an inhuman grimace, Franky swung his right arm back for a king hit. When he followed through, I slipped to my left and brought my hands up to deflect the blow. The unexpected move left him unbalanced, and he almost landed in my lap.

I grabbed Franky by the vest and slammed my forehead into his face. The satisfying crunch of bone was like a trigger unleashing the unforgiving savage within me. He cried out and his neck flung back as blood streamed from his nose and mouth.

The enforcers pushed off from the wall and fumbled for their guns. I stood and spun Franky so his back was to my chest, then clamped one arm around his neck in a tight choke hold. They'd have to shoot through their boss to get to me. Franky's legs kicked out in front of him, and he clawed at my arms.

Not nice being on the receiving end, is it?

Franky's pistol, tucked into the back of his pants, pressed between us.

Game on, assholes.

In one motion, I pulled the weapon, released the safety and put two bullets in the redhead on the left. Body shot; head shot. Before his corpse hit the floor, I aimed at the other guard as he raised his Glock. I fired one bullet through his pistol hand and the next through his head. Weapon and body hit the deck.

Franky made choking noises as he struggled. I shoved him onto the ground, face first. He scurried onto his back, gripping his throat and gasping for air. Crimson spittle stained the front of his gray vest.

I aimed the pistol at Franky's chest. "Cam, come on out."

She emerged from behind the pillar, her gaze darting around the room as she scanned the scene before her. Then her eyes met mine and she ran to my side. I tucked her under my spare arm and pulled her close.

Franky looked between the two of us, confused.

I aimed the pistol at his crotch. The expression of horror on his face was satisfying. "I have to know, Cam. Did he take advantage of you like he said?" Her cuts and bruises would heal, but if he'd forced her to do other things, she might never recover from that. And I would need to make someone suffer.

She shook her head. "No. He was bluffing."

I breathed a sigh of relief. He could keep his dick, but he wasn't walking away from this. I raised the aim of my weapon to his chest.

"Wait! We can make a deal." Franky's words flew out fast as he coughed and sat up.

"Stay down!"

Franky raised his hands in the air. "Twenty of my men are about to storm this basement. I'll tell them to stand down if you stop this right now. You can walk away and live, or fight and die. You can't take them all on and keep her safe."

The cunning bastard had a point. If I didn't have Cam to protect, I'd end Franky this second and go to war with his guys topside despite the risks. Landers was upstairs, but I wasn't sure how much I could trust him to back me up.

But if Franky and I went our separate ways, I could still follow through with my plans to get Cam out of the country and come back for him when I'd regrouped. After all, this wasn't a peace offering. It was a temporary ceasefire.

He winced and wiped blood from his nose. "All of you can leave. I give you my word." Franky leaned forward to stand, and a flash of silver caught my eye. He reached for a pistol strapped at his ankle.

I fired two bullets into his heart before he got it out of the holster.

Cam yelped as Franky's lifeless body slumped to the floor beside her. She kicked the pistol from where it lay near his outstretched arm. Franky let out one last wheezing exhale before his dark eyes took on a vacant stare.

Enjoy your one-way trip to hell, motherfucker.

Franky Russo's reign of terror had ended, but our fight out of here had only begun.

26

SHEP

I wasn't great at math, but with only three rounds left in this clip and a truckload of mobsters to dispatch on our way out, I figured we had a problem.

I checked Cam over. She seemed a little wide-eyed, but otherwise fine. "I'm sorry you had to see that, darlin'."

"Don't be sorry. I'm just glad you made him stop talking." A shiver rippled through her.

Listening to Franky explain how he planned on killing us couldn't have been easy for her.

"He wasn't lying about one thing. His guys are on their way. We have to move."

She nodded and helped me untie the bindings at my ankles before I fell on my ass. I grabbed Franky's pistol and handed it to her, then collected the weapons from the other bodies. It still wasn't enough.

Gunfire sounded above us. A lot.

Cam glanced at the ceiling. "What the hell is going on up there?"

I recognized one of the firing patterns. Double shots. Operator style.

I nodded. “That’s Landers.” At least it seemed like he was making good on his promise to help.

We climbed the stairs and paused at the door. Rapid gunfire cracked nearby. There were multiple shooters, and I wondered how many men Landers faced on his own. More than he could handle, I suspected. He needed my backup.

I checked over Cam’s pistol. Loaded, good. I took the safety off and handed it back. “That’s ready to go. Only use it if you have to. Don’t get fancy. Aim for the torso.” I tugged her to me for one firm, reassuring kiss. She held my face in her free hand and pressed hard against my lips. I pulled back but kept my eyes at her level. “Stay behind me. Keep close.”

She nodded and we were off.

The hallway offered little protection from the gunfight happening at the end of the corridor. I kept my weapon aimed at the opening up ahead where people flashed past, running for cover. No one looked our way, but if they did, they’d be dead.

We were close to the club floor, and I took in the chaos unfolding. Armed men took cover behind flipped-over tables. Screaming women clad in G-strings and glitter staggered in high heels to escape the building.

Landers, the clever bastard, had set himself and the waitress, presumably Sage, up in a prime sniper position on the top level. From the looks of it, they’d already picked off seven or eight of Franky’s guys. But they were being fired upon now and were pinned behind a large metal filing cabinet pushed up against the balustrade.

I had the element of surprise. No one expected another shooter to emerge at ground level.

Behind me, Cam hunched low with her spare hand covering an ear. I needed to get her somewhere safe while I dealt with this.

I directed her to an alcove where she’d have cover. The

gunfire was deafening, so I put my lips to her ear to speak. "Stay here. If anyone comes, shoot them."

She gave a sharp shake of her head. "I want to come with you. Let me help."

I cupped her face. "Darlin', I'll be distracted with you out there. Shit's gonna get crazy, and—"

Boom!

An explosion rocked the club floor.

That sounded like a grenade.

Cam's nails dug into my forearm. I gave her a pointed look.

She nodded fast, her face a little paler than it had been moments before. "Okay. I'll stay put."

I pressed a kiss to her forehead and set off.

With my pistol aimed ahead, I took steady steps as I advanced. *Slow is smooth and smooth is fast.* That was drilled into us during training. I'd lived and breathed this shit for so many years it was second nature, and I effortlessly slipped back into combat mode. And even though my head pounded from the beating, my instincts were sharp and my mind clear.

My first target was a guy with an automatic rifle spraying bullets at Ben and Sage. After taking him out, all hell broke loose. Some returned my fire, others ran for cover, which only put them back in Ben's range. He took the opportunity to dispatch a few more.

A guy launched over the bar with a shotgun. Sage moved fast and shot him straight through the heart. That was a surprise; she wielded her Glock like a pro.

Out of ammo, I found cover behind a booth. I swapped pistols, then got back in the game. A guy sprang from the curtained-off back rooms, belt buckle undone, firing twin pistols like some kind of wild-west outlaw. The booth protected me but erupted with splinters of timber and exploding chunks of foam. I counted the rounds as he shot them in quick succession, and when he'd exhausted his ammo, I emerged from my cover to take him out. Two shots. Body, head.

Dirt nap for you, cowboy.

While Landers fired, I dashed to another booth. From there, I took out two more thugs while they were reloading.

Between the three of us, Franky's guys had nowhere to hide. Those still breathing realized they were screwed, so they ran for the exit, firing as they went. Some got away, but we dispatched a few more before the room went silent.

I glanced at Ben who used hand signals to indicate that there were two more hiding behind the bar, determined to fight their way out.

Ben unloaded an entire magazine at the bar. Splinters flew, glass exploded, and liquor rained down on the pair still hiding. While Ben re-loaded, they broke cover to return fire. But I was ready for that. Two clean shots and they were down. The room became quiet again.

I walked through the club floor with my pistol raised and cleared the room like I'd done a thousand times while deployed.

"Floor clear!" I called.

A shot rang out from above. Lou, one of Franky's captains, staggered from an upstairs office, the pistol in his hand flailing like he was drunk.

I took aim.

Two shots were fired, but not by me.

Lou was hit. He collapsed onto the handrail, then tumbled over the balustrade, crashing to the club floor with a meaty thud.

I turned to find Cam holding her discharged weapon still aimed where Lou had been standing moments before. She lowered the pistol and her shellshocked eyes came to mine.

I went to her and pulled her against me. "Are you all right?"

"Yeah. I thought he was going to shoot you," she said on a ragged breath.

I hadn't thought it was possible for her to be more appealing, but seeing Cam take down Lou filled me with pride.

"For Christ's sake," Landers grumbled from his position. "He winged me. Should've shot his unconscious ass when I had the chance."

Ben wasn't seriously injured. A bullet to the arm wouldn't kill a tough bastard like him.

"Jesus, you're bleeding!" Sage dropped to her knees next to Ben, ripped off her apron and tied it around his bicep.

Landers watched while she fussed over him, more interested in the woman than the wound she tended to.

I took Cam's face between my palms. "It's done. You're safe."

She flung her arms around my neck and squeezed tight enough to cut my air off. She pulled back and did a head-to-toe scan, her hands running over my chest and shoulders.

"Are you hurt?" she asked.

"I'm fine."

"And Justin?"

"I don't know yet, but we should move. Eyes up while we walk through. It's kind of a mess in here." There wasn't much else I could do to prevent her from seeing the carnage. I took Cam's hand and led the way, but when we came to Lou's body, she stopped and dropped my hand. He was on his back with a pool of blood around his skull and one leg bent at an unnatural angle. Two bullet holes pierced his chest.

Her gaze roamed the corpse at her feet. "I'm glad he's dead."

My jaw clenched as I glanced between her and the lowlife on the floor. What had he done to her? That question would have to wait for later because Landers, Sage, and Cam's brother had made their way downstairs.

"Justin!" Cam let go of my hand and ran to her brother. Her arms went around his shoulders and he winced in pain.

I was glad to see Cam happy, but I wanted to throttle her brother. The logical part of my brain told me that was a bad idea, so I settled on imagining how satisfying it would be to have my hands around his throat. He must've noticed my murderous expression, because as soon as he made eye contact he looked away.

Cam approached the waitress next and pulled her in for a quick hug.

Landers took Sage by the hand. "To the parking lot, people. Let's hustle."

If the injury bothered him, he didn't show it. He must be hurting, though, which was satisfying. I planned on making him hurt a whole lot more once all this was over. But not today. I still needed his traitorous ass.

We followed his lead, the five of us now grouped at the door to the underground parking lot. Landers and I went through first to clear the area while the others stayed behind. Apart from six cars, the lot was empty. I directed everyone to come through before blocking the door with a dumpster in case any surprise heroes followed us.

Landers approached with a set of keys. He thumbed a button, and the lights on a black sedan flashed.

"That's Tony's car. He won't be needing it anymore." Ben tossed me the keys. "We go our own way from here."

I couldn't bite my tongue any longer. I fronted up to him with arms folded, if only so I didn't take a swing at him right away. "You want to tell me what the fuck's been going on with you?" It was only because of our history that I didn't shove him against the wall and demand answers. I'd give him this one chance to explain himself. I thought I knew Ben well. He'd always been a decent guy, so none of this added up.

He nodded, his lips pressed tight and eyes downcast. "I know this looks bad, but I needed to get Sage out of a situation with Dante."

Ben referred to Dante Moretti, Franky's nephew and heir to the Wolf Street crime syndicate.

He glanced at the nervous waitress standing next to his car. "When I found out both you and the Mob were looking for the McKenzie guy, I found my bargaining chip. I needed something valuable to offer Franky in exchange for Sage's freedom. I was desperate to get her out of that club." He exhaled a sharp breath. "And I knew you could handle yourself, but I never suspected you had a personal connection to that junkie. I thought maybe you were going to go after the money he'd stolen." He gestured to Justin with a look of disgust. "I swear I didn't know you had a woman who'd get dragged into it. You've always been on your own." He shook his head and thrust a hand through his hair as though he realized how close we'd come to death. "You've got to believe I always intended to help you deal with any blow back. I kept track of what was going on. That's why I sent the message to you at the motel, and it's why I shot the place up just now. I didn't expect things to go so wrong. I'm sorry, brother. For all of it."

"You could've handled this better." I pinned him with a stare that made grown men piss themselves.

"Agreed. Things have been a little... crazy lately." He shot another glance at his woman. "Look, give me some time to make sure Sage is safe, then you and I can hash this out, all right?"

A week ago, his explanation wouldn't have cut it, but if Sage meant something to him, like Cam did to me, I understood the lengths he'd go to protect her.

Ben could have left us in Franky's hands and taken Sage out of harm's way, but he stayed and got Cam and me out. He'd risked both their asses to save ours. Taking down Franky and his men on my own would have been tough even if I hadn't been tied up in the basement. Having Ben and Sage's help had been critical. Still, he only deserved credit because we were all still breathing. It could have gone the other way, and that would have rested squarely on his shoulders.

My teeth ground as I nodded, accepting his reasons, even though I wasn't ready to forgive him.

"Franky?" asked Ben.

"Dead. In the basement."

Ben nodded. "Good. Dante's still out there. You can have any of the others, but that asshole is mine."

Dante was a slick, intelligent bastard with his own army of paid private security contractors. He was on my list of threats that required immediate neutralizing and a difficult one to deal with, but if Ben had a personal issue with Dante, he could have him. I hoped he understood what he was up against.

I shrugged. "No objections from me."

"Good luck, Shep." Ben turned and headed for his truck.

27

SHEP

Police sirens wailed in the distance. Time for us to move. I led Cam and her brother to the black sedan.

"Get in." I told Justin and opened the back door.

He hesitated.

I spoke through gritted teeth. "Do anything stupid now and you and I are gonna have a problem."

He had the nerve to look pissed and like he wanted to say something which would end with my fist in his face, but kept his mouth shut and got in the car. Cam eyed our tense exchange before getting in the front passenger seat without a word.

Landers and the waitress had already split. A minute later, we were on our way.

The sirens drew nearer, but we had enough of a lead to drive away without drawing attention. Pedestrians were scarce. Perhaps the gunfire had sent them scrambling.

On the dark inner-city streets, we encountered the usual Philly congestion. I wanted nothing more than to hit the gas and weave through the gaps in oncoming traffic, but it was wiser to blend in.

Next to me, Cam gnawed on a fingernail or five. Her constant checks in the side mirror didn't calm her any.

Justin groaned in pain while adjusting his position in the back seat. "I'm sorry, Cammy," he panted. "I never wanted you to get hurt. I didn't think any of this would come back on you."

She spun to face him so fast I thought she might climb back there and slap him. "You hid Mafia drugs and money in my car!" she yelled. "What the hell did you think would happen?"

The fuck?

I turned and glared at the son of a bitch who was smart enough to shift away from my reach.

"I know. It was dumb and I'm sorry." He hissed and held his ribs. "I haven't been thinking right lately—"

"Because you're cooked all the time." Cam interrupted.

"I was, yeah, but I've been clean for five days. I'm done with all that, I swear."

Cam scoffed. "Spare me your lies. I've heard it all before." She flopped back in her seat and pinched the bridge of her nose.

"I needed money and didn't want to ask you again. Plus, I wanted to pay you back for all the times before. I made a stupid, messed-up decision in a moment of weakness. Once I realized what I'd done, it was too late to take it back. They'd have killed me for sure."

A horn blasted behind us, and Cam jumped. But it was nothing, only an impatient jerk.

She rubbed her red eyes. "When are we going to be out of here?"

"Soon. Not much further." I glanced in my rear-view mirror and continued to monitor for anyone tailing us.

Cam sighed and turned back to her brother. "How bad are you hurt?"

"Think I've got a cracked rib or two." His voice strained as he tested the injury. "And a couple of broken fingers."

"Did Ben do any of that?" Cam gestured at Justin's busted-up face.

"Ben? You mean Brandon?" He shook his head. "No, it was Franky's guys."

I eyed him through the rear-view mirror to find him grimacing in pain.

"Don't worry, we'll get you somewhere safe." Cam turned to me. "Won't we? Where *are* we going?"

"A rehab facility. It's discreet. People go there when they don't want anyone to know they're drying out or detoxing." I glanced at her. "They'll patch up the rest of him there, too. He'll be safe."

Justin piped up from the back. "You don't have to take me to rehab. I'll be fine on my own. Just drop me—"

"No!" I snapped. "You've misunderstood. I wasn't asking if you want to go. You're a liability to us out here on your own, so you'll go to rehab and you'll damn well stay there until I tell you otherwise." I glanced over my shoulder, narrowing my eyes. "We clear?"

He scowled, but nodded. I didn't know why he looked so pissed. Thought I was being pretty charitable.

Cam fidgeted in her seat. "Sounds expensive. I know you'll offer to cover it, but I'll pay you back."

I clicked my tongue. "I don't want your money, Cam. And I think you've paid enough for your brother's mistakes, don't you?"

Her eyes dropped to her lap while she chewed her lip. It would never stop unless he got himself clean.

The traffic eased once we moved further from the city. Cam's breathing slowed, and her movements were less twitchy. Justin kept his mouth shut in the back. Lucky for him because I itched for an excuse to make him hurt more.

I broke the silence. "You want to tell me what Lou did to make you happy to see him dead?"

She sighed. "Some awful threats against you and me. Plus, he was grabby and rougher than he needed to be. Jerk gave me this." She pointed at the purple swelling on her cheek and the cut on her lip.

I'd hoped the crash caused those injuries. At least Cam got to end him.

I reached across and cupped her jaw gently. "We'll get some ice on it soon."

We pulled into the entrance of the clinic. There were only a few cars in the parking bays because it was late and visiting hours were over. I stopped the car at the side of the building where we were away from security cameras and the lighting was poor.

Once out of the car, Cam hugged her brother. Justin winced, but put his arms around her, too.

She pulled back to look him in the eye. "Shep's right, you know. It's not safe for you out here on your own."

"What's going on, Cammy?" He kept his voice low, but his eyes darted to me with a look of disapproval. "Are you with this guy, or what?"

Justin was the second asshole in as many hours to remind me I wasn't good enough for Cam. It grated on me that they were both right.

"Kind of." She shook her head, her wavy hair falling around her shoulders. "It's complicated."

Justin's one good eye bugged out. "You saw the massacre at the club. He's even worse than the Wolf Street crew. You can't trust him."

I'd heard enough.

"Time for you to go." I reached for his arm, but he stepped away.

"No! Not until you tell me what you're going to do with my sister."

"I don't have to tell you shit."

Cam put a hand on her brother's arm. "Justin, please."

"Stay with me, Cammy. This guy killed a bunch of dangerous people without breaking a sweat. You can't seriously want to go with him?"

"She's coming with me," I growled.

"Why don't you let my sister make her own decisions?" Justin glanced at Cam. "Or is she your prisoner?"

"Justin. Shut the hell up," Cam ground out.

Justin ignored her. "You're not a cop. Who are you, anyway?" he said, jutting his jaw out.

Kid picked the wrong time to grow a pair. I was done holding back.

"Who am I?" I advanced on him. For every step I made toward him, he took one back. "I'm the man who killed your biggest enemy and helped get you out of that club alive. I'm the man who's been cleaning up your goddamn mess all week. I'm the man who helped your sister when you" —I stabbed a finger at his chest— "wrote her death sentence. I'm the man who would do anything, *fucking anything,* to keep her safe."

He brought his hands up in front of him when his back hit the side of the car. I grabbed his shirt and pressed him against it, hard. I wanted to break him. Take all my anger out on this oxygen thief and snap him in two.

"Your stupidity almost got her killed." I tightened my grip and showed him the whites of my eyes. "More than once."

"Okay, okay. I already said I was sorry."

Cam put her hand on my shoulder. "Shep, stop."

"You're sorry?" I snarled up close in his face. "You have no idea what your bullshit has put her through. The only reason I haven't killed you already is because I'm in—" I paused, rattled by what had almost slipped from my mouth. I blinked and changed my approach. "Because it would hurt her. And she's been through too much."

"That's enough!" Cam said. "You've made your point."

Had I? It didn't feel like nearly enough.

I released Justin and he slumped to the ground, panting. Spineless piece of shit.

I took a step back from them. As much as Justin deserved it, I shouldn't have lost my cool.

Cam squatted next to her brother and whispered quiet words. I turned from them, taking a moment to get myself together.

I'd almost admitted to something I hadn't even acknowledged to myself yet. I'd never been in love before. Is that what this was? It was such an all-consuming, overwhelming sensation, but it left me vulnerable in a way that made me uneasy.

Whatever this was, I decided I wasn't a fan. And besides, nothing good would come of it.

Light footsteps approached from behind. "He didn't mean to offend you. He's scared. We've all been through hell and he's worried about me."

I turned to her. "Don't you think it's a little late for him to be showing he gives a damn about you?"

She sighed and rubbed at her forehead, but ignored my question. "Look, I've spoken to him, and he's ready to go in without making a fuss."

"Fine, I'll take him. You still need to stay out of sight."

The siblings shared a hug before parting. I walked Justin in because I needed to see for myself he was admitted, and to take care of the financial details.

After I completed the paperwork, the nurse was ready to show Justin to his room. If she thought it was strange that we both looked like shit, she didn't say so. I supposed people might often turn up here at odd hours and looking rough.

Justin stood before me, hands stuffed into his pockets. He cleared his throat. "Cammy told me some things about how you helped her. What I said to you earlier, I was out of line. For what it's worth, thank you. Please, get her somewhere safe."

My jaw clenched as I stared him down. "Yeah, I'm working on it."

He walked through the security doors without looking back. It wasn't a reconciliation, but at least we could acknowledge we wanted the same thing.

When I returned to the car, Cam sat in the passenger seat, resting her head against the window. She looked lost in thought and beyond tired.

I slipped into the driver's side.

"How'd it go? Did he seem all right going in?"

"As good as can be expected. Hopefully what he's gone through will be enough motivation for him." I wasn't convinced Justin had the strength of character to fight his addiction. Time would tell.

I pressed the button to start the car.

Cam reached for my bicep. "Thank you for getting him where he needs to be."

I shrugged. "It's up to him now."

We drove out of the parking lot and headed north. Now that Justin had gone, I felt comfortable talking with Cam. Her profile illuminated as we passed under each streetlight.

"You holding up?" I asked.

She rubbed her eyelids as if she needed to erase the images behind them. "I guess. I can't even begin to process this day." Her hands came away from her face and she turned to me. "I'm not afraid of you, if that's what you're wondering. You did what you had to, to get us out alive. Actually, I'm kind of in awe of your ass-saving skills."

"You held it together when you needed to and saved our asses as well. We'd both be dead if you hadn't got down to the basement and got my cuffs off when you did. That took courage. And taking down Lou? Damn impressive."

She shrugged, but I noticed a hint of a smile playing on her lips.

We pulled into a self-storage facility.

"What are we doing?" Cam asked.

"I've got a unit here with supplies. We'll get organized and move on with the next phase." A phase I wasn't looking forward to. I needed to get Cam far away from here. Franky might be dead, but it was still too dangerous for her to be in Philly until I dealt with the fallout from the club shooting.

My unit sat in the blind spot of the on-site security cameras. I must be one of few people who didn't want their door to be under surveillance. I kept my face angled low as I punched in the access code. It was a large space, big enough to store my truck inside from time to time, so I drove the sedan in and closed the roller behind us.

The motion sensor activated the lights, which flickered, then illuminated the room. Cam emerged from the car and spun in a slow circle eyeing the contents of the unit with an odd expression on her face.

I imagined people stored all types of things in these units. Mine was well-organized with a large weapons cabinet and a chiller unit for various medications, sedatives mostly, against one wall. In the back corner was a bulk roll of black plastic, a spool of rope, and a ten pack of duct tape.

On an open shelving unit, I had a duffel bag with an emergency change of clothes, cash, burner phones, and a decent medical kit. Below that, a bunch of tactical gear: night vision goggles, body armor, plate carrier, holsters, flashlights. To me, this was all regular stuff; for Cam, it was anything but.

She scanned the room while rubbing goosebumps on her arms. Unsure if she was cold or freaked out by all the hitman gear, I handed her a jacket, which she draped over her shoulders. Maybe it was good for her to be reminded of who and what I was.

The first thing I wanted was weapons. Having them close calmed me, but not so much tonight. I loaded a bag with rifles, pistols, a shotgun, suppressors, knives, fake number plates, grenades and a ton of ammo.

Franky might be dead and the Wolf Street Mafia crippled, but a bunch of pissed-off mobsters still roamed this city. Those left alive would demand retribution for slain family members and for having their substantial pay checks ripped up.

I invited it. I was ready.

"What's the plan now?" Cam asked.

I zipped up the bag at my feet, then stood to meet her stare. "I'll find us a place to sleep, patch up our wounds, then get you on a plane first thing in the morning."

"Australia?"

"Not without a passport. I'm thinking west coast. San Diego, perhaps. With Franky out of the picture, it's safe for you to stay in the States. His men won't be concerned with tracking you across the country when they've got a bigger problem to deal with."

"I gather that problem is you."

I tucked a loaded Glock into the back of my jeans. "Yep."

She wrung her hands in front of her. "Maybe you don't have to go after them. What if they're happy Franky's dead?"

I nodded. "Some of them will want to jump into the top job, but I murdered a bunch of their friends and relatives at the club. I can think of several who are going to be coming for me and I can't be looking over my shoulder twenty-four seven." I moved to the shelving unit to grab more supplies. Cam followed close behind.

"You're not thinking straight. If Franky's guys don't get you, the Feds will. There'll be security camera footage and DNA at the club." Her voice wavered. "They'll come for you. You know they will."

I turned to face her. "I need to finish this, Cam."

She took a step closer and reached for my hands. "Come

with me. We'll get Ranger and leave together. Across the country. Across the world. Anywhere."

The hope flashing in her eyes cut right through me. I wanted nothing more than to pull her against me and say yes, that I'd follow her wherever she wanted to go. But I'd already spent plenty of time dreaming about what a life with Cam might be like. The problem was, I kept coming back to the same conclusion: I couldn't do that to her.

I withdrew my hands from hers and missed the warmth from them right away. "That can't happen." Grabbing the bag full of weapons, I stepped around Cam to make my way to the back of the car. She followed hot on my heels.

"Why not?" she demanded. "If I can disappear, so can you. Why can't we do it together?" Cam's feet shuffled behind me. "I know this sounds crazy, but we could still go to Australia. Find a small outback town, somewhere with plenty of land and hardly any people. It would be a quiet life, but we'd be happy."

I dumped the bag in the trunk and kept my back to her. "You won't be happy. Perhaps for a time, but that would change. There's so much you've yet to experience. I want you to have it all, but I can't give it to you. You should be with a guy who'll take you on dates, someone you can go to parties and concerts with. A guy you can introduce to your friends without them wondering which psych ward you plucked him from. A guy who doesn't come with so much baggage he turns into a killing machine every time he hears a car backfire or a helicopter pass overhead. You deserve so much more than a normal life, but I can't even give you that."

"Shep, stop. Please look at me."

But I didn't turn around because this was hard enough without looking into Cam's soulful eyes. "If I go with you, I know how it will end. Being with me will wear you down. It'll make you miserable until you're a shell of your former self. You'll hate me for it and then..." I exhaled a resigned sigh. "And then you'll come to your senses and leave. Let's skip all the nasty shit and save us both the trouble."

"That's a load of crap and you know it. Admit it. You're afraid of letting anyone get close. Well, guess what? So are most of us." From close behind, Cam scoffed. "You're a lot of things, Elias Shepherd, but I didn't think chickenshit was one of them."

I slammed the trunk closed and spun fast to face her. "Yeah, I'm scared. I'm terrified of ruining your goddamn life."

With eyes glaring and arms folded, she didn't back down. "You're not your dad."

"No, I'm worse. You think you know me because we've spent a few days together? Look around you." I swept my arms out wide, gesturing to the tools of my trade and the veritable armory surrounding us. "This is me. I'm not gonna change." I held her stare. "Do you have any idea how many people are dead because of me? I'm a killer. Always will be. You're a smart woman. You should know better than to get tangled up with someone like me. I'm as fucked up as those sons of bitches back at the club."

"How can you say that?" Her brow pinched. "What you did for me proves you're nothing like them." She leaned in. "Maybe you don't realize it, but there's good in you, Shep. So much of it. Why can't you see that?"

I ran a hand through my hair. "Quit trying to save me. I don't need it."

Her eyes narrowed. "You're so full of shit right now. You know that's not what this is about. Stop pushing me away. Come with me, please." She moved closer. I couldn't let that happen.

This last week, all my plans had unraveled. I never wanted to be drawn to Cam like an oasis in a scorching desert, never wanted to fall hard and put her in danger because of my screwups, and I never wanted to lie to her, even though I was trying to do the right thing.

"Don't you get it?" I snapped and her responding flinch was like a swift jab to my throat. But I couldn't pussy out now. "I was happy on my own before you came along and threw my life into chaos. You've complicated everything. Hooking up was a bad idea. It should never have happened."

She shook her head, eyes glistening. "You don't mean that."

"I promised you two weeks of safety and a one-way ticket out of the country, nothing more. There's no room in my life for a girlfriend, or a tag-along, or whatever you'd be. I fly solo, end of story. I did what I had to, to save your ass, and now it's over. There is no *us*." My heart cracked, ready to shatter into a million pieces as I let her go.

"Stop being a jerk." Her breath hitched. "I know this isn't you."

"It is. And this is only a small glimpse into the future you're begging for, so drop it."

In my entire life, I'd never been more of an asshole. I stepped around her to busy myself doing anything to escape the look of anguish on her face. It made me want to drop to my knees and beg forgiveness for what I'd done. I hated how I was hurting her.

Cam didn't realize it now, but I did this to save her one last time from a life full of regret if she was stuck with me.

28

SHEP

I changed the license plates on the sedan with a fake set. "Time to go."

Cam got in the passenger seat without a word, but she looked pissed. We drove in uncomfortable silence, which was better than getting into another argument.

When we arrived at the inn, I parked the sedan in the lot next door. The budget lodging near the airport would be our last stop for the night.

I went alone to check in at the small reception area. The old guy manning the desk almost had a coronary when I approached. I supposed I looked like trouble. I fed him a story about being a boxer from out of town and joked that my fight hadn't gone so well. That appeased him because his face returned to a normal color by the time he handed over the room key and wished me a pleasant stay.

I carried the duffel and weapons bags into the room and laid them on the floor next to the bed. Cam followed me inside but seemed unsure what to do with herself.

I pulled a spare T-shirt from the bag and handed it to her. "Why don't you get washed up, then I'll fix that cut."

Her hand went to her temple as though she'd forgotten the injury from the rollover. She nodded and headed for the bathroom.

I used my cell to book her a flight to San Diego, accommodation, and transport. I knew the city well, so it wasn't hard to do.

A short while later, Cam emerged with wet hair trailing down her back and wearing my white tee. It reminded me of the first time she'd bathed and dressed in my clothes at the cabin. I looked away because seeing her like that stirred up unwanted feelings.

I patted the bed next to me. She could probably patch herself up, but the instinct to take care of her was still strong.

You did a shitty job of taking care of her earlier, asshole.

I wasn't proud of the way I'd treated Cam at the storage unit, but I didn't see any other way to make a clean break. If she thought I didn't want her, she'd move on quicker.

Cam sat and faced me, back straight, eyes penetrating. Without saying a word, she conveyed how disappointed she was in my behavior. I hoped one day she'd understand why I had to cut her loose.

I cleared my throat and dabbed the wound at her temple with antiseptic. As I worked, I scanned her face. Since this would be our last night together, I wanted to memorize every breathtaking feature. Her feline green eyes, the smattering of freckles over her nose, those perfect lips. Now, all I could think about was that I'd never get to taste her again. Holding myself back was even harder now that I knew what I was missing. I had to look away, so I rummaged through the medical kit for steri-strips. It was difficult to keep my hands steady while I applied them. As I put the last strip on, Cam's hand came to rest on mine.

"This is stupid," she said. "Please don't be like this. Talk to me."

I kept my eyes on my work. *Coward.*

"There's nothing more to say." I stood and headed for the bathroom, grabbing the medical kit and a clean pair of boxers on the way. "Why don't you try to get some sleep? The bed's yours."

Showered, wounds tended to, and more tired than a Himalayan pack mule, I exited the bathroom in my boxers to find Cam tucked into the huge bed. She watched me go to the closet and remove a spare pillow and blanket. I headed for the sofa.

"You won't fit on that thing." She sat up and pulled the covers back. "Get your ass over here."

I paused and stared at the empty side of the bed. Cam was right. The couch was tiny and looked uncomfortable, but she didn't realize what she asked of me. I wasn't sure I could handle sharing the bed and not tucking her against me.

Why couldn't she hate me like I needed her to? She should throw a desk lamp at my head and tell me to sleep on the cold bathroom tiles, not demand I lie next to her.

I could do this. I *had* to do this because I was so exhausted I thought I might fall asleep standing.

I moved to the bed and slid between the sheets as far from Cam as possible. Satisfied I'd done what she asked, she returned her head to the pillow and got comfortable.

I could still smell her from here. I laid on my back with one hand propped behind my head and stared at the ceiling, suddenly not as tired as I thought I was. Being near her made my body resonate as if there were static electricity building in the space between us. I shut my lids and focused on taking slow breaths.

She shimmied toward me.

My eyes shot open. "Cam," I warned.

"Quit being such a baby. This won't kill you."

Wrong.

She leaned her head on my shoulder, and one hand came to rest on my bare chest. The brush of her fingertips sent a charged shiver through me.

I swallowed hard. "This is a bad idea."

"I disagree." She snuggled closer and her fingers trailed south.

Sweet Jesus. I snatched her hand and held it in place. "Stop it. You don't know what you're doing."

"Not true." She sat up fast and threw a leg over my hips, straddling me. "I know *exactly* what I'm doing."

Cam's hands went to my shoulders, and she moved against me. I gripped her waist to hold her still. My body was already reacting to her.

Stunned by her actions, my top brain came to its senses and I tried to shift her to the side. Judging by the grip of her thighs, she wasn't having any of that.

"Don't!" Her eyes flared.

"We're not doing this." My raspy voice didn't sound as convincing as I'd intended.

"You promised me." She jabbed a finger at my ribs. "Back at the cabin you promised you'd be whatever I needed until this thing was through. And until I get on that flight tomorrow, it's not through. Not yet." Her voice caught, and it made my chest ache. "Please," she went on, moisture pooling in her eyes. "I need this with you one more time. After everything that happened today, I want to be close to you more than anything. This wall you've put up between us is killing me."

If she cried now, I was done for.

"I know I said that, but doing this won't change anything."

She blinked back unshed tears. "You've convinced yourself we shouldn't be together. I get it, but I still want this with you tonight." She pulled the T-shirt over her head and threw it to the floor.

The sight of her naked body above me stole my breath. This wasn't playing fair. I couldn't hide my hardness as she rocked against me.

I wished we could be something more. Cam and I were never meant to breathe the same air or walk the same path. I should put an end to this now, but I wanted her, the selfish asshole that I was, and all my willpower couldn't prevent my hands from moving over her skin. Up the smooth expanse of her back, then down her front, caressing her breasts and tracing her hips. My eyes roamed every inch of her. Even with her injuries, she was still the most beautiful thing I'd ever laid eyes on.

Before I could stop her, she'd freed me from my boxers and tried to lower herself onto me.

I sucked in a breath. "Cam!" I hadn't expected her to move things along so fast. It was as though she wanted to hurry things in case I called it off. I supposed I'd given her reason to think I might.

"Wait," I told her.

She gave a defiant shake of her head and continued to move.

"No, I mean, slow down, darlin'."

The truth was, I didn't want to rush this. Cam deserved better. And now that we were tangled in this bed together, I wanted to savor every moment. If having her one last time screwed with my head, so be it. It was already a mess.

Her body relaxed into my hands when she realized she'd won. I thought I called the shots here, but I didn't have a clue. This woman held more power over me than anyone.

I sat up with her in my lap and pulled my boxers all the way off. "We do this, we're gonna do it right." With our faces an inch apart, I weaved my fingers through her damp hair. Her warm breath on my skin was intoxicating.

She nodded and clung to my shoulders. "Okay." Her eyes shifted to my mouth.

And that was it. I had to have all of her. I crashed my lips to Cam's and groaned at her taste. She moved her hips and her soft, wet folds slid along the length of my cock.

I flipped her onto her back and stared at the angel below me. I wished I was a different person. Someone who could make her happy for the rest of her life. Perhaps she could tell where my mind had traveled because she wrapped her legs around my waist and pulled me nearer, ripping me from my dark thoughts.

"I need you now, Shep. Please."

I needed her, too. I pushed inside her because every part of me demanded it. Being like this with Cam felt incredible, except it was hard to look in her eyes without expressing how much I truly cared for her, how much she meant to me. So I put my lips to her slender neck and kissed a trail to her ear.

Grabbing her ass, I tilted her hips up and pressed deeper, harder. She moaned as her nails raked down my arms. I didn't care if she drew blood.

"Goddammit, Cam. See what you do to me? You drive me fucking crazy."

I wanted to tell her other things. That she was clever and brave and the most amazing woman I'd ever met. That she was so beautiful I could hardly think straight when she was around. And most of all I wanted to tell her I was sending her away because I loved her, not because I didn't want her. Never that. Instead, I kept my thoughts to myself because it was the only thing I could do to make this easier on her once she left. I needed her to move on with her life, so the less she knew about how I felt, the better.

We took things slowly, each of us focused on the other. Our

lips and hands explored what we'd never have the chance to again. These memories would have to last for the lonely months and years ahead.

I moved inside her, over and over until Cam writhed and moaned below me. She cried out. Her release rolled through her in waves as her core clenched around me. When I came, she clung to me like if she held on tight enough, maybe we would never part.

Our chests heaved and a light sheen sparkled along her brow. I brushed a damp strand of hair from her neck and pressed my lips to hers. Her mournful eyes held mine, and I wondered if she thought the same thing as me: how much it hurt that we'd never have a moment like this again. I didn't share that with her though, because I hadn't lied when I'd told her this wouldn't change anything.

I rolled off and maneuvered myself to spoon her. No point trying to put physical distance between us now because I didn't think she'd let me get far.

Cam squeezed the hand I had splayed over her breastbone. "Can we please talk about this?"

I pressed a gentle kiss to her shoulder. "Say what you need to."

She rolled in my arms to face me; her palms on my chest. She shook her head. "I don't want to leave you. If you won't come with me, then I want to stay."

"You know that's a bad idea." I tucked a lock of hair behind her ear before cupping her jaw. "Once all this is over, it'll be safe for you to come back home and get on with your life. But it won't be with me." The lump in my throat made it difficult to speak. "You need to let me go, Cam."

She held my stare and must've realized I meant those words because she broke down in my arms and cried. Watching this strong woman fall apart was difficult. All I could do was hold her tight and hope to hell I hadn't made the biggest mistake of my life.

She sniffled. "Promise me you'll be all right." Her hands on my shoulders squeezed hard. "Promise me." The desperation in her tone told me she needed to hear my reassurance, even though she knew it was a lie.

"I promise." I kissed her forehead.

The week I'd spent with her would forever mark a defining moment in my life. From here on there would be *Before Cam*, and *After Cam*. Our time together would be something I'd treasure always. And as much as I was reluctant to admit it, she had changed me. Who knew I was capable of opening myself up and caring about another human being?

The downside was she'd leave me with scars so deep they'd stay with me forever.

29

CAMERON

We stood among the morning rush at Philadelphia Airport. I barely registered the people moving all around us. Some hurrying, others killing time. My eyes remained fixed on the man before me.

Shep held a relaxed stance with hands in pockets. He scanned the area in a way that didn't draw attention. To onlookers, we might appear as a normal couple sharing parting words.

We were anything but that.

He handed me a boarding pass and a new model iPhone. "Leave the cell off until you get to San Diego." He kept his voice low while issuing my final instructions. "When you arrive, there'll be a driver waiting with a sign. He'll take you to your apartment. And if you notice a scary looking blond guy with a beard and tattoos hanging about, that's Kane. I've asked him to watch out for you. You can trust him."

I tucked the cell into my backpack and nodded, struggling to pull my brain from the fog clouding it since I woke. Everything was moving so fast.

Shep didn't suffer the same problem. He'd been up well before dawn taking care of business, including breaking into my house to retrieve my ID so I could pass airport security. He'd also hit the mall to buy me clothes, a backpack, and makeup to conceal my cuts and bruises.

This morning, I'd made difficult phone calls. The first was to the police to have myself removed from the missing persons register. Shep said it would make traveling less troublesome. I told the cops I'd left Philly in a hurry to help my brother and apologized for causing any trouble. After verifying my identity with a bunch of questions, they told me to report to the Philly PD. I declined, telling them I was out of state. I wouldn't risk it. That station was too corrupt. And as far as I knew, I hadn't broken any laws.

The harder call was to Tom. It broke my heart hearing the relief in his voice. I couldn't imagine what he must've gone through. He already suspected I'd been dragged into Justin's problems, and although I couldn't elaborate, he knew it was serious. He had plenty of questions I couldn't answer, but it was necessary to protect Shep and Justin.

Tom worried when I told him I had to stay out of Philly for an unknown amount of time. I apologized for the trouble it would cause him at work. I felt awful leaving him understaffed. And even though he assured me I'd have a job whenever I returned, I knew he'd soon have to hire someone to replace me.

I still had so much to ask Shep, so much I wanted to say before I left, but I was running out of time.

I adjusted the backpack on my shoulder. "Can I call you? How long do I have to stay in San Diego? Should I look for a job?" The questions came out in rapid fire.

Sensing my anxiety, he placed both hands on my shoulders. "Just take some time to decompress from everything you've been through. And when you're ready, get out and explore a little. San Diego's nice."

It seemed ridiculous that I should vacation while Shep dealt with all the nasty things here. It also didn't seem fair. But there'd be no arguing about the situation with this stubborn beast.

He dropped his hands from my shoulders. "And it's probably best if we don't keep in contact. If the Feds or the Mob are monitoring me, it could lead them right to you."

I'd thought as much and was glad for Shep's logical reasoning because I didn't want to feel the sting of his rejection again.

I cursed myself for getting carried away. He felt something for me, I was sure of it. But not enough to take a leap of faith and let me into his life. What had I expected? He'd told me all along he preferred to be on his own and didn't do relationships, so why had I foolishly looked for a way to keep us together? I didn't blame him. He'd never led me on. I'd set myself up for this fall, and it hurt like hell.

He might believe he was like his dad and unworthy of love, but I didn't buy it. Shep had shown me far too much kindness over the last week to think he'd be a neglectful partner. I wished I could've made him see that. I wished I had more time to try.

Gripping the boarding pass in my hand, I glanced at the gate as the last few passengers made their way through.

Shep exhaled a deep breath. "It might take a few months before it's safe for you to come home. I'll send word through Kane. And if things don't go as planned, I'll leave instructions with him for that, too."

I didn't like that Shep had a backup strategy. He'd always appeared confident of beating the odds and coming out on top. Why the uncertainty now? A heaviness settled in my stomach.

Shep's eyes roamed my face. "I'm sorry it has to be like this."

He wasn't talking about sending me to San Diego. He meant the end of us.

"Me too." I blinked back tears because I didn't want to fall apart here.

The final boarding call was announced and my heart rate sped up. This was it. I wasn't ready to leave him. I threw my arms around him, holding on tight and pressing my cheek against his chest. The firmness of Shep's embrace told me this was difficult for him as well. I closed my eyes and inhaled one last deep breath of his scent.

I pulled back first and took Shep's face in my hands. His hazel eyes flickered between mine as his jaw tensed beneath my palms. I kissed him, a firm press against his lips to soak up his warmth one final time, then rested my forehead against his. "Thank you," I whispered. "I love you."

Without waiting for a response, I released him and turned for the gate.

I meant those words, but they weren't reciprocated, so my steps were fast and I didn't look back.

30

CAMERON

La Jolla, San Diego

I walked inside the apartment and dropped my backpack on the sofa. Following a quick glance around the modern open-plan living space, I spotted one area I had to check out first.

The moment I pushed open the enormous glass sliding doors, the sound of waves greeted me, and when I stepped onto the balcony, my skin cooled from the mild brine-tinged breeze that blew straight off the Pacific Ocean. Tall palm trees, which stood evenly spaced alongside the quiet street, were the only things separating my lodging from the rugged coastline.

The car ride from the airport had been filled with a one-way conversation as my chatty driver provided a run-down on San Diego. He said La Jolla was one of the nicest and safest beach areas in the city. Now that I'd arrived, I believed him.

I closed my eyes on the expanse of blue before me and let the afternoon sun warm my skin. This would be my home for the coming weeks or months. And even though my heart was full of melancholy, I couldn't deny the beauty of this place. The view from the balcony, both peaceful and revitalizing, was what I needed to recharge my depleted batteries.

My man did good.

Ugh, when would I stop thinking of Shep that way? I lifted my lids and steadied myself against the glass balustrade when I swayed on unsteady legs.

Like living on an active fault line, my life had been shaken many times this last week. The walls of my world had crumbled around me as Franky and his men tried to bring me down. With Shep's help, I stayed strong and emerged from the rubble intact. But the thing that had shattered my foundations and brought me crashing to my knees was finding love with the unlikeliest of men, and then losing it.

I rubbed at the ache in my chest as my breath hitched. Tears pooled in my eyes. I'd somehow remained composed on the flight and during the car ride here, but now that I was on the other side of the country, far away from the man I loved and would never have, I fell apart. Perhaps that had to happen before I could piece myself back together.

I needed to start letting go of everything that had happened since the night Shep took me. How the hell did I begin rebuilding when I wasn't sure if I could ever go home? Even though I was out of harm's way, my life was still a mess. I had no family here, no friends, no job, not to mention my heart had been ripped from my chest and stomped on.

"Fuck!" I thumped my fist on the balustrade.

Fuck Franky, Lou, and Pauly for being murderous, wretched assholes. Fuck Justin for being a monumental screw-up. And fuck Shep for making me fall in love with him, but being too stubborn to love me back.

I didn't care if the neighbors or beachgoers saw the crazy lady having a breakdown on her balcony. I needed this.

If Shep were here, he'd tell me I was trying to process it all at once when I should be taking it step by step. God, I missed him. I decided to take his advice and tackle each hour as it came.

Thinking about the things I was grateful for helped. My brother and I were both alive, and Justin had the medical support he needed. My heart was still heavy, but maybe one day it wouldn't ache so much. Not anytime soon, though. I wiped my face and went inside to look around my new digs.

It was a narrow apartment, decorated in a nautical theme of white, gray, and cerulean blue. The inviting living space was furnished with a linen sofa and a huge TV mounted above a fireplace. Upstairs, the large master suite had a luxurious white marble bathroom complete with jacuzzi and an open shower with not one, but three shower heads. I'd never seen anything like it and wondered how much Shep had paid for this place. No doubt it was way out of my budget. I'd have to find somewhere more economical to stay when my booking ended.

I flopped onto the sofa and removed a half-drunk bottle of water from my backpack. Then I remembered the cell Shep had given me. As soon as I switched it on, it chimed with messages. My pulse raced when I realized they were from Shep.

The first one contained contact details for Kane Daniels, the guy tasked with keeping an eye on me. Whatever that entailed.

The second message said:

If you need anything, call Kane.

I was a big girl and able to look after myself, but it was nice to know there was someone in this city to help should I need it.

The next read:

Rent paid for a month. Will extend if required.

Kitchen stocked with supplies (check the freezer).

That piqued my interest, so I went to inspect. Sure enough, the pantry and fridge were filled with groceries. When I checked the freezer, I found tubs of ice cream in a bunch of flavors. I smiled, even though my chest tightened. There was only one thing to do at a time like this, so I grabbed my favorite flavor—peanut butter—and returned to the sofa. The only thing I'd ingested all day was coffee on the plane. I still wasn't hungry, but since when did you need an appetite to eat ice cream?

I checked the last message. It explained how Shep had set up a bank account and provided details on how to access the funds. He told me to use the money for any expenses until I returned home. That was thoughtful of him. I wouldn't get far with my dwindling savings. At the bank's website, I followed the log in instructions and almost choked when I saw the balance.

I sat upright and swallowed the cold mouthful. "Sweet Jesus!"

He'd deposited one hundred thousand dollars into the account. I fell back onto the sofa and covered my open mouth with one hand.

Wait, I had his number! I typed a return message thanking him for everything and asking if he was all right. *Text Message Failed* bounced back right away. Disappointment echoed through me, but I wasn't surprised. Either his cell was off, or he'd already ditched it and unboxed a new one. That man went through burners like nobody's business. I tossed the cell on the sofa and shoveled another spoon of peanutty goodness into my mouth.

I was going to need it.

31

SHEP

Appalachian Mountains, three weeks after the shootout

I returned to the mountains to collect a few favorite weapons and to check on Ranger who convalesced at Debbie's home. The vet assured me he continued to make solid progress, although needed more rest and rehabilitation before he'd be back to normal.

Visiting my boy had been bittersweet. Our first reunion since I'd left him at the clinic, he'd greeted me with an enthusiastic wiggle of his butt, his stumpy tail working overtime with excitement. The sight of his shaved chest and healing wound renewed my determination to finish the job I'd started. Since I still had a few loose ends with Franky's crew, he couldn't come with me yet, but soon.

I'd done a lot of thinking in the last few weeks. The hitman business was a murky game. Sure, I took out human filth, but to what end? Every time I eliminated a cartel or gang member, retaliation followed and the cycle continued. Innocents got caught in the crossfire, street wars intensified, and hatred grew.

Perhaps I wasn't fixing the problem at all. Perhaps I added to it. None of it made sense to me anymore.

Being back at the cabin for the first time in three weeks didn't bring the sense of relief I'd hoped for. Everywhere I looked were reminders of Cam. The coffee table she'd sawed through, her discarded clothes strewn on the bedroom floor, the tangled sheets from our lovemaking.

Determined to torture myself, I picked up her pillow and inhaled. My chest clenched and a goddamn knot constricted my throat.

Idiot.

I didn't make the bed. Didn't pick up her clothes or drag the ruined coffee table to the workshop. I left it all untouched because changing anything felt wrong. Like if I washed the linen and tidied the house, all traces of Cam would be gone forever. And then what? It would be as if she'd never been here at all, and she'd be lost to me.

You've already lost her, fool.

I headed for the deck to get some air. The mountains had always held answers for me. Perhaps they'd have some pearls of wisdom now.

The floor creaked beneath my boots as I made my way to the railing. Taking several deep breaths of clean icy air, I stared at the snow-capped mountains.

Cam's parting words at the airport echoed through my mind.

Thank you. I love you.

She might as well have thrust a hunting knife under my ribs.

I dragged a hand through my hair. I didn't want to be here, not without her. The cabin, this property, they weren't my peace any longer. Cam was. I didn't deserve her, but she loved me, and I loved her. Yet I'd thrown that love away as if it were meaningless. As if it weren't the most precious thing in the world to me.

No, I hadn't thrown it away. I'd *destroyed* it.

I regretted those awful things I'd said to Cam. Not a day went by that I didn't wish I could take them back. The pained look in her eyes during those moments haunted my dreams.

Goddammit. I'd fucked up. I gripped the timber handrail so hard I nearly ripped it from the deck.

How could I have been so stupid to let her go? Aside from Ranger, Cam was the only good thing to come into my life, and I'd sent her away. All because she'd somehow achieved the impossible feat of bringing my stone-cold heart back to life. When I was with Cam, that muscle in my chest pumped red-hot with purpose, and I felt more alive than ever.

My old man never loved my mom. He did the right thing by sticking around to help raise me, but neither of them held any genuine affection for the other. So why did I think I'd treat Cam the same way he'd treated Mom? We weren't the same, at least not in that way.

Leaning against the railing, I closed my eyes and bowed my head. It was too late. I'd screwed everything up. And that beating thing beneath my ribs grew icier by the minute.

32

CAMERON

San Diego, six weeks after the shootout

Most mornings, I ran along the sidewalk by the beach. It helped a little. I slept better if I could physically exhaust myself by the end of the day. Even with the exercise, I woke often and had disturbing dreams of being chased, the car crash, or being back in that basement with Shep, only we didn't get away. When I sat up in bed, terrified and alone, I missed my bossy hitman more than ever.

Today as I returned, sweaty and wheezing, I spotted a familiar black Harley Davidson parked in the driveway and Kane sitting on the steps below my front door. He rose to greet me, flashing one of his stellar smiles. He might look like a modern-day, badass Viking warrior, but when he beamed, it was a thing of beauty.

Despite being out of breath, I managed a smile for him as I approached. "Hey, Kane."

"Girl, did you run to LA and back? You look like you're dying." He walked toward me and leaned down for a hug, even though I smelled awful.

"Just added an extra mile to my loop." I wiped the sweat from my brow.

He rested his hands on his hips and gave me the same stern look Tom did when he worried about me. "You still not sleeping right?"

I shrugged and headed for the door. "Sometimes. Nice hickey by the way." I gestured to his muscular neck, exposed because his shoulder-length blond hair was pulled into a low pony.

His brows shot up and he rubbed the bruise. "Really?"

"You bagged yourself a wild one last night." I laughed and unlocked the apartment door.

Kane followed me in. "Damn. Should've got her number. And her name."

It didn't surprise me he did well with the ladies. Although bearded, built, and covered in tatts, Kane was sweet and deceptively charming. The women he bedded had no clue he was an ex-SEAL and the best sniper stateside. I'd weaseled those details out of him suspecting Kane was one of Shep's Team Zulu buddies. But like Shep, he kept his military career private and didn't let anyone get too close.

Kane and I had become friends even though he'd tried to resist. One day early on, I came out of a supermarket and spotted a guy matching his description sitting on a Harley. I'd noticed him a few days before because although I was heartbroken, I wasn't blind, and Kane was a damn fine sight seated on his black beast.

On a whim, I dialed Kane's number and watched as the man on the Harley checked the screen of his cell, then looked right at me. When he kept staring, I waved, walked over to his bike, and invited him over for coffee. He declined because he'd been warned not to fraternize with his client. What a load of horseshit. I wondered if Shep thought Kane might be a rebound distraction for me. Not likely. Another man was the last thing I wanted.

Every time I spotted Kane, I'd made a point of starting up a conversation, and despite his protests that Shep would murder him in his sleep, he caved and accepted my offer of coffee. We'd been hanging out ever since.

At first, my intention had been to push him for information on Shep, but Kane's laid-back attitude and roguish sense of humor had sealed our friendship.

Kane tossed his leather jacket on the sofa, and we headed for the kitchen.

"Your usual?" I asked over my shoulder.

"Yeah, thanks."

He sat at the breakfast bar while I made an espresso using the apartment's fancy machine. I took a bottle of water for myself.

"Any news from back east?" I scanned his face for any telltale signs as I placed the strong black in front of him.

He shook his head. "Cam, you know I'm not supposed to say anything."

"Yeah, but you know I've got to ask." I gulped down water. "He's still alive, right?"

Kane nodded.

"And I've seen nothing in the news about Shep being a suspect for the shootout investigation. So that has to be good, yeah?" I didn't know how he'd managed it, but so far, Shep had stayed off the cops' radar.

Kane shrugged and held his palms up. "I don't know, maybe. He doesn't talk to me about that stuff."

I braced my hands on the white marble counter. "What *does* he talk to you about?"

Does he ask about me?

He folded his tattoo covered arms. "Cam," he grumbled in warning.

“Can you pass on a message for me?”

Kane lowered his chin. “I already told you a bunch of times that’s a bad idea.”

“Okay, fine.” I held my hands in the air. “I know I’m supposed to give up on him, but I can’t. I wish it was as simple as that.”

He scrubbed a hand over his bearded face. “He really did a number on you, didn’t he?”

I bit down hard on my bottom lip to stop from tearing up and stared at the shimmering blue waves over Kane’s shoulder. My chest still constricted whenever I thought about Shep. I needed way more time.

Kane sighed and pointed in my direction. “See? This is exactly why I don’t get attached. It’s too goddamn messy.”

“You might be on to something there.” I tossed the plastic bottle in with the recyclables before leaning against the kitchen counter.

He sipped his espresso. “You need to get out more. Start having a life again.”

“I will. I’m looking into some short courses at a local college.” I wasn’t ready to start doing normal things, but I also knew it was important to try.

“That’s good.” Kane finished the coffee and took the empty cup to the dishwasher. “Everything else okay? Is there anything you need?”

Only the man I love and my old life back. I scrunched my nose and faked a grin. “Nah, I’m good.”

“See you tomorrow then.”

“Sure.” I followed him to the door and locked it after him.

~

AFTER KANE LEFT, I showered and dressed in ripped jeans, a white tank, and a warm, gray, knitted sweater. Winter in San

Diego was milder than Philly, but December was its coldest month. I'd bought some basic wardrobe items when I first arrived, but had otherwise only purchased essentials. I didn't need much and hadn't touched the money Shep left me. Last week, I splurged and bought a tablet which I'd been using to research courses. I sat on the sofa filling in an online application for a photography class.

The doorbell chimed, startling me. I was still a little anxious since everything had happened. It was probably Hannah who lived next door, but I checked the security camera to be sure.

I covered my mouth as I jumped back from the image before me.

I blinked and checked the screen again. My chest pounded and I froze.

Move your feet, girl!

With tingling limbs, I walked to the door, then wiped my sweaty palms on my jeans. What was I waiting for? I steeled myself and opened the door slowly, trying not to let nerves get the better of me.

My heart stuttered at the sight of Shep. I hadn't seen or heard from him in six long weeks.

I'd forgotten how much his presence dominated when he was near. His towering height, those muscular arms and broad shoulders. The black fitted tee he wore outlined an impressive torso, and his large hands were jammed into the pockets of faded blue jeans.

Shep looked... good. Better than good. He looked delicious, and I wanted to drag him inside and climb him like a tree. Instead, I stood motionless and mute, staring into his unreadable hazel eyes.

"Hey." He scratched the back of his head while eyeing me with uncertainty. His light brown hair had grown so long he could almost tie it back.

My stomach fluttered at the sound of his gravelly voice. I'd missed him so much.

"Hey." I rested one hand on the doorframe to steady myself.

Emotions warred inside me. Every cell in my body urged me to leap forward, throw my arms around him, and never let go. But things had changed since we were last together. Self-preservation was a priority nowadays because I'd finally gotten myself to a place where I could function without crippling heartache. The thought of being rejected by Shep again scared the crap out of me.

"What are you doing here?" I needed to know that more than I needed the air in my lungs. Hope was a dangerous thing to have when your heart was as fragile as mine.

He glanced at the ground between us before his eyes returned to mine. "I just... I needed to see you."

He seemed odd, nervous even. Did he have bad news? Was he here to tell me I had to go on the run again because one of Franky's crew had found me? I folded my hands around my belly where a sinking sensation grew. "Is everything all right?"

"There's no trouble following us, if that's what you mean."

I exhaled a deep breath, not realizing I'd been holding it in.

Shep looked over my shoulder into the apartment beyond. "Are you alone?"

"Yeah." I opened the door wider, my grip on it firm to stop my hands from shaking. "Do you want to come in?"

"Actually" —he hooked a thumb over his shoulder— "there's something I want to show you." He turned and walked down the path.

I wasn't expecting that, but followed him to the driveway, anyway. Parked out front was a shiny black pickup, a newer model than the one that got wrecked.

"You... got a new truck?" Great, but not worth coming all this way to show me.

"Well, yeah, but—" He gave a whistle and a familiar brown head with floppy ears popped up in the front seat.

"Ranger!" I ran to the truck and ripped open the door. The pointer leapt down and almost floored me when his front paws met my chest. I let him snuffle my neck with wet-nosed kisses while I gave him a cuddle.

As I rubbed his coat, I smiled so hard my cheeks hurt. "I missed you, boy." His butt wiggled with excitement, so I gave it a scratch. "And I never got the chance to thank you for saving my life."

Shep eyed our reunion with one brow arched and arms folded across his broad chest. Was he jealous? I guessed I hadn't greeted him as warmly as I had his dog, but I still wasn't sure why he was here.

Ranger's nose went to the ground. It led him to the mailbox where he cocked his leg and relieved himself.

I laughed and glanced at Shep who covered his face with his hands before dropping them to his hips. "Sorry. He's been stuck in the car since Phoenix."

"Perhaps we should take him to the beach to stretch his legs. Is he fully healed?" The hair on Ranger's chest was a little shorter than the rest of his coat, and there was a bald patch around the scarring.

"I'm increasing his exercise gradually, but he's coming along well. The vet said it wasn't a good idea for him to fly yet since the bullet messed up his lung pretty bad. The pressure in the cabin can cause problems. That's why we drove."

We crossed the road to the beach and made our way to the firm sand by the shore. There weren't many people around because of the cool weather, even though it was a sunny day. Ranger ran through the shallows and stalked sea gulls as Shep and I walked.

I was painfully aware that he hadn't once tried to touch me.

That hurt. Plus, he seemed anxious, which wasn't like him. What was going on?

"You've driven a long way to get here." I swept my windblown hair from my face. "What's on your mind?"

"I needed to talk to you, and it's stuff that shouldn't be said over the phone."

Right. Being monitored must still be a concern.

"How have you been?" Shep asked.

I shrugged. "I've been better." He didn't need to hear how I was heartbroken and still a mess. But I'd toughened up since he saw me last. I wasn't about to grovel and beg him to take me back. "And you?"

"Okay, I guess. Things were kind of tense after you left. Took me a while to deal with the fallout from the club, but it's done."

From the tight set of his shoulders, I sensed he didn't want to talk through those messy details.

I rubbed my arms to stay warm. "And the cops? The Feds?"

"We're in the clear thanks to Landers. He wiped the club's security hard drive and stopped the cameras from recording before the shootout. And later, he screwed with the DNA evidence by hacking into the system. The whole thing ended up looking like a botched investigation because of him."

Relief washed over me. Shep and Ben had some serious skills, and I was thankful for it.

"I've got some good news for you," he said. "I got your car back."

I stopped walking and my jaw dropped. "You did?"

Shep nodded like it was no big deal. Perhaps he underestimated how much Helen meant to me.

My grin transformed into a wide smile. "Oh my God, thank you." I took a small step toward him, then halted. If he was keeping his distance, I should, too. I shoved my hands in my pockets instead. "Is she all right?"

"A little dirty, but otherwise fine. Found her in a workshop at the rear of your aunt's house in Illinois. Still had Franky's gear on board. I destroyed the dope but kept the nine hundred large for you."

"Nine hundred grand?" I did a slow blink. "Wow. I don't even know what to think about that."

"You don't have to decide what to do with it right away, but I'd say it's a small compensation for the nightmare you've been through."

I supposed I could use it to pay for Justin's rehab. I called my brother weekly and was impressed with his progress. Addiction would be a lifelong struggle for him, but I remained cautiously optimistic.

We continued walking.

"And I wanted you to know I'm done with being a hitman. I don't want that life anymore."

"Really? That's great news!" I reached across to give his arm a squeeze.

Shep's gaze focused on my hand as if it were burning a hole through him. Hadn't I told myself I wouldn't touch him? Or get carried away by his presence? I tore my hand away and fidgeted with the cuff of my sweater, hoping I hadn't overstepped some unspoken boundary.

"What will you do now?" I asked.

"I'm not sure." He relaxed his stance and scratched the stubble on his jaw. "Think I'll take some time out to start with. Get Ranger one hundred percent so we can go hunting again. Might make some improvements to the cabin. I've fixed the front door, but there are a few other things to mend."

I winced. "I still feel crappy about destroying your stuff."

"Don't," he said. "It'll give me a chance to get familiar with my tools again before I take on bigger projects." He shrugged one large shoulder. "But I'm done with all the killing. I think my time will be better spent creating things rather than ending them."

Shep had done some serious soul searching since I'd left. It was everything I'd wanted for him—a peaceful life without violence—except I'd hoped it would be with me. Still, I was proud of the decisions he'd made, so I tried to bury my disappointment at not being able to experience the journey with him.

I sighed. "Well, it sounds like it's safe for me to head home, and you and Ranger can return to the cabin." Where he had the isolation he craved and no risk of forming any unwanted attachments. "I guess everything worked out the way you wanted." I hated how bitter my words sounded. I should be content that we'd all come out of this with our lives intact.

But I wasn't.

Not even close.

He stepped in front of me, blocking my path. The action surprised me, and I pulled up fast.

"Dammit, Cam, it hasn't." There was an intensity to Shep's stare as he considered his next words.

This was it. This was why he'd driven thousands of miles to meet with me face to face. My chest clenched with anticipation.

"Before you left, I said some things I regret. They were hurtful and cruel. I wish I could take them back, but it seems those words found their mark."

He thought I was standoffish because of what he said in the storage unit? I supposed that was better than him thinking I'd been a lovesick wreck this whole time.

Shep continued. "I hated upsetting you, but I thought it was the best way to get you to move on. I'm so sorry I hurt you like that. Do you think..." He paused, struggling with his words. "Do you think you could ever forgive me for being such a jerk?" He held his breath while he waited for my answer.

My heart sank. He'd only come here out of guilt. Shep was

taking this *new man* thing seriously and wanted a clear conscience before starting the next phase of his life. I'd been wise to rein in my enthusiasm at seeing him on my doorstep.

"Is that why you're here, Shep? Because you want a pardon for pushing me away and breaking my heart?" A lump formed in my throat, something I'd become familiar with these last six weeks. "If you need that to move on, then fine, I forgive you. How could I not after everything you've done for me?"

"That's not why I'm here. I mean, yeah, I want to make things right between us, but not so I can move on *from* you. I want to move on *with* you."

Wait. He what?

"I've had a lot of time to think about what happened between us at the cabin. You've practically consumed my thoughts since we parted."

My pulse thrummed through my veins. He'd come here in person not because of phone taps, but because this was important to him. I guessed that went some way toward explaining his nervousness since he turned up on my doorstep.

He shook his head. "I fucked up."

"Yeah, you did." I folded my arms.

"And I'm sorry."

I let the silence linger before narrowing my eyes. "Is that all you've got to say for yourself?" He wasn't getting out of this hole so easily.

He raked a hand through his hair. "I was scared, all right? Being with you made me so damn happy all I could think about was how unbearable it would be to have you, then lose you. I mean, how does that even happen in the space of a week when I've never felt that way in my entire life? And it was stupid, I know that now, but I pushed you away because I was afraid of hurting you, and having you resent me. Please believe me, Cam, I never meant those things I said. I want to be with you more than anything."

His words melted me. My heart kicked into overdrive, and I worked hard to maintain a neutral expression.

"And?" I arched a brow.

Yeah, I was asking him to dig deep, but he needed to get these things off his chest as much as I needed to hear them. Getting Shep to open up was difficult, so we were doing this, no matter how hard he found it.

"And… I thought feeling something for another person was impossible for me. From the moment I laid eyes on you, that changed. I was living in a dark place before you came along. Somehow, you pushed the shadows away. It's like everything is… vivid when I'm with you. Everything makes sense. And what I thought made me vulnerable only gives me strength, gives me purpose."

Shep moved toward me. His hazel eyes dropped to my hands as he reached for them, and when his warm palms surrounded my own, my stomach went into freefall.

"I've missed you like crazy. I want us to be together, and I want to build a life with you. I know this makes me a selfish asshole because I still think you can do so much better than me, but I want to be the one taking care of you, and I want to be the lucky son of a bitch who gets to wake up next to you every morning."

He moved closer still and cupped my jaw, his touch igniting my skin. The yearning in his gaze almost undid me. I struggled to draw breath, but when I did, I couldn't help but lean into his palm and inhale his scent, which I'd missed so much.

"I love you, Cam. Been wanting to tell you that for a while now. You almost killed me with those words when you left. Please, darlin', what's it gonna take for you to give me another chance?" His brow creased as the moment drew on.

I couldn't believe this was happening. Shep wanted me like I wanted him. I needed someone to pinch me, or in this case, kiss me. And I craved that more than anything, so maybe it was time to let him off the hook.

I rolled my lips together to hold back a grin. "I guess you can start by building a workshop for Helen. And all that healthy junk in your kitchen won't do, so I'll need candy in the pantry and ice cream in the freezer. And"—I held up my index finger—"Ranger gets to sleep on the bed with us three nights a week."

His strained expression vanished as he rested his forehead against mine. "Goddamn, you had me worried there."

"You kind of deserved it." A smile spread across my face, but Shep still appeared anxious.

"I promise, Cam, I'll try to be the man you deserve. I'll do anything to make you happy, but if I screw up, you gotta kick my ass and let me know."

Shep held a deep-seated fear of messing things up between us. I had my work cut out to make him believe otherwise. Yeah, he was different from any guy I'd ever met, and he had his quirks, but none of that scared me. It only made me more appreciative of the generous and kind person he'd become, despite what he'd been through.

My hands clasped the powerful lines of his neck. "I'm not an expert, but no relationship is perfect. If something comes up, we'll talk about it and deal with it together. Just don't lock me out again, all right?"

He nodded. "I won't."

"And I don't want you to change and try to be this person you think I deserve. I love you, Shep. Exactly as you are."

The words had barely left my lips before his mouth hungrily met mine. His arms enveloped me, clinging to me as though making up for lost time. I closed my eyes and basked in the warmth, taste, and feel of him.

This wasn't a dream. He was alive, he was here, and he was in love with me.

He's freaking in love with me!

Being with Shep was intoxicating. He overwhelmed my senses by demanding more with every eager caress of his tongue and every gentle nip at my lips. I gave it gladly.

This was as monumental as our first kiss, only this time it marked the beginning of something real. Something I wanted with all my heart and now had in my grasp. I'd never let him go.

One hand went to my ass, squeezing firmly as he pulled me against him. Heart pounding, every nerve ending sparked to life. I moaned into his mouth and my legs would have buckled if he hadn't been holding me so tight.

He drew back, and both of our chests heaved from the ferocity of our kisses. The heat in his gaze had the butterflies in my stomach frenzied.

He rubbed his thumb along my bottom lip. "I've had six long, lonely weeks to think about all the things I want to do to you."

"Oh yeah? And how's that imagination of yours?"

Shep's lips twitched into a smile. "When it comes to you it's thorough" —*kiss*— "creative" —*kiss*— "and a little dirty."

My eyes widened at his playfulness. "Really?"

"Mmm hmm, but if I lay you down in the sand and show you what kinds of things I'm talking about, we're gonna get arrested real fast."

This man. This thoughtful, caring, overprotective, pig-headed, hot-as-sin man. It might surprise him, but I had a few things dreamed up for him as well.

I flashed him my most wicked grin. "Then we'd better hurry back before we get into any more trouble."

He twined his long fingers through mine and pressed a kiss to the back of my hand.

Not a single shadow lurked behind the bright smile Shep aimed at me. I longed to see more of them, and I was sure that I would.

EPILOGUE

SHEP

Two Years Later, Appalachian Mountains

I snuck Cam's present into our bedroom before heading to the workshop.

"Cam?" I came around the barn doors and found her waxing the already gleaming Camaro. Ranger sat nearby, keeping a close eye on our girl. He rarely left her side these days.

"Darlin', why are you cleaning Helen again?" It was the second time she'd done it this week, and the car hadn't even left the workshop.

She smoothed a rag over the sleek black lines of the hood before standing. A smile lit her face when she rested one hand on her belly, which was... well... pretty darn huge at thirty-eight weeks pregnant. Our little peanut had grown into a watermelon.

She shrugged. "I think this must be my version of nesting."

When Cam had first put it to me that she wanted us to start a family, I'd needed time to think it through. Honestly? It was something I never thought I'd have. The idea of raising a child and screwing it up scared the hell out of me. It concerned me my only role model for fatherhood was my old man, and I didn't want to be like him.

But I wasn't my dad. Far from it. Cam had helped me see that. And when we'd stared wide-eyed at the little blue positive symbol on the pee stick, my heart swelled bigger than I thought possible. All because of her.

I put my arms around her shoulders, drawing her in for a hug. She relaxed into me.

"You should be resting." I tucked a loose strand of hair behind her ear and searched her eyes for weariness. I found none. She was taking this pregnancy in stride and looked beautiful.

"I'm fine." She laughed and slapped me on the chest. "Stop fussing over me."

My eyes ran over her. The freckles across her nose were a little darker, cheeks a little fuller, boobs a *lot* fuller, and those long, wavy locks were more lustrous than ever.

Gorgeous.

"I've got something to show you. Come with me." I took Cam by the hand, leading her into the cabin and down the hallway. We stopped outside our bedroom, but Ranger headed right on in and jumped on the bed.

"Close your eyes."

She did as I asked before I brought her into the room.

"You can open them."

Cam sucked in a breath. "Oh my God, Shep. It's incredible!" She approached the rocking chair I'd been working on in secret for weeks, shaking her head as she took in every detail.

From the moment we'd returned home from San Diego, Cam had kept me occupied with projects. First up had been an extra workshop big enough for her to work on her car and others in time. And when we'd found out she was pregnant, she asked for an extension to the cabin. Four more bedrooms. I guessed building things wouldn't be the only task keeping me busy.

Working with my hands relaxed me. I didn't miss being a hitman; I was glad those days were done. I was more than happy to turn my attention to making a life with the beautiful woman before me and the baby boy we'd soon be bringing into this world. I did my best to make sure Cam lived the sweet life she deserved, and I felt more peace than I'd ever known, so we were both enjoying our life together in the mountains.

Cam eased her frame into the chair and tested the gentle rocking motion, her hands gliding over the smooth armrests. "It's perfect. All of it. You're amazing." She beamed as she looked around the room at the crib and changing table I'd finished months ago. I'd never been so proud of my work before that moment.

This fatherhood thing was growing on me.

She stood with effort and approached me. Her palms pressed against my chest as she smiled and gazed into my eyes. "You're going to be a great dad. I hope our little man turns out just like you."

I placed one hand on her belly, in awe of the growing life inside of her, and wondered if maybe that wasn't such a bad thing.

The End

AFTERWORD

Thank you for reading *The Hit*. If you enjoyed it, please consider leaving a brief review on Amazon.

If you'd like to continue the Team Zulu series, you can read Brandon and Sage's story, *The Payback*.

And don't forget to download your free copy of *The Rescue, a Team Zulu Christmas novella* from my website:

www.julieweaverbooks.com

Julie

TEAM ZULU SERIES READING ORDER

The Hit

The Payback

The Heist

Scarred Souls, a Team Zulu Duet, Book 1

Ravaged Hearts, a Team Zulu Duet, Book 2 (coming soon)

The Rescue, A Team Zulu Christmas Novella (Standalone)

ACKNOWLEDGMENTS

There are two talented, amazing women who have become the backbone of my author support network.

Hollee Mands, not only are you the conjurer of beautifully written books, you're also incredibly kind and generous with your time. I appreciate your brutal honesty, and your author pro-tips are absolute gold.

And Kelley Luna, editor extraordinaire, Team Zulu cheer squad, and all-round gorgeous person. You've made the tough editing phase a dream. It's been great to chat books with you and marvel at the endless differences between Australian and US English.

A big shout out to my ARC team. Thank you for the positive feedback and your early reviews.

A special mention to those who posted on social media for The Hit and The Payback. If you tagged me in, I definitely saw it and I'm grateful for the love.

Thanks to my husband and sons for your encouragement and for understanding I sometimes need extra hours at the keyboard.

And lastly, thank you to my readers. I hope you'll continue on this journey with me.

Jules

ABOUT JULIE WEAVER

Julie lives in Mandurah, Western Australia, where she writes spicy romance books with morally grey characters who do very bad things for (mostly) good reasons.

She's a boy mum, dog mum, ex-mechanical engineer, and an unashamed coffee slut. She'd rather stay home so she can read, binge watch her favourite series, or plot her next book.

facebook.com/julieweaverauthor
instagram.com/julie.weaver.author
tiktok.com/@julie_weaver_author
amazon.com/author/julieweaver
bookbub.com/authors/Julie-weaver

Printed in Dunstable, United Kingdom

77133306R00194